I0668587

UNDERCOVER WITH THE ENEMY

SHARRON MCCLELLAN

This book is a work of fiction. Names, characters, places, and incidents are the product of the author's imagination or are used fictitiously. Any resemblance to actual events, locales, or persons, living or dead, is coincidental.

Copyright © 2015 by Sharron McClellan Camaratta. All rights reserved, including the right to reproduce, distribute, or transmit in any form or by any means. For information regarding subsidiary rights, please contact the Publisher.

Entangled Publishing, LLC
2614 South Timberline Road
Suite 109
Fort Collins, CO 80525
Visit our website at www.entangledpublishing.com.

Select Suspense is an imprint of Entangled Publishing, LLC.

Edited by Tracy Montoya
Cover design by Fiona Jayde
Cover art by iStock

Manufactured in the United States of America

First Edition August 2015

For Sue Bringen. You taught me to sail, that a day on the water always ends with cocktails, and how to not scream like a little girl when a sailboat heels onto its side. Thank you!

Chapter One

"Entrance of the Gladiators," the big-top circus theme, played in Holly's head as she stood on the roof of the Waltham Office Complex eyeing her target—the building across the alley. Swinging a galvanized cable attached to a grappling hook in a circle over her head, she let it go as its momentum peaked. It arced across the twenty-foot gap, landing on the rooftop of the other building.

She tugged the cable, the metal grapple scraping loud against the cement in the still night. "Come on."

The hook caught on the ledge. She yanked. Hard. It held. "Nice."

Decision time. Tightrope or swing across? She assessed the distance, the wind, and whether she felt like swinging—crashing, really—into the side of the building, then scrambling up to the roof or walking across empty space with the possibility of falling to her death.

Either was dangerous, but given a choice, she preferred

walking the rope. It was more fun.

Keeping tension on the metal cable, she used her customized carabineer system to latch the other end onto a thick metal pipe that followed the perimeter of the Waltham roof, then stood back to survey her handiwork. Not as taut as she would like, but enough to keep the grapple engaged and herself from swaying.

"Time for a status update, Holly." Kane MacMillan, her by-the-book mission leader, broke her concentration, his voice coming in through her ear bud. She rolled her eyes. Maybe if she didn't answer, he'd go away and let her do her job.

Dressed in black tights, tank top, hoodie, leather gloves, and a silky black ski mask—what she considered traditional apparel when thieving—she did a quick gear check. The drop to the pavement was sixty feet, and carelessness could be a death sentence.

All tight. All secure. She hopped onto the ledge and put a delicate foot on the cable, taking a test step to make sure the grapple still held.

It barely twitched. "Excellent."

"Status, please."

Dammit. "In a minute," she replied, not bothering to hide the irritation in her voice.

With the moon and the glow of the city as her only sources of light, and the big-top theme still playing in her head, she took the first full step onto the cable. It shimmied beneath her feet but nothing more.

Another step and she stood over the empty space. She tossed apprehension out of her head and focused on the walk. Raised in the circus by a mother who was a self-professed psychic, she'd been performing since she was old enough to walk. Of course, she'd never be skilled enough to do the more advanced moves—those were left up to the kids born into the family that claimed the tightrope act, but she'd been allowed to play at it.

She'd learned, and now she could walk the rope. It wasn't much, but for what she did, it was enough.

Deep breath. Easy. Exhale.

"What the hell is going on? Do we have a situation?" Kane asked.

She stilled, arms still outstretched as her concentration broke. "I'm a step away from death. Can you please shut up?"

"Next time, check in as scheduled and give an update. Why do you have to make everything harder than it needs to be?"

She didn't, but there was something about him that brought out the rebellious teenager in her. "Whatever."

"No. Not whatever. Check in. On time."

Or you'll do what?

She managed to keep the comeback in her head, promising herself he'd pay later. Refocusing her attention on the task, she hummed the circus theme as she took a second step. She was out of reach of the ledge now. No turning back.

Adrenaline rushed, and she took a deep breath, channeling the heat and the energy.

"Da da dadadada da da da dum."

"Is that necessary?" Kane's voice cut in.

She swayed, thrusting her arms out to keep her balance. "Are you trying to get me killed?"

Hesitation. "Dammit. I'm—"

Holly reached up and tapped the earpiece, cutting him off in mid-sentence.

Kane. Why did it have to be him?

With a well-muscled six-foot-two frame, eyes the color of a stormy sky, and pale brown hair that begged to be tousled, he was the kind of man most women fantasized about being with. A small part of her imagined that being held in his arms offered an unexpected feeling of safety.

All-in-all, a sexy package that was everything a woman desired.

Until he opened his mouth and revealed himself to be the biggest stick-in-the-mud that ever walked the earth.

Holly bobbled on the wire and realized that she had to get him out of her head or she'd end up splattered on the pavement below. Humming louder, she used her feet to feel her way along the cable, keeping her gaze on the ledge of the other roof. One step. Two. Three.

The world fell away as she crossed the void. There was nothing but the slight breeze, the humming in her head, and a goal.

No big-top audience. No stage lights. No Kane.

Nothing.

She'd never admit it to anyone, but this was where she felt most at home. Where she didn't have to be anything or anyone other than herself. Holly Milano, thief extraordinaire.

Her feet landed on the cement ledge of the Waltham building, and she blinked. That felt faster than normal. She glanced at her watch. Seventy seconds. A new record.

But long enough that Kane was probably having a conniption fit. She tapped the earpiece. "What did I miss?"

"What the hell?" the masculine voice on the other end

growled. "I thought you fell off the damned rope."

"It's a cable."

"Do not turn off the earpiece again," he said, ignoring her correction.

This was why she didn't like working with him. He was so by-the-book, he left no room for the unexpected. In her line of work, there had to be wiggle room and a bit more. Not allowing for the occasional "off plan" experience could get her caught or killed.

Not that he cared. She'd learned that two years ago when they'd worked their first op together. She'd improvised when a door that was supposed to be open had turned out to be locked. The lock was complicated and cracking it would take time—time she didn't have. Instead, she'd entered an un-locked office next door, gone through a window, and scaled the outside of the building to the target to retrieve the files they'd been after.

Instead of being thrilled with the fact that she'd gone above and beyond, and got away with it, Kane-the-Pain had cited her for "insubordination" in his report to Temperance Smith, the V. P. of the West Coast branch of High Risk Se-curity—a for-profit security agency that offered everything from rescuing kidnapped victims to recovering stolen items.

The complaint had become a black mark on her record. Plus, she'd had the added thrill of a lecture on the value of teamwork—given by Tempe, herself.

He really was *Kane-the-Pain*. She snickered at the nickname.

"What's funny?" he asked, his voice brisk and low.

"Nothing."

"Then get moving. The security cameras won't remain

deactivated forever."

"On it, boss."

"I'm not your boss. If I were, you wouldn't be here."

Kane the Pain. She didn't laugh this time. There was nothing funny about his snarky comments. "Then don't distract me when I'm in the middle of *not dying*."

"Agreed," he replied.

He hadn't changed. Holly jogged across the roof-top garden—a small area with benches, trees, and even a fountain—toward the door to a stairwell. She pulled on the handle. Locked.

"Holly?"

She reached up to switch off the earpiece again then stopped, her hand hovering for a breath before dropping to her side. As much as she'd love to ignore him, she didn't need him to tattle on her again. "What?"

"I didn't know you were already on the cable when I interrupted. Sorry about that."

An apology? Unexpected warmth followed the adrenaline that still coursed through her veins. "Thanks." Maybe he wasn't so bad. Sometimes.

"If you would check in, then I'd know what was going on."

The warmth vanished as quickly as it had appeared. "Of course." She shook off the agitation, knowing it would only hinder her. "The stairwell is locked." They were running tight on time. "I'm using the secondary route." She walked to the three-foot by three-foot metal lid that capped the main roof vent for the building's HVAC system.

"Roger that," he replied.

Flipping open the metal cover, she tied one end of a

static rope to the door handle of the stairwell, tossed the remaining length down the ventilation tube, and stared into the blackness. It was going to be a tight fit. Not impossible, but she was glad she'd forgone dessert at dinner.

Being careful for any sharp edges, she dropped into the shaft and lowered herself into the darkness.

• • •

The rules were in place for a reason. He knew she wasn't ignorant, so why did she keep flouting them at every given opportunity?

Sitting in the back of a non-descript delivery van with the name "Ramona Bakery" painted on the side along with the picture of a smiling muffin, Kane tapped a pencil on one of his video monitors as he watched the blip that represented Holly make her way into the building. He'd hoped she'd outgrown her childish desires to bend the rules at every given chance.

It was the only reason he'd agreed to the assignment with her. He'd seen what she could do the last time they worked together. Her combination of fearless gymnastics and street smarts made her one of the best retrieval specialists that HRS had ever hired.

But her inability to adhere to any plan—no matter how simple—made her a nightmare to work with. He'd heard her say that she preferred to work alone, and a part of him wondered if she were capable of working on a team. With him.

The dot that was Holly stopped its vertical movement, then continued on horizontally.

"Are you on the fourth floor? Or did you attach your

GPS to a dog and run in the other direction?" Kane asked, hating that he even had to broach the question. Anyone else and he wouldn't even bother.

But with Holly, she would be off the agreed-upon path in mere seconds if she thought it would add to the excitement of the operation.

"Just as instructed, O captain my captain," she replied, affecting a slight New England accent. He ignored her attempt at humor, wondering if the inflection was real. It was hard to tell. In addition to being an excellent thief, she could perform an array of accents, making it impossible to judge where she actually came from.

There were rumors that she'd been raised in a circus, which would explain a lot of her abilities, but he ignored them. He didn't gossip and didn't appreciate people who did.

Besides, people ran away to join the circus. Not from it.

With her blonde hair, big china-doll-blue eyes, and over-the-top optimism, it was more probable that she'd been a cheerleader before arriving at HRS. The kind for whom a pyramid of people was never enough. He could imagine her in one of those tiny skirts, pompoms in hand as she worked the crowd, and he grinned, in spite of the irritation she caused.

"Okay chief, I'm at the office," she said, the Massachusetts in her voice even more pronounced.

"Checking the perimeter," he replied, swiveling in the chair so he could check his link to the security cameras. The single guard was still at the desk, watching something on his smartphone.

"The guard is right where we left him," Kane said. "You have thirty minutes until his next round."

"I'll only need three."

A shiver raced up his spine. He wasn't a superstitious man, but a leftover sliver of magical thinking from his childhood whispered that she'd jinxed the mission. "Less chatter. More doing," he said, then winced at the holier-than-thou sound in his voice.

Dammit, but he had a difficult time maintaining his composure around Holly. And he knew what it was—the flamboyant showmanship. Her lack of substance. But mostly, her refusal to follow any of the rules—HRS's or society's. He never knew where she stood on anything, except for the fact that she'd be in opposition to him more often than not.

And then there was her ability to lie with no hint of subterfuge.

How could he trust someone like that?

He ran a hand through his thick hair, frustrated at being stuck with such a pain-in-the-ass partner. It wasn't like she needed help. Not for this. It was a simple job. Get in. Get the file. Get out.

The building wasn't even high-security.

Leaning back in his chair and balancing on the back legs, he watched two of the monitors. One showed Holly's location per the tracker, and the other displayed the visual of the guard, courtesy a quick hack of the security camera across from his desk.

Movement caught his attention. On the black-and-white monitor, the guard answered the phone. Kane zoomed in, reading his lips as best he could, considering the angle was off.

Something about pizza. A break? The guard put the phone down, picked up his nightstick, and stood. Kane straightened in his chair, the front legs hit the van floor with a thud.

He didn't need to read the entire conversation to know that someone was bringing the guard dinner, which meant he would be making his rounds early. The shiver that had raced up his spine a moment ago made an encore. "The guard's on the move," he said. "Stand by."

"Don't you mean work faster and get the hell out?"

And there it was—her inability to play well with others. "I mean stay where you are until I can ascertain where he's going."

He had to be sure before he made a decision on what to do. Perhaps the guard was going to the rest room, though Kane's gut told him otherwise.

"Do you copy?" he asked. Holly didn't respond, and he could only imagine what she was doing. The guard dropped off the screen, and Kane flicked on another set, following the man's movement as he skipped the bathroom and headed for the elevator.

Kane frowned. Dammit, he hated being right. They didn't have much time. From the files, he knew that the guard would start his rounds by heading to the rooftop garden and working his way downward.

Holly could hide a lot of things but not the open duct or the cable that spanned the buildings. "We're blown," he said. They could go back for the files but not if they tipped off their mark and he moved them. "Get out. Do not break into the office. We'll go at this from another angle."

"I can do this," Holly said. "I'm standing outside the door."

Kane pressed his lips tight, keeping his frustration at

bay. "I said, get out."

"Too late," Holly said. "I'm in."

"Dammit," he snapped, the dam on his annoyance breaking. "If I told you to break in, would that have made you leave?"

"Possibly." She chuckled in his ear, the sound throatier than he expected.

It was done. There was no choice but to finish. "Just get the info and leave before he sounds the alarm."

"See you in sixty," she replied. "Side alley. Be there."

• • •

Setting the timer on her watch for sixty seconds, Holly strode across the room.

According to HRS's intelligence, the photos were in the filing cabinet. She grinned both at the simplicity of the job and the fact that people assumed their valuables—from files to diamonds—were safe once they locked the door behind them.

But a filing cabinet? She chuckled, took out a screwdriver, slid it into the small gap between the drawer and the frame, and torqued it. Seconds later, the locked popped open.

"Bingo," she said.

She took a quick glance at her watch. Fifty seconds to go.

She opened the bottom drawer.

Hidden beneath a stack of manila folders was a two-inch thick, dark brown accordion folder—just like their client had described. She opened it and took a quick glance at the contents.

Pictures. A toddler dressed in pink lace. Their client and her daughter on the beach. Lazing on the couch. A whole perfect suburban life in color prints. She dug deeper. There had to be more. "Come on. Come on."

In a corner at the bottom, she found two small flash drives. Each bore a small label citing Grace.

Bingo. The digital copies of the pictures in the file. The soon-to-be-ex-husband had stolen the pictures of his deceased daughter to use as a bargaining chip in the divorce proceedings.

What an ass.

Fortunately for his estranged wife, she was a wealthy CEO who earned more than enough to hire HRS to get them back. Jobs like this were usually a cakewalk for HRS operatives—who often extracted people and valuables from war-torn countries or high-security prisons in hostile nations—but they paid the bills.

Holly tucked the entire file into her backpack, went to the window, and opened it. Wrapping a second rope around the leg of the heavy, oak desk, she tossed the other end through the gap.

Fifteen seconds left.

From her vantage, she watched the van barrel down the alley toward the meeting point. She made a quick rappelling harness using the rope and jumped out the window. Kane was waiting, lights off and engine running.

She counted off the last seconds with each push off the building.

Four. Three. Two.

She landed feet first in a flower bed, crushing a patch of yellow mums.

"And one to spare," she said, untangling herself and running to the van. Flinging open the back door, she jumped in. Kane started driving even before her feet hit the floorboards.

Sitting in the back, Holly watched the building on the monitors as they sped down the street. It remained quiet, but she knew it wouldn't last. The elevator had reached the top floor by now, so the security guard would be on the roof. She changed the channel to find him.

There. The security guard was on his phone, pacing and looking rather panicked. It wouldn't be long before he called the police.

Backpack in hand, she turned off the monitors and went to the front of the van, plopping into the passenger seat.

"Mask," Kane said.

She had forgotten she was wearing it.

Her hair cracked with static as she pulled the ski-mask off and tossed it behind her.

"I take it you got the file?" he said.

"Of course," she said, buckling in. "What kind of person treats his wife that way? Even an almost-ex. What kind of person uses pictures of his dead daughter as leverage?"

"The worst kind," Kane replied.

He gave her a sideways glance. She knew that expression—the furrowed brow, deep frown, and the silent *tsk tsk*.

Combined, they screamed disappointment. She sank into the seat with a sigh.

"What?" Kane asked, turning his attention back to the road.

"You're angry, aren't you?"

"The job was to get in and get out, and you did it."

"But?" she asked, wishing she could let it go, but that

one little word hung in the air, impossible to ignore.

"I am running this op, and you ignored my orders."

"I got it done. I have the file," she said. What more did he want?

"I know, which is why I didn't say anything."

Until now. "You're still pissed."

"Not pissed. Frustrated," he said with a shake of his head. "But it highlights why I don't like to work with you. You don't have any idea of how to be a team player."

She flushed at the reprimand and was glad it was dark. As involuntarily as the sudden heat in her cheeks, her hands clenched into fists. He didn't know anything about her or her ability to work with others. She did it all the time when she was home. She worked, played, and hung out with an entire freaking circus. She'd been part of a team her entire life.

Not that she planned to tell him that.

"You don't know me," she said, keeping the rest to herself.

Ahead of them, flashing blue lights lit up the road. Kane pulled over to let the cops speed past—going to the office building no doubt—and put the car in park at the curb. "You're right. I don't know you, but that doesn't matter. I should be able to trust you when we're working together."

She hated it when he was right. "You can trust me," she said, but the words sounded less than sincere despite her desire to prove otherwise.

He turned in the seat to face her, his square jaw made sharp by the play of light and shadow. "If we do things your way, yes. But what about when I'm calling the shots?"

She hesitated, not sure what to say.

He stared at her, gray eyes turned black by shadow,

making him difficult to read. His sandy-colored hair was perfect, as always. Her fingers itched to run her hands through the strands and test the texture. Silky or coarse? She guessed silky, but she kept her hands in her lap, resisting the urge.

Finally, he shook his head, put the car into drive, and steered the van back onto the main road, pointing them in the direction of HRS. "That's what I thought."

Chapter Two

"Do you think they know it was us?" Holly asked, watching the lights of the cop cars responding to the robbery recede in the mirror.

"Hope not," Kane said.

She kept watch in the side mirror. The flashing blue lights reflected in the windows of the surrounding buildings, growing more distant, before they stopped and changed direction. The cops were coming back, and intuition told her that she and Kane were the marks.

"They know."

"Dammit," Kane replied. He turned a corner and hit the gas. In seconds, the company van—a vehicle that was designed to blend in with soccer-mom suburbia but could outrun almost anything on wheels—was doing over sixty and climbing.

"Not even going to try and talk our way out of this?" Holly asked, grabbing the "oh hell" handle above the window.

"Have you seen yourself?" He had a point. In her black-on-black cat suit ensemble, she was dressed like a walking cliché when it came to burglary. While she was good at talking her way out of a bad situation, the mission would be a bust if the police took the pictures as evidence. "What next?"

"We need cover. That means traffic."

"This is L.A. That shouldn't be hard to do." Even at this hour, the 405 was almost guaranteed to be a nightmare.

"One would think," he replied, his attention alternating between the road in front of them and the police behind them. "I'd like to not put others in jeopardy."

They were getting closer to the populated areas now. The buildings were getting taller. There were more concrete and billboards. More vehicles parked on the side of the road and fewer parking lots were visible. Ahead of them, a car cut them off, and Kane cranked the wheel.

She squeezed her eyes closed and braced herself for impact.

There was no crash. No sensation of anything other than a jerk to the left and back, and then speed. When she peeked through her lashes and into the side mirror, the car was falling back behind them.

But the blue lights of the pursuing squad car grew closer with each passing second.

"It's only going to get worse," Kane said, but it sounded more like he was talking to himself. His jaw tight with a grim set, he reached over to a panel between them, flipped a switch, and adjusted a few knobs. Seconds later, the sounds of a police scanner emitted from the radio in time for them to catch the tail end of a conversation…*westbound on Los*

Felix Boulevard. Requesting backup.

She wiped her hands on her thighs. She was good at many things, but sitting back and waiting for an outcome wasn't one of them.

"I need you to take the wheel," Kane said.

Her heart lurched into overdrive. "What?" A tightrope was one thing, but driving in a high-speed pursuit? That was out of her realm of experience.

"Just keep it on the road," he said. Unbuckling his seat belt, he reached over to do the same to hers. "And don't hit anyone."

Her mouth went dry, but he was halfway out of the bucket seat.

"Come on," he demanded, almost shouting the words.

You can do this. Hands shaking, she wiped them on her legs again, took the wheel, and slid over Kane and onto the seat, her backside nestled against him for a split second before he slid out from beneath her and slipped to the back of the van.

This would be erotic if it weren't for the cops and impending jail time.

The flicker of thought sped through her mind, vanishing just as quickly.

Breathe.

She focused on the task at hand. Ahead of her, the road seemed to stretch for miles, but she knew that was an illusion. At the rate they were going, they'd reach the populated areas in minutes.

When that happened, they were in trouble, because population in L.A. meant traffic jams. She was a decent driver, but she wasn't Kane. His ability to weave in and out of traffic could almost be classified as a super power.

No more cars. No more cars.

The plea went through her mind like a chant or a child's song, but it wasn't enough to keep her growing fear at bay.

Using the rearview mirror, she watched him at the computer console. "Don't let them get too close," he said, his fingers flying over the keyboard. "This will be easier if we can keep distance."

"I'll try." She forced her attention back on the asphalt stretching out in front of her. "What are you doing?"

"Don't worry about it. Just watch the road."

She managed a quick glance at him. He was smiling.

Smiling?

They crested a small hill, and ahead of them, perhaps a half-mile away, she spotted the green glow of a traffic light. To the sides—low beams of cars glimmered. Her stomach did a full somersault and possibly a cartwheel. "Whatever it is you're doing, you should hurry," she said. "We're running out of road."

"On it," he said. Slipping on a headset, he held up his index finger—the international signal for "be quiet."

"Assistance is on the way," he said, his voice echoing over the police scanner. He lowered his finger. "That should help."

He hacked the cops' radio signal? Impressive, except she was less than thirty seconds away from getting them both killed. The light turned red.

Two hundred feet.

"What do I do?" Her voice trembled. Should she stop? Run it?

"Keep going."

One hundred feet.

She swerved around another car, and whatever moisture that was left in her mouth evaporated.

Fifty feet. She gripped the wheel, forcing her foot to remain on the accelerator. The light turned green seconds before she blazed through the intersection.

There seemed to be cars everywhere. And roads. And decisions that she wasn't prepared to make while driving a one-ton vehicle. "What do I do?" she asked, wishing she were home. When it came down to it, being shot out of a cannon was a hell of a lot easier than trying to navigate L.A. traffic at high speeds.

"Just go straight," he said.

She swerved around a Mercedes and glanced in the mirror. The green light was now red. The police car slowed down, beacons flashing as people scrambled to get their cars out of the way. Another traffic light ahead of them turned green as she grew close. Then red as soon as she was through.

The clacking of the computer keyboard caught her attention. Was Kane making the lights change?

"Take the next right," he said, typing like their lives depended on it.

She slowed as much as she dared and took the turn, praying they didn't flip. They made it, but there was more traffic, and she had to either slow down or start hitting cars.

"You're doing great. Take the next left. Then turn off your lights but don't stop." He turned on the headset. "They're heading east on Beachwood. Will intercept at Scenic."

Beachwood. The road they had left two turns ago.

"Don't slow," he snapped.

"Sorry." She hadn't realized she had taken her foot off

the gas.

"We need to get lost. And fast." Then he was at her side. "Turn here." He pointed toward a winding road, and for the next ten minutes, she followed his directions as he took her through the Hollywood hills and to safety.

• • •

Holly tossed the backpack with the photos and the flash drives on Temperance Smith's desk.

It was almost midnight, but the V.P. of HRS had waited up for them. The company was her life, and she treated all operations—no matter how small—as if they were the most important op in the world.

Tempe unzipped the pack's compartment and dumped the contents onto her desk. At the top of the pile lay a picture of their client and her daughter during bath time—the toddler almost lost in a sea of bubbles. They had the same dark brown curls. The same smiles.

Marriages ended. Things went wrong. But how did they go this wrong? Holly wondered.

"This all of them?" Tempe asked.

"Unless he stashed more elsewhere, yes," Holly replied. "If so, I'd be happy to go back and get them on my own time."

Kane cocked his head, catching her attention. He stood at the window, his gaze on the city below them. To the casual observer, he might appear disinterested in the conversation, but the slight movement combined with the tense muscles in his broad shoulders told her otherwise.

"Same here," he said, confirming her observation.

Tempe gave a solemn nod. "Understood."

"Thanks," Holly said, ready to go home and sleep. With the clock hands pointing at midnight, it was later than she liked, and she wanted to get to the gym in the morning. HRS had a new hand-to-hand instructor, and she'd heard his seven a.m. class was not to be missed.

Besides, it had been a long night.

"A minute," Tempe said. "We need to talk."

Holly stopped mid-step, hesitated, and took a seat. That wasn't something she wanted to hear.

Kane followed suit, his puzzled expression a reflection of her own confusion. "Is there a problem?"

"How did it go tonight?" Tempe asked, her expression unreadable.

Holly glanced at Kane. Did Tempe know about their encounter with the police? She fought the urge to fidget. She could lie, or keep a secret, under most circumstances, but dealing with Tempe was different. The V.P. might only be two years older, but she sported the same, penetrating stare as Holly's mother, Madam Sarah.

"Why do you ask?" Kane asked before she could either confess or hide the details of their high-speed pursuit.

"It's been a while since you two worked together, and I wanted to see how that went."

Tempe didn't know about the chase. Holly held her breath. Waiting. Would he tell?

Kane continued, "There was a bit of an altercation with the police, but nothing we couldn't handle."

Of course he would, she exhaled with a little groan of annoyance. He was incapable of lying.

Tempe's eyes widened. "Plates?"

"They didn't get them, but I'd change them anyway. Perhaps a new paint job. If they're motivated, they might pull the traffic cam info."

Tempe's eyes returned to normal, and after a few seconds, she gave a nod of approval. "Anything else?"

"We're professionals," Kane said. "It went well. Holly can be a little hard-headed, and she has issues following directions but otherwise, fine."

"Hardheaded? I'm right here," Holly said.

"I know. I wanted you to hear it."

Jerk. She'd rather work with Tempe than deal with Kane and his inability to do anything besides follow the plan to the letter. It was partners like that—men and woman who couldn't adjust—that made her job harder than it needed to be.

She wasn't going to tell Tempe that and prove Kane right or brand herself a whiner. "Like he said, we're professionals."

"Good," Tempe said with small nod of approval. Uncrossing her arms, she took a glossy, white binder from one of her desk drawers, but instead of handing it over, she placed it in the middle of the table as if daring either of them to try to take it. "You are my two best agents when it comes to recovering stolen property, but the last time I paired you together, you blew it."

Holly's cheeks heated as she remembered the almost-botched job. They'd been going in for files and had barely gotten away. "We recovered the data."

"By dumb luck. It sure wasn't because you functioned as a team."

The heat in Holly's cheeks deepened. She wondered if Kane felt the same shame but didn't dare check.

"So, what was the point of pairing us again?" Kane asked. "To test us?"

"Exactly," Tempe said. "You passed. I've always thought you two would be a good match in the field and was disappointed last time. I'd hoped things had changed, and it seems I was right."

Weren't they past being tested? Holly snuck a look at Kane. His face was almost as unreadable as Tempe's, but the set to his jaw told her that anger boiled beneath the cool exterior.

She couldn't blame him.

What was done was done, and Tempe never did anything without a reason.

That reason was in the binder Tempe had just taken out of her desk.

"I take it that's our prize for succeeding?" Holly asked. Whatever the notebook contained, it had to be special for Tempe to go to all this trouble of setting up her and Kane.

"It is," Tempe replied.

"Did you call the guard?" Kane asked, apparently still stuck on the news that they'd been subjected to a test. "Get him to make his rounds earlier?"

"I did. Sorry about the pursuit, but I thought you'd get out faster." A small, unexpected smile flitted across Tempe's face. "No harm, no foul."

She'd done it on purpose?

Tempe nodded toward Kane. "I'm surprised you figured that out before Holly. I think I underestimated you."

Holly's brows arched in surprise. Was Tempe saying he was as good as she? An onsite test was annoying but tolerable. But to say that Kane was her equal at reading people?

Unacceptable. She was trained by the best—her mother.

In the long run, being the circus' second psychic wasn't her calling, and her mother had understood. The rest of the family hadn't been as forgiving, but eventually, they'd accepted her decision to leave. Of course, that she sent them money every month didn't hurt. It was hard to stay mad at someone who took care of those she loved.

"Glad you trusted us to manage, but I don't like being set up," Kane said, rising partway out of the chair.

Holly's eyes widened in shock. She'd stood up to Tempe on more than one occasion, but she'd never said anything so brash. The V.P.'s expression morphed into annoyance, and she tapped the binder with her index finger. "I don't ask your permission. Now, do you want to move on or argue?"

Kane hesitated then sat. "What's the assignment?"

She slid the notebook across the table to Kane. "Open it."

He flipped it open but left it flat on the desk so Holly could lean in and read the contents.

There was the usual contract. This time, the client was a woman named Mira Burke, from Savannah, Georgia.

"Tim Burke's ex-wife?" Kane asked.

He knew them? Kane was one surprise after another.

"Yes," Tempe replied. "Do you think they'll recognize you?"

"If they recognized anyone, it would be my father. Not me. Besides, it's a different social circle. The Burkes are politicians. My family was religious. They're close, since one tends to support the other, but not that close."

Holly's interested piqued. She'd discovered more about Kane in the last ten seconds than she'd learned in two years.

He was closed-mouthed about everything, which was why he worked the ground-control portion of his assignments. To play a part took skills he didn't possess. Like acting. Being both open and impenetrable at any given time.

Kane was only impenetrable. A fortress of a man with no discernable emotions.

"Good," Tempe said. Holly flipped the page. There was a color picture of a necklace. A gaudy combination of diamonds and rubies in the shape of a turtle, the pendant seemed more suited to Hollywood and the red carpet. Not on a Southern belle's neck. She didn't bother to ask if this was the item to recover. Why else would it be in the folder?

"It's a family heirloom," Tempe explained. "Mira was supposed to get it in the divorce, but it never arrived. He said it should have."

The usual, petty *he said she said* that seemed to accompany divorce. Holly shook her head. Why did people have to make it so difficult?

Of course, if they didn't, she'd be out of a job, since most of her retrieval gigs centered on high-profile broken marriages. She flipped to the next page. More pictures. A gray-haired but distinguished older man, sporting what was probably a custom tuxedo, had his arm around the waist of a big-haired blonde wearing an emerald-green sequined gown that made her look like a mermaid. His other hand was raised up in triumph.

At first glance, most people might assume the younger woman by his side was his daughter. Holly honed in on the eagerness in his eyes and satisfaction at winning in hers. The way he held her just a bit too close.

"Is this the mistress?"

"That's Tammi Lynn Burke," Tempe said. "She was the other woman and his assistant until he married her a few months ago."

Tim and the new wife had the necklace. There was no way the blonde was letting it go, and if Tim Burke was like every-other politician she'd read about, he'd keep it out of spite.

"What's the new wife say?" Kane asked. "Does she deny having it?"

"Of course," Tempe replied. "He bought a beach house for her right after they married and claimed it was lost in the move. We're fairly sure it's there."

"Do you know where inside the house?" Holly asked.

"No. Which is why you'll need this." She opened her desk drawer, pulled out an envelope, and handed it to Holly. She opened it. Inside was an invitation. Hand-drawn calligraphy. Gilded. Heavy linen paper.

Very chichi, as her mother would say. She opened the invitation and leaned toward Kane so he could read it with her. He smelled like soap, and she took a deep inhalation before she could stop herself.

Get a grip, girl. This is Kane.

She focused her attention on the paper.

Save the Date

For your next Senator, Tim Burke

Summer weekend at Tim's private estate on Hilton Head Island, S.C.

Fishing. Golf. Auction. Dinner.

Requested contribution:

$20,000 Saturday Only

$50,000 (Friday, Saturday, Sunday)

It continued on with contact info, location, and what to wear.

A weekend at a mansion? On the beach?

Holly's feet almost danced at the idea. Now, that sounded like fun. Of course, her black cat suit would be not be considered proper attire with this crowd unless they were into that sort of thing.

Unlikely.

"I'll need some new clothes," she said, trying to keep the excitement from her voice.

"I take it we're going as a couple?" Kane asked.

Her excitement ebbed as he brought her back to reality. This wasn't a weekend gig that involved a little larceny. It was a weekend gig with Kane.

Kane the Pain.

He sounded less than thrilled.

"Not you. I need you to run the op," Tempe said. "You'll be Holly's assistant, since it'll give you an excuse to use your computer and question the staff. We're pairing Holly with Michael Bravo."

"Michael?" Holly's heart pounded as she tried to keep the enthusiasm out of her voice. Jet black hair. Blue eyes. He was six-feet three inches of super-hot agent.

They'd worked together before, and it had ended up with them in bed and one of the best nights of sex she'd ever had. She hadn't seen him since, but he'd crossed her mind on more than one occasion.

She'd get to sleep with him again and steal a necklace?

Best job ever.

Except for one thing, or rather, one person.

Kane.

• • •

Michael Bravo? Kane frowned. The man was an ass.

It wasn't his skills. Kane had worked with him more than a few times, and the agent always did as he was told. Never deviated from the plan, and if the situation changed, he spoke to Kane for direction. More of a follower than a leader, Bravo was a helluva lot easier to deal with than Holly.

Away from the field, Michael bragged about his work and used it to get laid. More than one new recruit had ended up in the man's bed, and from the look on Holly's face, he'd bet money she would be next on the list if she hadn't slept with him already. He glanced at her carefully blank expression.

She had.

He didn't know how he knew, but he did, and he wished he didn't. Disappointment washed over him. He'd hoped she was smarter than that.

She caught his stare and scowled in return. Kane didn't care. She was probably mad that he was going to be on the op and ruin her fun.

Let her be angry. This was work. Not a tea party. "The event starts this Friday," he said. "That only gives us twenty-four hours to prep and arrive onsite, and once we're there, we have just three days to find a piece of jewelry with no intelligence on where it might be."

"Doable," Holly said.

If we're lucky. But he didn't contradict her. Not now and not in front of Tempe. He turned his attention back to their boss. "Do you have the cover stories set up?"

"We do," Tempe replied. "It's a rush job, so they're not as deep as I'd like, but this is politics, and nothing is what it seems. I think you'll manage despite the short notice."

She held out a flash drive. "This gives you everything you'll need to know. Names, itineraries, etc."

"Thanks." He pocketed the drive.

"This is for Holly," Tempe said, fishing in the drawer. Pulling out a credit card, she handed the plastic to his partner.

"Clothing?" Holly asked.

"Yes, but no sequins."

"I can do conservative," she insisted.

She could try, Kane mused. But Holly could wear a dress made of burlap and still seem more vibrant than the rest of the world. More alive.

More everything.

"Got something you want to say, *assistant*?" Holly asked.

Was he that obvious? "Just that you might need some help. You could wear a sack, and you'd still stand out."

Tempe rose. "Just be ready. Both of you. The company plane leaves in twenty-four hours. A red-eye into Atlanta." She waved them out.

Kane toyed with the drive in his pocket as he headed for the door. *Awesome.* He hated red-eyes. He slid a glance at the agent beside him. She alternated between bouncing and stalking down the carpeted hallway. Either way, she was as flamboyant as a gilded peacock feather.

"I don't need you telling me what to wear," Holly said once they turned a corner and Tempe's office disappeared from sight.

Kane glanced down at her, "It was a compliment, in case you missed it."

She flushed. "Sorry. That sounded less antagonistic in my head."

She didn't look apologetic, but he'd take her at her word, or they might not make it to the plane, much less run another successful operation. "Don't worry about it," he said. "We're both tired."

"Thanks." She followed him down the hall to the locker room. Because the room was co-ed, his locker wasn't far from hers. She faced her locker as they both stripped out of their work clothes.

"It sounds as if you ran in these circles once upon a time. Can you at least give me a few store names?" she asked, the rustle of cloth catching his attention.

He stopped himself before he shrugged off the question. She was trying to get along. He would do the same. "Just Google 'stupidly expensive stores in L.A.', and you should get a list."

She snickered, and he chuckled. First smile. First shared laugh.

What else would they discover about each other on this op?

"Nothing too Hollywood," he continued. "East coast and old southern money makes style a different beast. You want class. Not flash. Nothing too sparkly. Or low-cut—"

"—I know," Holly cut him off. "I've traveled. A lot."

"I noticed," he replied. "The New England accent earlier was dead on. Can you do Southern?"

"Of course I can, bless your heart," Holly said with an accent so thick it sounded as if she grew up south of the Mason-Dixon Line.

Silence reigned as they continued to strip out of their

work clothes. Sitting in the van always left him stiff. Wearing nothing but his boxer-briefs, Kane stretched, arms overhead. That helped, but a sauna would have been better.

With a groan, he reached for his shirt, and glancing in the mirror he kept on the shelf in his locker, he saw Holly watching him. Her eyes were on his calves, then his thighs. She hesitated, and he knew what she was staring at—

The scar that traveled up his left thigh, ending on his hip bone and out of her sight. Thick and ugly, it was impossible to overlook.

Ignore her, his smarter inner voice said. *Get dressed*. He remained frozen, unable to take his eyes off her as her gaze traveled up his body.

She reached his shoulder. Then a few more inches. Their eyes met in the mirror.

The heat rushing to her face was immediate and visible. She whirled away. "Sorry," she muttered. "I saw the scar and wondered…"

Of course, it was always about the scar. It was the first thing most women wanted to talk about, and they all fantasized that he got it by doing something heroic. Maybe shark wrestling to save a seal pup. Climbing the metaphorical castle to rescue a damsel in distress. Whatever they thought, it all came down to a singular courageous act.

But it wasn't a badge of honor. It was a mark of failure.

He looked away as his thoughts turned to his ex-partner and lover, Danielle, and how he couldn't save her.

"There are worse things that happen when you fail a mission than pissing off your boss."

Chapter Three

"That's not a house. That's a hotel," Holly said as their town car came to a stop in front of a three-story, white and yellow beachfront home that could board her entire big-top family, plus a few more.

"Seventeen bathrooms. Sixteen bedrooms. Almost seventeen thousand square feet," he said, giving her the stats as he held the door open for her.

She hesitated. This was sheer opulence, and even though she was dressed to impress in tan linen slacks, a cream-colored silk blouse and understated gold hoop earrings, she felt as if she should have worn something better. Nicer. Perhaps diamonds.

No chance of that. Not now.

She and Kane had arrived at the Savannah airport minus Bravo—he was flying in later from New York where he'd completed a job two hours ago. Kane had insisted on talking shop while he drove to their destination. She'd given him half an ear and scoped out the area as it sped by, making note of the small bridge that separated the island from the mainland.

Easy to run if needed.

Otherwise, it was a golfer's paradise. Bike paths paralleled the road. They even passed an organic farmer's market, with Mercedes and BMWs parked in the adjoining lot. When golfing greens disappeared, cypress trees, marsh grasses, and an array of flowers—both manicured and wild—took their place.

They reached the driveway—gated to keep out the riff raff—and presented the guard their invitation. He gave them a bit of side-eye, and she assumed it was because they were late—the plane had been delayed in Houston. But she didn't apologize or offer explanation, since she was playing the part of a woman too wealthy to care what the staff thought.

He waved them through, and the house came into view. Now, here she stood. Staring like a yokel.

"Are you getting out or do you plan to sit and gawk all morning?" Kane asked.

Heat rushed to her face, and Holly swung her feet to the pavement, being careful not to scuff the patent leather of her tan pumps. Kane held out his hand. She hesitated. How did he appear so crisp after a red-eye flight combined with the long drive from the airport? Both his pressed white shirt and gray slacks were still wrinkle free. He could walk into any meeting in the world, and no one would think he'd been awake since midnight.

Neat trick.

He gave an almost imperceptible shake of his head, breaking her concentration. "Take it. I'm your assistant, so let me assist."

The warmth of his skin penetrated hers as he helped her to her feet.

"Thank you."

"Of course," he replied, his voice low.

Two men dressed in matching navy blue jackets and tan khakis trotted down the stairs, took the keys from Kane, opened the trunk, and proceeded to empty it of luggage.

Holly hoped she appeared less uncomfortable than she felt. She'd played a lot of parts in her time at HRS, but this was new. She wasn't used to affluence and felt more out of place than normal.

It didn't help there were no other cars in view. No people. No nothing.

It doesn't matter, her inner voice scolded. *It's a show, like anything else, and the show must go on.* "Looks like we're not the only ones running late," she said, in her best southern drawl. "Are you sure we're at the right place?"

"According to the GPS, yes. Then again, it's been known to send me to a trailer park when I wanted a steak house."

Was that a joke? It was hard to tell, since he didn't smile. If he were kidding, he was the best straight man she'd even seen. "Good enough," she replied. "Though, I hate being late to the party." It was easier to blend when she didn't have to make an entrance in a crowded room.

"Don't worry about it. We'll find them later. In the meantime, we can finish going over the plans," Kane said, following the attendants as they hauled the luggage up the stairs.

He seemed to be in full it's-about-the-job-and-nothing-else mode, so not a joke. Maybe later, when Bravo arrived, she could spend some time with him instead. Anyone was more interesting than Kane. Still, she kept in character and offered him a small, indifferent shrug as a reply as she scaled the stairs into the foyer, letting Kane open the door for her.

"Wow," she whispered, the word loud enough for only herself and Kane to hear. A giant crystal vase, bursting with orchids, was the focal point in the middle of the vast foyer. Marble floors led to a wide staircase that wound its way upward.

"Close your mouth," Kane said, his mouth barely moving. "You're gawking again."

She snapped her jaw tight as a petite woman in a conservative blue jacket and tan skirt, not unlike the valets, walked toward them, a clipboard in her hand. "Hello, you must be…"

"Kane Buchanan. This is Holly Kennedy."

She shook their hands. Her grip firm. "Welcome to Mr. Burke's home. We're so glad you could join us. I'm Mary Beth. I'll be assisting the host and hostess this weekend."

Another woman wearing the same suit trotted up and whispered something into Mary Beth's ear. Panic washed over perfect, petite features before disappearing almost as fast. "I hate to be rude, but we're just cleaning up after lunch and—"

"Not at all. We're late," Kane said, cutting her off with a wave of his hand.

"You're not the only one, trust me," she said with a quick nod of thanks as she handed him an envelope. "Keys to your room, and the itinerary for the weekend. The rest of the guests are at the marina, having cocktails before sailing. The path is on the far side of the house."

She turned on her heel and disappeared down the

hallway, her pace quickening until it was almost a trot.

"Shouldn't I be the one talking?" Holly asked.

"I'm the assistant," Kane countered. "You look pretty and act dumb."

"I can't believe you said that." That had to be a joke. Right? She glared at him, but his deadpan delivery gave nothing away.

"Your mouth is open again. You might want to watch that," he replied.

She cocked her head, staring. Not sure if she should be laughing or holding back from giving him a smack. "If you're joking, you should give me a sign. Blink. Wink. Something."

He did neither. Holly snatched the envelope out of his hands and pushed past him.

Ass.

• • •

Did she think he was serious? Kane watched Holly stomp up the stairs to the second floor, wondering how someone who was so amazing at reading people couldn't see humor when it was right in front of them. Hell, he'd thought she was joking when she told him to give a sign that he was kidding.

With a sigh, he followed her, wondering what else was going to go catawampus. He was good at reading people, but something about her made assessments more difficult— sometimes impossible. But her ability to hide her true motivations also made her great at her job, he realized. Why she could do what she did with such ease.

The flex of her thighs beneath her slacks caught his attention. She was graceful as hell, he thought, watching her climb the stairs ahead of him then saunter down the hall. A mysterious combination of silk and steel that made him curious to learn more.

"It looks like this is my room," Holly said, interrupting his thoughts. She had stopped at an oversize oak door.

Kane gave a tight nod, grateful for the interruption. Best to not think of Holly in any way erotic. It was only inviting trouble. Besides, she had her sights set on the idiot man-child due to arrive this afternoon, which told him more about her than any file.

"Where's my key?" he asked.

She upended the envelope, and a piece of paper fluttered to the floor but nothing else. He picked it up. It was their itinerary for the weekend.

"Don't know. Don't care," she said, opening the door.

He followed her in. If she wanted to be difficult and surly, let her. It seemed to be how their relationship functioned.

The room was as stunning as the rest of the mansion. Decorated in varying shades of turquoise and sand-colored accents, the ambiance screamed "beach." A queen-sized white wicker bed dominated the room, and white sheer curtains billowed as a breeze blew in from the partially opened French doors.

Next to the bed was their luggage and an unopened bottle of Cristal.

"What are you doing?" she asked.

He took a seat in a small sitting area in the corner. "What do you think?"

"Like you're making yourself comfortable in my room."

He tapped his nose with his forefinger. "*Ding. Ding. Ding*," he quipped, pointing at her even though his inner voice told him that teasing her was the wrong thing to do. She was already pissy—probably because Bravo hadn't arrived—and seemed to have left her sense of humor in L.A.

She glared at him. "Go ask Mary Beth for a key. You're my assistant. It isn't appropriate for you to stay here."

"It's entirely appropriate," he replied. "What would be worse would be to draw attention to myself while the staff is busy. Give it a few minutes, and I'll go hunt her down so you can untwist your knickers."

"How about searching the other rooms? Sounds like most of the guests are gone."

If only he could be sure. "Tempting, but some haven't arrived. Plus, we don't know the staff's routine. Let's take a few hours and then we can make an actual plan. One that won't get us busted."

Her lips pressed tight.

He mirrored her expression, exaggerating it in an effort to jolly her out of her bad mood, but her mouth remained scrunched and pissed.

Dammit but she was cute when she was angry. He ducked his face to hide a grin then rose. Time to make peace.

Striding over to the champagne, he tore off the packaging and untwisted the wire that held the cork down. "I'll pour you a drink and you can relax on the balcony. I'm your assistant. I'll unpack."

"Really? Or are you messing with me?"

The cork shot out of the bottle. Quickly, he poured a glass and held it out, giving her a wink at the same time. "Really."

Her shoulders relaxed, and a small smile turned the corners of her mouth upward. "Okay. Thanks," she said, taking the drink. Her fingers brushed against his, and his breath caught in his throat at her touch. For a flicker, he wished he wasn't running the action but was in the middle of it.

Champagne in hand, she strolled out through the French doors. He could see her through the sheers, leaning against the railing. Sexy in an understated way and looking every-inch the wealthy debutante.

He tossed a suitcase onto the bed and opened it. Her clothes were folded into neat stacks. Shirts. Skirts. Panties. Even her bras. He picked one up. Lavender satin with lace edging. Of course.

What would she look like wearing it?

The visual made him catch his breath, and he dropped the tiny piece of lingerie back in the suitcase with a reminder that this was work. Only work. "I didn't think you could be this organized," he said, more to himself than to Holly, as he tried to refocus his thoughts on the op.

There was no reply. He went out to the balcony and saw that it extended past their room, running the length of the back of the building and wrapping around to the sides of the house, allowing all the rooms access.

Holly was nowhere in sight.

Frustrated, he ran a hand through his hair as the reason he needed to stay focused became clear—she never did as she was told. Someone had to keep her on target.

That someone was him.

. . .

Holly walked the length of the verandah, taking a quick glance into any rooms with open curtains. Whoever designed the walkway must have had thieves in mind, she mused.

The creak of a door, subtle and almost lost in the sound of the wind through the trees, made her ears perk up. Out of habit, she pressed herself against the house. A woman giggled.

She knew that laugh. Someone was doing something they shouldn't. Setting her champagne glass in the dirt of a potted bougainvillea, she stayed low and peeked around the corner.

Tammi Lynn. She recognized her from the picture.

Their hostess stood in one of the doorways that opened on to the balcony, kissing a man who was not her husband. His hand ran up her thigh, hiking up her dress.

She wasn't wearing panties.

She slapped his hand and giggled again.

Holly sunk back into the shadow of the house, picking up her glass as she rose and waiting to see which way their hostess would leave. The wooden planks vibrated with movement, and Holly stepped around the corner to see them descending a set of stairs at the far end where the balcony met the front of the house.

Holly hurried toward the room they'd left. There was no time like the present to start work. If she were lucky, she'd find the necklace and could spend the rest of the weekend enjoying herself with Bravo.

She tried the knob. Unlocked. *Perfect.* She slipped inside.

"What the hell are you doing in here?"

Holly whirled around. Kane stood in the doorway to the balcony, one hand on the doorknob and the other clenched at his side.

"My job," she replied, flipping back the edge of a rug to

see if the Burkes had installed a safe underneath. Nothing but an expensive cherry wood floor.

He glanced around and then entered, shutting the French doors behind him. "If you're caught here, you'll blow our cover."

"Then *we* better not get caught," she said. "Unless you want to leave and let me get on with my work."

"What I want is for you to stick to the plan. Let me do my job. I will find the safe. I don't need you sneaking into random rooms and taking unnecessary risks."

If I stuck to every plan given to me, I'd be the worst thief ever.

With all the players and political intrigue in play at the party, she'd bet dollars to donkeys that this weekend was going to require agents who could improvise—her specialty.

Even if it didn't, a little bending of the rules wouldn't hurt, and being an alarmist only took away from the thrill. "Your way takes too long," she muttered, lifting the corner of a frame from the wall.

Nothing. Again.

"My way is why I'm in charge," Kane whispered.

"Why are you whispering?" Holly asked. "No one can hear us. They're all downstairs."

He straightened. "Oh."

He looked guilty as sin. He wasn't lying when he said acting wasn't his forte. She checked another picture to see if it covered the safe.

Still nothing. She let go of the picture, and the frame hit the wall with a dull thud.

"I told you. Let me do this," he said. "It'll be faster and a helluva lot safer."

She hesitated.

"The safe is probably in either the office or a master suite," Kane continued. "And this room is neither of those things."

"It is," she assured him. "Our hostess just left it, and she wasn't just checking up on the maid."

"That doesn't mean anything," he replied.

Did she have to spell-everything out? "She was hooking up. With a guest."

"I don't care. You're putting this mission in jeopardy."

Control freak. "You don't know that this isn't her room. Look at it. It's enormous." She twirled in a slow circle, arms outstretched. "Entire families live in houses with less square footage."

"It's not," Kane insisted. "The master suite is above our room, which you would know if you'd listened to me in the car."

Her cheeks warmed at being corrected. "Well, she still came out of here, so you might be wrong," she countered, but the argument sounded weak.

"Are you doing this to impress Bravo?" Kane asked. "To show him what an awesome thief you are?"

With a click, he locked the French door and strode across the floor to confront her on the other side of the four-poster bed. "Are you hoping that if you can get this done, you'll get to spend the weekend having fun?"

The heat was slow this time. It began in the pit of her stomach, working its way up her chest, then neck, and settled in her face.

"He's an ass, Holly."

She flashed back to yesterday when Tempe said Kane

was as good at reading people and intent. She'd have to re-member that. She did not need Kane prying into her private thoughts. Not now. Not ever. "There's no need to make ac-cusations. Let's leave."

He opened his mouth as if to reply, then snapped it shut. Good.

She shoved past him when voices in the hallway caught her attention, and she paused mid-step. The voices drew nearer and stopped in front of the door to the room.

Then there was the sound of metal on metal—a key in the lock.

"Crap," Kane whispered.

Her heart beat harder. She and Kane simultaneously sprinted for the balcony door. She grabbed the handle and turned. It jammed. "Dammit."

"Turn the bolt," Kane said, trying to reach past her scrambling hands to do so.

The lock to the main door clicked, and they were seconds from being caught. Her mind spun, seeking a reason that they might be in a locked room that wasn't theirs. Only one idea came to mind.

"Follow my lead," she said as she pushed Kane onto the bed. Landing on top, she kissed him.

He stiffened, then melted into the kiss. His mouth was hot. Eager. She found herself opening her lips, letting him taste her. He wound his hands through her hair, messing her braid.

She shivered at his touch as he rolled her over until he was on top, pinning her down with his weight and his kiss.

"Excuse me?" a quiet, feminine voice asked. "Excuse me?"

Holly stopped mid-kiss. Kane looked at her in surprise,

and she wondered if she sported the same startled expression.

"Excuse me," the voice said for a third time. "I think this is my room."

"Let me handle this," she whispered. "I'm the better liar."

He gave a quick nod then moved so Holly could sit up. She smoothed her hair. A young woman stood in the door. About her age. Dark hair. Doe eyes. A blue sundress and sandals.

Holly flashed a sheepish smile. Kane rose, offering her a hand as she stood.

Quite the gentleman.

"Excuse me?" Holly replied. "Are you sure? I think it's ours."

"Positive," she replied. "See, here's my luggage."

Holly took a step back, making sure to widen her eyes. "I am so sorry. We were in the car all day and just thought—"

"No need. I understand." The girl gazed at Kane as if he was chocolate, and she hadn't eaten in hours.

"Thank you," Kane said, sounding as mortified as he appeared.

Holly giggled, acting like the silly girl she'd never had the chance to be growing up.

The dark-haired girl held out her hand. "I'm Elizabeth Bowler."

"Holly Kennedy."

Elizabeth's eyes widened, and Holly giggled again. "Not those Kennedys."

"Of course." Elizabeth focused her attention on Kane again, appraising him and, from the gleam in her eyes, liking what she saw.

Smile plastered to her face, Holly hesitated to introduce

him. She sure as hell couldn't say he was her assistant. Not now. If she did, then all eyes would be on her this weekend, and she'd never get a chance to retrieve the necklace.

There was only one reasonable reply, and knowing she'd brought this chain of events on herself tasted as bitter as a pill.

Despite the anger, she let the smile reach her eyes. "This is my fiancé, Kane."

Dammit.

Chapter Four

"What were you thinking?" Kane said. "You never listen, Holly. Never. Frankly, it's getting old."

Holly walked down the path to the marina, wishing she could steal away from her "fiancé," but she was stuck. After they'd retreated from Elizabeth's room to their own, they'd changed their clothes in silence, with Holly taking refuge in the spa-like bathroom. Five minutes later, she emerged wearing a pair of cream-colored linen walking shorts, periwinkle T-shirt, and white sneakers. Kane stood by the door, dressed in khaki slacks, a green and white rugby shirt, and deck shoes.

He didn't say a word. Just opened the door and escorted her outside and to the path that led to the marina. It wasn't until they were clear of the house that the current scolding had begun.

A scolding she deserved. As much as she hated to admit it, she should have listened to Kane—at least this time.

Instead, she'd come close to botching the mission, and worse, she was now stuck with Kane as her fiancé—not that she planned to tell him that she was disappointed in the latter.

She was already in enough trouble.

Holly plucked a gardenia as they passed the glossy-leafed bush and put the fragrant petals to her nose. Under better circumstances, she'd stroll through the lush landscape and take in the scents and sights.

These were not those circumstances.

Scattering the petals on the path, she picked up the pace, trying to outrun both Kane and her embarrassment, but Kane matched her speed, and her embarrassment only grew with each passing moment.

"Are you going to answer me?" Kane asked. "Or do you want to ignore the problem you created?"

Ignore, please. She slowed. She wasn't getting out of this conversation, even if she broke into a sprint. "I'm sorry. Okay?" she replied, telling herself that despite the change in plans, she'd done a good job covering for her mistake.

Liar.

He snorted in what she assumed was disgust.

Leave it to Kane to not let her off easy. Steeling herself, she raised her eyes and met his hard gaze. His gray eyes were the color of flint, as if reflecting his mood. "I was wrong," she admitted. "I should have done as you asked and left as soon as you told me to. I didn't listen and nearly botched the mission."

Kane slowed mid-step and then came to a halt. His brows furrowed together, and his lips were pressed tight. Still angry, but she also saw a bit of surprise in his eyes.

He couldn't hide his emotions, she realized. Everything

showed on his face. *Everything*.

"Thanks for admitting it," he replied. "And you didn't botch the mission. There's a change in plans, but it's still a go."

"That's sweet, but notice I said *nearly*."

He chuckled. "So you did."

She glanced at him. He seemed sincere. She smiled, the knot in her stomach loosening but not disappearing. She and Kane might be fine—for now—but there was still the matter of their cover. "Now, the question is, how do we fix this?"

Voices sounded on the path behind them, and she glanced over her shoulder to see a group of four coming toward them. Kane aimed her down a side path that ended in a small sitting area bordered with jasmine, gardenia, and roses.

"We don't fix this," Kane replied once the others passed them and were out of earshot. "We play this as is. Bravo will be our assistant. You and I are engaged."

"They know myself and Bravo as the couple," she said, regretting her actions. Sure, she'd screwed up by calling Kane her fiancé, but only one person knew about it. That didn't mean they both had to suffer for an entire weekend. He was the brains, not an actor. To have him play the part of the man she loved was going to tax them both.

She looked him up and down. He might be easy on the eyes, but he'd have to act like she mattered to him, and she didn't see that happening.

"If anyone mentions it, we'll laugh it off as a screw-up," Kane assured her. "Better that than the rumor mill whispering that you're a cheater. You'd draw too much attention."

The knot tightened. She could try to lie to herself, but he was right. She sighed and took a seat on a worn, marble bench, mentally kicking herself. "Agreed" she said with a tight nod.

Kane sat next to her, hands on his knees and oblivious to her remorse. "Think you can convince them of that? That someone made a mistake?"

She could convince them the moon was made of cheese if needed. "Of course. The question is, can you?" she asked. She tucked her foot under her knee so she could face him. "I hate to say it, but you're not a good actor."

He sighed. "I know." Now he was the one looking disappointed. She'd screwed up the op for both of them, she realized. He wanted to play her fiancé about as much as she wanted him to.

Why didn't he want her?

It was one thing for *her* to not want to pose as his lover, but she didn't like getting the same from him. She crossed her arms, surprised at the sudden heat rushing through her body. "You can't lie. You suck at it," she said, the words harsher than she'd meant them to sound.

He didn't seem to notice. "Which is why I will be relying on you to help me. Carry the conversation. Step in if you see me struggling."

Great. "Think you'll struggle?"

"Let's hope not. The operation is already in jeopardy."

And it was her fault. She uncrossed her arms. "Stick to the truth as much as possible. It helps. Plus, it's easier to remember."

"Thanks," he smiled at her, and for a brief beat, she believed the caring and energy behind the grin. He continued, "I know you don't want to do this. Neither do I, but we'll get through it."

He didn't want to do this?

The simmering anger flared again. Why did it matter what he thought of her?

She knew the answer even as she asked herself the question.

Her past. The years of travel and being home-schooled. When she was twelve, the troop had taken a two-month hiatus, and she'd asked to attend "real school." Her mother hadn't liked it but had finally agreed.

It had been awful. She didn't fit in. Her clothes were wrong. Her speech wrong. She didn't have a dad—and it wasn't because of divorce. That would be normal. It was because he was dead. Died when she was a toddler and his magic act went horribly wrong—the breakaway handcuffs didn't break. So instead of escaping the "Box of Doom," also known as a small water tank, he drowned, breaking her mother's heart and leaving her with only vague memories of a man who used to make her laugh.

When their troop had left the area, it had been a relief. It wasn't until high school that she'd tried again, but this time she played it smart. She watched the popular clique. Dressed like they did. Copied their mannerisms.

As ashamed as she was to admit it—she'd even teased the same people they did.

Teased people like her. *The real her.*

It wasn't long before she'd become cool. Girls wanted to be her. Boys wanted to date her.

Of course, that was until they met her family and realized she was a freak who hadn't fallen far from the freak tree.

But the stratagem she'd used in high school had been the beginning of her true calling.

Now, here she was, annoyed that Kane wasn't falling over his feet like a high schooler. That he didn't admire her. Her animosity was illogical. Foolish.

And it wasn't going away.

God help her, she wanted Kane to like her.

• • •

Holly stared at him like he'd grown horns, and he had no idea why.

What he did know was that her blue-eyed stare was unnerving as hell.

He retrieved his phone, hiding his confusion. It had taken him this long to get the upper hand on Holly Milano, and he had no plans to lose it anytime soon.

If she glimpsed an inkling of sympathy, she'd use it against him.

"Calling Bravo?" she asked.

"Texting. He's in the air." Which was a blessing—he wasn't in the mood to go over details.

"What are you going to say? That I'm an idiot?" she asked with a forced laugh at the end.

Holly worried about what Bravo thought? He'd been hoping she was better than that. "I'm telling him there was a change in plans. That he's the assistant and to please read that section of the mission op. And that we'll see him later."

"Oh. Thanks."

Kane paused in typing. "Do you think I'd tell Bravo that this was your fault?"

She took a step back. "No, of course not."

"Good." He hit send and rose. Too much alone time

wasn't a good thing when it came to him and Holly. It only seemed to lead to disagreements and misunderstanding.

She hesitated. "What about Tempe?"

"What about her?" he asked, already knowing what Holly was going to say—because it was what he was thinking.

"Are you going to tell her what happened? Not telling Bravo is one thing, but leaving Tempe out of the loop is," she hesitated, "unwise."

Bingo.

He knew the answer—he should.

But he didn't want to. It wasn't that he was going to be alone with Holly on a nightly basis, though he had no illusion that being in her bed and not touching her was going to be easy. Holly was a beautiful, adventurous woman, and the very male part of him wondered if that translated in the bedroom.

That frustration he could handle.

What he doubted was his ability to play the part of her fiancé. The affection. The kissing. Acting as if the engagement was real.

He wasn't the actor she and Bravo were.

They all knew it, and no one more so than Tempe. She'd abort the mission, and that would be a first.

A mark on his record he'd rather avoid. "All Tempe wants is for us to complete the mission. How we accomplish that is my job."

"She said—"

"I know what she said, but since when did you do as you were told?" he replied.

"Now you *want* me to break the rules?"

"Just try not to screw up again," he replied, smiling so

she would know he was joking.

She gave him a wary look.

He stuck his hand out. "Deal?"

Her eyes locked with his, and she took his hand in hers. "Deal." Her palms were calloused, and her fingers strong as they wrapped around his. He imagined she gave one helluva massage when she was inclined.

He shut down that train of thought as they shook on the agreement.

He let her go, not sure if he should believe that she'd live by the bargain, but it was a start. Besides, he had his own issues to deal with—like wanting to kiss his partner and wondering how he was going to keep his hands off of her when they were alone in the bedroom.

This weekend was going to be torture, he realized.

"You know, in hindsight, this might work out for the best," Holly said.

"How so?" he asked, grasping at the change in topic like a man grasped a life preserver.

"If he gets here while everyone is still sailing, Bravo can start asking questions, and he might even have the opportunity to case the house, since most of the people will be gone," she said.

Kane took out his phone and texted the other agent the plan as they walked toward the marina.

The path ended at a boardwalk, and beyond that was a wide wooden pier with rows of sailboats moored on each side. Near the entrance, a group of people milled about a small tiki bar.

He spotted Elizabeth in the crowd. "Those must be the other guests."

He headed toward them, but was stopped short when Holly grabbed his hand. "Can't we sit on the dock and watch?"

"You haven't sailed before, have you?" Kane asked when he noticed her eyes on the boats and not on the crowd.

She shook her head.

He wished he could accommodate her trepidation, but if he and Holly wanted to be part of the crowd, then they had to play by their rules. That didn't include sitting on the sidelines. Besides, the more he sailed, the less he spoke and put the mission in jeopardy.

A win-win for all.

"Don't worry about it," he said, squeezing her hand. "I'll take care of the sailing part."

"I won't be much help," Holly bit her lower lip, drawing his attention.

What would she taste like? The strawberries or the champagne?

Dammit. He wanted her out of his head. "You don't have to be. I know enough to get us from point A to point B. Don't worry about it."

"So, I can shut up and look pretty?"

His head swiveled in her direction, all attention on the beautiful blonde as he prepared himself for a repeat of the earlier fight.

Instead, she smiled at him. Her blue eyes laughing.

Say what you wanted about the best thief at HRS—she didn't hold a grudge.

He found himself grinning back, glad to see the smile on her face and knowing that, for once, he was the one that put it there.

• • •

By the time they arrived at the dock, the party was already breaking up and the people were dispersing to their assigned boats. Another young woman—wearing the household uniform of a tan suit—met them on the dock, shoved a piece of paper in Kane's hand, then ran off to intercept another couple.

"We're on the *Blind Ambition*, slip fourteen," Kane said.

Holly took in the competition as Kane led her to the far end of the small marina. It took less than three beats of her pulse for her to size up the group.

Rich. Bored. Ambitious.

The sum of why most of these people had arrived this weekend. What else were they going to do? Not that she faulted them their motivations. Paying attention to politics was one of the ways the rich stayed rich. Not that she cared. Politics wasn't an interest for her, and from what little she understood, most of the people involved were bigger thieves than she would ever be.

She and Kane found their small vessel and boarded. It wasn't big—twenty feet by her estimate. Maybe twenty-two. There was a small, open cockpit with the wheel and the tiller at the back of the boat. Cushioned, fiberglass benches ran the length of each side, giving her ample room to sit. Opposite the wheel, and on the other side of the cockpit, a set of stairs led to a cabin with a combination seat/bed, dorm-sized refrigerator, cupboards, and little else.

Not that she planned to go down for further investigation. She visualized the boat capsizing—trapping her inside—and shuddered.

She patted the fiberglass bench in the cockpit. Nope. She'd stay right here.

"I'll get us ready to go," Kane said. "Why don't you open up the cooler and make us a couple of drinks?"

He descended the stairs into the berthing area, and it bobbed on the water in reaction to the new weight distribution.

A small squeak of fear slipped out of her throat, and she grabbed the railing. *Get a grip*, she told herself, *or you'll never make it out of the dock. Just stay on the boat. That's all you have to do.*

"I take it you don't sail," a feminine voice asked.

She tore her gaze upward. On the small vessel next to them, a redhead wearing denim shorts, an emerald green bikini top, and an unbuttoned gauzy white shirt sipped something with limes.

"Is it that obvious?" Holly asked with a small, half-frightened laugh.

The redhead's eyes slid down to Holly's death grip on the railing. "Not at all," she lied. "The boats are all rentals, but I'm sure they're sea-worthy."

Rentals? Holly wasn't sure if the redhead was trying to be sympathetic or sarcastic.

Possibly both. Slowly, she unclenched her fingers then shook the blood back into them. "Thanks."

"Not a problem." The redhead toasted her with the now half-empty glass. "I take it you're the engaged couple?"

How would she know that? The hair on the back of Holly's neck rose. "We are. What gave it away?"

"I'm friends with Tammi Lynn," she replied.

Tim Burke's trophy wife.

The redhead continued, "Apparently your fiancé, Bravo, called and paid for a lovely bottle of champagne to be waiting in your room."

Dammit. "Bravo is my assistant," Holly corrected. "That's my fiancé up at the front of the boat, Kane."

The redhead gave a sigh of indifference that Holly knew all too well. She didn't care about Holly or Kane or any of it. Hell, the drink in her hand held more interest for her than Holly ever would.

Insulting but for the best, considering the circumstances. The prickles on Holly's neck calmed. "And you are?" she prompted, refusing to be ignored.

"Rachel and Enzo," the redhead replied, sounding even more bored.

"Hi." An awkward silence fell over them, and Holly bent to open the cooler. Drinks, she reminded herself. Kane had asked for drinks.

"When's the big day?" Rachel asked.

"April first," Holly replied. If she ever did get married, that was the date she wanted. Had always wanted.

"April Fool's Day? I have to ask, why?" The corners of her mouth curled up in a small sneer.

"Weddings can be so serious, don't you think?" Kane answered for her, coming up the cabin stairs to the cockpit. "All giant dresses and tuxedos. We thought it would be more fun to have a bit of a laugh. You know—finding a giant plastic ring in my pocket instead of her diamond."

Holly took his hand and squeezed, grateful for the rescue. "It might even light up," she added.

"To each their own, I suppose." Rachel tipped her glass and finished the last of her drink. "Enzo and I were married in France at a vineyard."

Holly mirrored back the sigh of indifference Rachel had given her earlier.

"Enzo?" Kane asked.

Holly stiffened, catching an undercurrent. Something was wrong. Did he know this man?

"My husband." A man wearing khaki pants and a polo shirt the same green as red's bikini emerged from their cockpit. His thick, black hair was buzzed short, and his deep tan told her he either lived near a beach or used a tanning bed and liked to pretend he did. "Ready to kick some ass, babe?" he asked.

She grinned at Holly, but there was no kindness behind the smile. So, it had been sarcasm earlier—good to know. Rachel was the "mean girl" of the group.

"Morning," Kane said, drawing the man's attention. "We're the competition, Kane and Holly."

"They're getting married on April first," Rachel said in a stage whisper, as if the information were either a secret or something to be ashamed of.

"Competition? Really?" Enzo replied.

Kane took a seat on the built-in bench and opened the cooler. "Just kidding. This is supposed to be a fun weekend." He handed Holly a plastic glass. "Want a Dark-n-Stormy?"

"Sure," she replied, surprised at Kane's calm demeanor. She sensed it wasn't because his acting ability had grown exponentially since they arrived.

It was his knowledge of the boat, she realized, thinking back to Tempe's comments. He knew this life. This was Kane, or an earlier version of him.

"Competition is fun," Enzo replied.

"It can be," Kane said, pouring a combination of ginger beer and dark rum into Holly's glass. "Today, I want to sail and just enjoy it."

Enzo gave a snort of derision. "Planning on coming in last?"

"Not at all. I don't see you as a threat," Kane replied. "So, this isn't a competition."

Holly stared across the cockpit at Kane. Where had that come from?

"Your mouth is open," he said under his breath.

She clamped it shut.

"See you on the water," Enzo said, dragging Rachel down into their cabin.

To conspire, Holly was sure. But unless they controlled the weather, there wasn't much they could do besides be better sailors.

"How good are you?" she asked, taking a sip of her drink. The sweetness of the drink flooded her throat, then went to her head when she swallowed. She'd have to be careful, or she'd fall off the boat.

"Better than him," he replied, nodding at the boat next door.

"You sound sure of that," Holly replied. "From your earlier, sour-puss expression, I take it you know him?"

He leaned closer, elbows on his knees." When I was a teenager, I raced boats for a while, and our paths crossed a few times."

"Any chance either of them will recognize you?"

"No. He took racing a helluva lot more seriously than I did. His focus was on the finish line and berating his crew. Besides, my parents didn't have enough money to appear on his radar of 'people to pay attention to.' I could have had dinner with him and Rachel, and I'd still be nothing more than a blank face. Unless you're 'above them'," he air quoted the phrase, "they won't remember you, nor will they care."

The animosity in his voice didn't shock her, but the pain behind it did. Her stomach churned. What kind of world had he lived in before he landed at HRS? Tempe had alluded to the fact that his family had money, but that tidbit, combined with this encounter, told her little other than he seemed glad he'd left that life behind.

Of course, if it had been occupied by people like Enzo and Rachel, she couldn't blame him.

Her family might be a giant pain in the ass at times, and a little strange, but they loved her and supported her, and they'd never treat her as if she didn't matter.

"Good," she said, taking another generous swig of her drink and suspecting she might need more before the end of the race. "But there's something you're not telling me."

"What makes you say that?"

She shook her head. "I can't put my finger on it, but my gut tells me that there's something else. I never ignore my gut."

He hesitated, then took a gulp of his drink. "Enzo's full name is Raul Enzo Pascua, and his father is a leader in the Unione Corse."

"The what?"

This time, Kane tipped the glass back and finished his drink. "The mob. Or one of them."

The mob? Holly's gut told her that the mob arriving at the same time they were sent to steal the necklace wasn't a coincidence.

So, what had Mira Burke neglected to tell them, and how was the mob involved?

Chapter Five

"Beautiful day to be on the water, isn't it?" Kane asked.

After the revelation about Enzo, they'd both been quiet, and she suspected his train of thought mirrored hers. Still, he didn't say anything, and neither did she. Not yet. She needed time to watch and listen.

And besides, the terror of being on the water—*so much water and who knew what lurked beneath the surface*—got in the way of her normal thought processes.

"It's gorgeous," she replied as she gripped the edge of the bench seat and tried to appear relaxed despite the terror that raced through her every time Kane adjusted a line or the sails flapped. For what she was sure was the hundredth time since they left the dock, she wished she had a lifejacket on. None of the others wore them, and if she wanted to fit in, she needed to suck it up.

Kane seemed oblivious to her fear, and despite her snafu and the encounter with organized crime, this was the happiest she'd ever seen him. Periodically, he closed his eyes and held his face to the sun, oblivious to the fact that the wind had blown his hair into an unrecognizable mess. Almost humming with pleasure, he nudged their rudder into a better position.

Yes, happy. It was unnerving and appealing, and she hated to admit it, but if he had longer hair and a tri-corner hat, he'd be the hottest commander on the water.

"Want to take the tiller?" he asked.

She, on the other hand, would have been the passenger who didn't know jack about the water. Didn't care about the water. And wanted to do nothing more than stay in her cabin and ignore the vast amounts of H_2O surrounding the boat. "No thanks," she said, toasting him with her drink. "I'd probably wreck us."

"On what?" he asked, arms open wide. There were a few small islands off the port side, and the other boats trailed in their wake, but none were within striking distance.

She could see herself managing to hit something anyway. "We might lose."

"Who cares?"

"We might lose to Enzo."

"Good point." He adjusted the tiller. The front sail caught the wind, and the boat sped up, rising on its edge.

Holly squeaked again before she could stop herself.

"You okay?"

She nodded. "I'm fine. I'm fine. Just do what you have to do."

"You're not enjoying this," he said.

What gave it away? Her grim smile, the white knuckles, or the way she squeezed her eyes shut when fear overwhelmed her desire to be brave. "I'm fine," she managed to say.

His right brow rose. "I might believe you if you hadn't said, 'I'm fine' three times."

"Just get us to the buoy and back in one piece."

"Wow. Now that's a ringing endorsement for the joy of sailing," he said, adjusting the tiller so the boat slowed, and the edge fell, sloshing water over the railing and onto them both. "Better?"

"Suit yourself." But she breathed easier. Not that she planned to admit it, because she'd have to confess about her inability to swim.

You. Are. An. Idiot. The voice inside her head told her.

She had to fit in, and she needed Kane to fit in—not watch out for her. She could take care of herself.

Shutting her eyes, she let the warmth of the late afternoon sun seep into her muscles until the tension eased. One more deep breath and she opened them again, ready to work. She looked over Kane's shoulder at the competition trailing behind them. Enzo and Rachel were gaining.

"Can we go any faster?" she asked.

"If you were a sailor—maybe," Kane replied.

"Sorry."

"Don't be. I'm on the water. There's drinks. I have half-decent company—"

"Gee. Thanks."

He continued as if she hadn't spoken—"and I don't have to pretend to be something I'm not. This is as close to perfection as it gets."

"As as you're happy," she said. Enzo was closer now, leaving the other six boats far behind as they caught up to the *Blind Ambition*.

She wished she wasn't scared. She wished she could swim.

Enzo and Rachel came alongside. "You said you could sail," Enzo shouted over the wind.

Kane shrugged as if he didn't have a care on the world, but Holly knew better. No one liked eating crow—especially an HRS agent. His hands tightened on the tiller, making the muscles in his shoulders and neck stand out. It was his eyes that made her gasp. They'd gone to flint again.

Not a commander, she reassessed her earlier opinion. *A pirate.*

But he held both his temper and the lead until Enzo edged closer, his boat inches from theirs.

"What the hell are you doing?" Kane shouted, adjusting the rigging so the boat veered away from the *Glory*.

Enzo followed, eyes narrowed. Rachel sat in the cockpit, her pale skin almost gray.

She was scared, Holly realized. If Rachel was frightened, then Enzo was out of control. "Be careful," she shouted. "He doesn't seem stable. Maybe we should speed up."

"You think?" Kane adjusted the sails again, keeping ahead of the other boat, but barely.

Enzo didn't let up. Gaining an advantage in the breeze, he left them in his wake. Holly let go a sigh of relief. "I thought he was going to be stupid."

"Don't underestimate him."

Despite the heat of the day, a shiver raced through Holly's spine. She stole a glance behind them. The other boats were almost out of sight. "Do you think he'd hurt us? He seems determined to win."

"This a political fundraiser, and he must have an agenda, so I'd like to say no, but still… Coming about," he shouted.

Holly ducked as the boom swung over her head. The main sail reversed direction, snapping when it filled with air again. "What are you doing?"

"Heading back to port. Never underestimate a mobster's ability to be a competitive idiot."

As much as she hated losing, Kane was right. Besides, this wasn't a pleasure trip. This was work, and antagonizing another guest was only going to make them stand out.

As if on cue, the *Glory* came about as well, trailing in their wake but gaining.

"Hang on," Kane said, the boat rising on edge as he spoke.

Holly grabbed the rail as the wind whipped hard and her braid loosened. Strands of her hair beat against her cheeks.

"It's okay. It's okay," she whispered the chant. "Please don't wreck. Please don't wreck."

"Watch out," Kane shouted, but Holly sensed it wasn't directed at her.

She peeked through her lashes to see Enzo on their tail.

"Coming about," Kane shouted. Holly ducked, and the small boat took a sharp tack toward a cluster of small islands they'd spotted earlier. Enzo smirked as they sailed out of his path.

Maybe this was enough. Maybe he'd leave.

Her gut told her otherwise. Kane had challenged him, and someone like Enzo took that as a personal affront that had to be dealt with. The thought no sooner flickered through her mind than their adversary tacked to follow.

"What an ass," Kane said, hands clenching and unclenching.

"What now? Race back?"

He shook his head. "Not with you in the boat. We hide."

Holly watched as the other boat rounded the far side of one of the bigger islands. "I think he's leaving."

"He's not. Hang on." The boat lifted on edge for a third time, and they headed between the small specks of land.

Holly swallowed down the fear that rose in her throat. "Are you insane?" Her fingers ached from gripping the railing. "This is a boat. Not a car."

"I've seen Enzo wreck a boat so he could win. He tried to cut off a competitor, miscalculated, and ended up with his bow in the side of their boat."

"We're not even in the race anymore."

"He won't care. We pissed him off and, to Enzo, that means payback. He won't be happy until he scares the hell out of someone."

"How can anyone get away with this kind of behavior?"

"Money. Power. Take your pick." He pointed at a small island to the left. "I'm not putting you in danger over a race. We need to get ahead of him, and I think we can conceal ourselves over there."

Kane was scared, she realized. He was scared for her.

That frightened her more than Enzo. She'd seen her partner nervous. Annoyed. Pissed. But this was new.

Her mouth went dry, and she started searching for the life jackets. No sign of Enzo as Kane angled the boat toward the small sanctuary.

"Faster. Faster," he muttered under his breath.

She lifted up the top of a plastic crate next to her bench seat. Grease-coated rags. A jumper cable. No lifejacket.

The *Glory* rounded the end of the other island, her main sail open as far as possible—her keel so high that both

Rachel and Enzo sat on the edge of the boat, legs hanging downward into the cockpit.

"Kane!"

"I see them."

They were impossible to miss, since they were on a crash course with *Ambition*.

The *Ambition* jerked as Kane dodged the other vessel.

"Coming about," he shouted over the flap of the sails.

Holly ducked and slid to the other side of the boat, but as their boat cut through the water, there was the sound of splintering and the *Ambition* ground to a halt, tossing Holly to the rear of the cockpit and against Kane.

What the hell? Had they hit something?

A metallic screech cut through the confusion, and with a groan, the mast swayed forward. Backward. Forward again. Holly stared in wide-eyed horrors as it fell toward them.

Before she could scream, Kane picked her up and tossed her into the Atlantic.

• • •

"Holly!" Kane yelled her name as he surfaced, spitting cold ocean water. He'd tossed her overboard as the mast came down, then followed. The last thing he'd seen before he hit the water was Enzo's face. Mouth open and eyes wide in shock.

Kane heard a shout and caught a glimpse of his partner on the other side of the listing boat. She looked panicked, but otherwise, she seemed unhurt. Better pissed and soggy than a concussion from being brained by a steel mast. Out of the corner of his eyes, he caught a final glimpse of Enzo as he sailed away.

He was sure the mobster hadn't meant for them to wreck, but that didn't mean he was going to stay and help. In Enzo's pea-sized brain, that might mean accountability—not something people of his affiliation were known well for.

Heat rose from Kane's core, radiating outward and keeping him warm in the frigid waters. Screw the mission. Once he and Holly were back at the mansion, he was going to kill Enzo if he ever got hold of him.

Holly's shout became a shriek, and he put the need for retribution on hold. He had bigger worries. He rounded the bow and spotted her flailing in the shallow water, gulping saltwater in her panic.

He side-stroked over, his feet touching the bottom on the third pull of his arms through the water. There was rock beneath his feet, and he noticed the abrupt change in the color of the water from a dark blue to lighter blue—indications of a shallow peninsula of the edge of the tiny piece of land.

Well, that explained what happened. They'd hit bottom.

Holly continued to scream and thrash.

Good grief. "Stand up," he shouted, making his way to her side.

Somewhere in her fright, she must have heard him. The thrashing ceased, and she rose, the water coming to her shoulders but no higher. She stared up at him. Blond hair sticking to her skin. Blue shirt floating about her with her eyes wide and wild. Her breath came in small gasps.

"Are you going to live?" he asked.

She took a single, deep breath, and the fright disappeared with a speed that made him wonder if he'd misread her. Before him was the confident partner that he knew and sometimes wanted to strangle.

"What do we do?" she asked. "Can we call for help?"

He shook his head. "No mast. No antenna." He pulled his soaked cell out of his pocket. "Is yours onboard?"

She shook her head. "Back in the room. I didn't want it to get wet. Someone will see us. Right?"

If they'd been on the edge of the island chain and facing the sound, perhaps. That wasn't the case, and there was the issue of them being off course. "Maybe, but it's going to be hard with the sails down."

"I take it Enzo isn't going to let anyone know what happened?"

Enzo? He was an ass, and once they were rescued, Kane planned to beat the crap out of him for putting Holly in danger. "Not today. Tomorrow. Probably."

Any longer and the mission would be over.

Next to them, the boat groaned, listing sideways. Enough talk. Unless he acted fast, they wouldn't have any supplies for the night. He grabbed one of the ropes hanging over the edge. "Get to shore. I'll be there in a minute."

"We can't stay here? The boat's dry."

"See how she's leaning?" he asked, pointing toward the wrecked craft. "She's on the edge of a drop off, with a hole in her hull and filling fast. One wrong move and she'll slide into deeper water. So no."

"I can help," Holly said.

The boat slid toward them, the weight pushing her on the slick rock.

"Shit." He dragged her out of harm's way. "Get. To. Shore."

"No. We're partners."

Now she choose to play with others? Figured. She never listened, but now wasn't the time to argue. "Wait here, and be ready to catch." Using the tangle of sail and rope hanging over the side of the boat, he scaled the craft, landing in the cockpit.

The boat slid again, this time tilting toward the deeper water.

Hurry. Hurry. Hurry.

He did not want to be onboard, or anywhere near her, when she sank. He tossed the remaining food into the small, plastic ice chest. "Heads up," he shouted, tossing it over the rail toward Holly.

There was a splash. "Got it," she yelled.

Making his way down into the already flooding cabin, Kane located the few blankets provided. They were wet.

"Dammit." He jammed them under his arm anyway. With luck, they could start a fire and dry them. The ship slid a few more feet.

Grabbing the first aid and rescue kit from the storage space under the bench seat, he made his way back to the deck. The ship tilted. This time, there was no stopping it. He jumped overboard, landing next to Holly.

"Is that it?" she asked.

"It is. Now go. Go. Go."

The panic in his voice set her in motion, and he followed her as she struggled through the water, the growing suction of the boat lifting her off her feet. He leaned against the current and caught her by the waist before she was swept toward the sinking craft. She didn't argue but kept one hand on the cooler and the other around his neck.

He had to get them out of the water. His focused on the

shore still thirty feet away and pushed forward, not daring to look backward.

Slowly, the water level dropped as he walked. Behind them, the boat gave a final groan and rumble as it sank, expelling the remaining air.

He stopped mid-step, a maelstrom of emotions warred within. Shame at losing the boat. Regret he had let Enzo get to him. Relief that Holly was safe.

"You can put me down now," she said, her voice muffled by his shoulder.

He tightened his hold on her, letting the final emotion win the battle. This was what counted, he reminded himself as the warmth of her skin touched him through the chill of the water.

"Kane?"

"Of course." He set her on her feet.

She released her hold around his neck, but instead of letting go, her hand slid down his arm, and her fingers laced through his.

Hand in hand, they waded to the shore. Once her feet were on dry land, Holly set the cooler down, released her grip, and flopped into the dark sand. Kane took a seat beside her, setting the supplies he'd saved between them. There was nothing around them but water and a few pieces of land that were barely large enough to qualify as islands. No sign of the other sailboats.

From his vantage, the "island" they landed on appeared bigger than the others. Spanish moss hung from a small forest of dogwoods and sugar maples, and a trail of paw prints—raccoon or maybe possum—skirted the edge where water met land.

Not the worst location, but either way he sliced it, they were stranded.

Idiot.

He knew what he had to say. "Sorry I got you into this."

"It's not your fault," Holly said with a shrug.

It didn't work that way. "I'm the captain, so actually, it is."

"It was a race that involved drinking. How were you to know that Enzo took it so seriously?"

No excuse, though he wished it were. "He's a rich boy with no sense of right and wrong. That should have been my first clue. Even if he wasn't, I shouldn't have let him push me into this situation."

"I think you did the right thing," she said, patting his thigh. "If he'd hit us farther out, the boat would have sunk over deeper water, and we wouldn't have had the chance to save anything."

He smiled, glad that she could see the bright side even if it was hard for him to do so. "Thanks," he replied.

"We lived. It's a good day," she said, lowering herself to her elbows, her face pointed toward to the sinking sun.

A good day? What was a bad one in her rose-colored world?

Shaking his head, Kane opened the rescue kit. There wasn't much. Medical supplies. No matches. A thermal blanket.

And under the blanket—a flare gun.

Finally. He held it up like an award.

Holly shot upward. "Yes! How many cartridges?"

He dug inside the kit again. "One."

"Better than nothing," she said. "Let's get out of here."

More than anything, he wanted to get her to safety, but instead, he put the gun and cartridge back in the kit. "We can't. Not yet."

"Why?" she asked, not bothering to hide her disappointment.

Before he thought to stop himself, he pushed a strand of wet hair from her cheek. Her skin was still cool but warming up. "No one will be looking for us for a few hours. We need to wait until we're somewhat sure there's a rescue party in the vicinity."

She blushed beneath his touch, and her throat worked as she swallowed hard. "You know how this type of crowd operates. When do you think that might happen?"

Slowly, he pulled his hand back. What was he thinking? Was he trying to comfort her or seduce her? He mentally admonished himself and refocused back on the task at hand—survival and rescue. "When we don't arrive back at the dock, they'll wait a while. Best guess is late tonight or more likely, tomorrow morning."

"You have got to be kidding me," she replied, exasperation overriding the optimism of a few moments ago.

"I wish I were," he said, the guilt growing.

Next to him, Holly got up, dusted the sand off as best she could, and yanked her shirt over her head, leaving nothing but a pink, satin bra to cover her perfect breasts.

• • •

Striding up the small beach, Holly hung her shirt on a branch. They only had a few hours of sun left. She hoped it would be enough to dry the saturated cotton. Sliding off her shorts, she hung them up next, leaving herself wearing only her undergarments and sneakers.

"You should dry your clothes," she said, turning around. "It's going…" The words died on her lips when her eyes met Kane's.

She knew that expression.

Desire.

A flush of heat washed over her in response.

Not good. This is by-the-book Kane, she reminded herself. *What you're feeling is the last of the adrenaline. Nothing more. Save the sexy for someone who you actually like. Someone like Bravo.*

She snapped her fingers, for herself as much as for Kane. "Hey, up here," she said, motioning for him to look at her face and not her half-covered breasts.

"Um. Sorry. I wasn't expecting you to strip," he said as a blush lit up his face.

"I'm not naked," she countered, though she was starting to feel that way despite the material that covered her. "It's a bra and panty set. I wore less on my last beach vacation and didn't get this reaction."

"I doubt that," Kane muttered.

Not helping, but she smiled before she could stop herself. Refusing to give in to modesty, she sat next to Kane and flipped open the cooler. "Drink?"

"Why not?"

"You should get out of those clothes," she said, pouring the combination of dark rum and ginger beer into the single plastic cup that had made it into the cooler.

He hesitated as if mulling over the idea then rose, taking the damp blankets with him as he followed her lead of walking up the beach to the nearest tree. A minute later, he tromped back through the sand. "Want to explore?"

Shielding her eyes from the sun, she looked up. His thighs were muscular. Stomach flat. A swirl of damp hair defined a path from his chest to the waistband of his dark gray boxer briefs.

Her pulse pounded in her veins, and she found herself staring at the outline under the thick, gray material.

"Hey. Up here." Kane snapped his fingers.

Dammit. She took a swig of the drink to hide her rising blush. "So, what next?" she asked, handing him the glass and ignoring his smart-ass attitude.

He took a sip and handed it back. "The top three needs for survival. Shelter first. Water if we can find it. Then food."

Made sense and sounded like something she'd heard on a reality show. "We have food," she said, tapping the cooler.

"It's not much."

"Do you think we'll be here that long?" Overnight would be bad enough. Much longer and they'd lose the window to find the necklace.

"No, but we need to hope for the best and prepare for the worst."

An agent's mantra, and under the circumstances, appropriate.

He offered her a hand, and she took it, letting him help her to her feet. A part of her wanted to hold on, but she released him instead. "Where to?"

"For now, we follow the shore. We might find something we can use."

"Sounds good," she replied, as he set off along the water's edge. Drink still in hand, she let the water wash over her feet as Kane dodged the waves. "You might want to let your shoes dry out," he said as a bigger wave went all the way to her knees before receding.

As terrified as she was of drowning, she liked the sound of the waves and the feel of the water as it swirled around her ankles. Still, she angled up the beach to join her partner. "How do you know so much?" she asked.

"About what?"

"Survival. Were you a Boy Scout?" It wouldn't surprise her if he was—he seemed like that kind of guy.

"Classes."

"HRS?" They'd learned a lot at the academy, but for her specialty the focus had been on escaping an ambush—not how to camp with no tent and almost no supplies.

"Some, yes," he replied.

"When you were a kid?" she pressed, ignoring his short, almost curt, answers.

"Yes."

"Where?" Didn't he realize that not answering made her only want to know more?

"Were you raised in the circus?" he asked, attention darting to the treeline and then back to the shore. Searching. Watching. "That's the rumor."

Holly stopped. "Excuse me?"

Kane waited, arms crossed. "Were you in the circus? That's the chatter. That you were raised doing acrobatics and crap. Is it true?"

"We don't talk about our pasts unless offered," she snapped. It was an unspoken rule at HRS. No one asked about an agent's history. Family. Schooling. Travel. Love. Nothing. Information could be offered, but to pry was beyond rude.

"I know," he replied, foot tapping as if waiting for her to connect the dots.

She realized that's exactly what she'd been doing. "Sorry."

She handed him the drink, and he took it, finishing it off as they continued to follow the beach.

"My dad made me take outdoor survival classes when I was thirteen," he said, surprising her. "He said it would make me more of a man."

"More of a man?"

"I went shopping with my sister and her friends. Once," Kane said. "I tried to explain that I did it because I liked being around the girls, but he sent me anyway."

"Sounds like a peach of a human being," Holly said, surprised to find herself angry at someone she'd never met.

"That was the general consensus," he said.

She didn't miss the subtext of the unspoken sentence telling her that his father was anything but that. "Sorry."

"Don't be. After all, I know how to build a shelter, so that's something. Maybe not as useful as walking a tight-rope…" He let the words die and flashed her a wicked smile.

"Smartass," she said, giving him a shove. He stumbled backwards, and she caught a glimpse of something behind him. Something linear and manmade.

"There," she said, pointing past him to the edge of the tree line. "What's that? A house maybe?"

"Too small." Kane peered through the trees. He pushed branches aside. "Wait here while I check it out."

Not likely, and she followed him into the woods, staying a few feet behind him as he pushed through the foliage. They entered a small clearing. In the center stood a shack. "I think it's abandoned," she said, her voice low as they stood outside the weathered door.

"Not abandoned, empty," he replied. "There are still windows. The place may be a piece of crap, but someone takes care of it." He eyed the worn, mismatched boards that made up the walls and the rusted roof. "Kind of."

"Well, let's hope they left some supplies. Maybe a radio."

"It's probably a meth lab," Kane said, testing the doorknob. It turned, unlocked. He hesitated.

"What are you waiting for?" she asked.

"This time, stay put. If it is a meth lab—or something dangerous—one of us needs to stay safe."

It made sense, but that didn't mean she had to like it. "Fine."

He gave a short nod of approval. "Step back into the trees."

She did as he asked, then peered around the trunk, watching as he opened the door and crossed the threshold, disappearing into the building.

Chapter Six

"It's a bar," Kane yelled from the dark interior of the shack.

Holly frowned. A bar? What was a bar doing on an island in the middle of nowhere? He had to be wrong.

She trotted to the door and stepped inside.

Kane stood behind a wide wooden counter. In nothing but his tight shorts, he looked more like a male stripper than an HRS field agent, and she found herself wishing she had a few dollar bills she could tuck into the waistband of his briefs.

Focus. She spun a slow circle. On the walls hung fish nets, glass buoys, and a wooden sign with the name, The Boatyard, burned into it. A scattering of chairs and a single table were spread out over the small, twenty-by-twenty area. A few empty liquor bottles littered the floor.

"Maybe," she said once she faced him again.

"And then there's this. The final clue," he said with a flourish and a told-you-so tone, as he held up a bottle of dark rum like they'd been drinking on the boat.

"Fine. It's the proverbial nail in the coffin," she teased, trying both not to smile and to sound unimpressed at the same time. "Find any food?"

"No. No radio, either."

She knocked a wooden-backed chair out of her way as she crossed the floor, then took a seat on a bar stool. "Who would set up a business out here?"

"Not a real bar," Kane said. "My guess is that the local teens hang out here."

"And drink rum?"

"Weren't you ever rebellious?"

For her, rebellion had meant attending a traditional high school. "Not really. And don't you think this place looks a little too nice to be a hang-out for kids?"

"It was probably already here and might have been a real bar at some point. I've seen them in weirder places." He opened the bottle and took a swig. "And I used to be one of those teens. We all had money, sailboats, and not enough supervision. If I'd known about a place like this, I'd have been here as much as possible."

More information about his past? She wanted him to elaborate, but to dig would make herself subject for scrutiny. Confirming that she had, indeed, been raised in the circus would just give him more ammunition. It gave most guys more ammunition. Or a reason to run for the hills.

Instead, she swiped the bottle from his hand and took a drink. The rum burned her throat, and the heat it left in its wake went all the way to her head.

She took another drink. Getting a little tipsy wasn't a bad idea under the circumstances. "Now what?" she asked once she could speak.

"We wait for rescue," he said, taking the bottle back.

"Tomorrow. If we're lucky."

"No, definitely. I just realized—we have Bravo."

She'd all but forgotten about the other agent. He would be wondering where they were, and it was doubtful that he'd believe Enzo's story. Of course, by the time they were missed, it would be too late, which meant she likely had to spend the night with Kane. Probably pressed together to keep warm.

The thought made her heart pound and her mouth go dry, and she wasn't sure who worried her more—herself or Kane. *Focus.* "Okay, you're the one trained in survival. What next?"

"We should stop drinking," he said. Capping the bottle, he put it back under the bar. "It might be the south in the summer, but we're right off the water, and it's going to get chilly. Getting hammered, or even tipsy, isn't going to keep us any warmer."

She nodded in agreement, already feeling the effects of the alcohol. "How do we keep warm? Our clothes are wet."

"I said chilly. Not freezing. We'll be warm enough as long as we stay close to each other."

He said the phrase like it meant nothing, but she'd seen the desire earlier. It was going to be a long night.

But this is Kane, she reminded herself. He isn't that kind of guy. He isn't Bravo.

Kane was the guy a girl took home to meet her mother.

Heaven help them all, her mother would love Kane. He was hot. A goody-two shoes. And saved her daughter from drowning.

Oh, yeah, Mama Milano would take one glance at Kane

and start planning a wedding. A giant, gaudy wedding that probably involved the entire big-top.

There was no way Madam Sarah was ever meeting him. Holly would never hear the end of it.

Nope. Not going to happen.

"What isn't going to happen?" Kane asked.

Holly clapped a hand over her mouth. Did she say that out loud?

Damned rum.

"Nothing." She needed to take a walk before she said something she shouldn't—or leaned over the bar and kissed her partner to see what happened next.

Knock it off. She stood, the bar stool tipping over and falling with a clatter.

"Do I need to cut you off?" Kane asked, eyebrows arched.

"I can handle my liquor, thank you," she replied, regretting that last swig.

He came around the bar, picked up the chair, and nodded for her to sit.

Yeah, her mother would love him.

"It's been a long day," he said. "Wait here. I'll get our gear, and we'll get settled."

She nodded, then breathed a sigh of relief when he disappeared out the door. A few minutes away from Kane was what she needed.

Shutting her eyes, she took a deep breath, wishing she had some water. Perhaps the ice in the cooler had melted.

A crunching outside the window at the back of the shack made her sit upright. "Kane?" she whispered, but knew it wasn't him. He was getting their supplies.

Maybe it was help.

Then why hadn't they made themselves known?

The crunching traveled from the back to the sides of the building. Someone, or something, was approaching the front door.

What if Kane was wrong? Maybe it was a drug dealer.

Or a bear.

Holly slid off the barstool and picked it up. Person or animal, she was going to defend herself.

• • •

Hands full, Kane took his time heading back to the cabin, stepping over branches and avoiding the rising waters. The beach would be lost to high tide soon, or he'd suggest they try to start a fire in the sand. They could try to start one in the cabin, but he didn't want to take a chance on burning down their sanctuary.

Stay close together. He hadn't meant it to be anything more than suggesting they use body heat to stay warm, but her shocked expression told him that she'd heard a different proposition.

Idiot.

Using the broken branches as an indication of the path he needed to follow back, he headed inland to the shack. As he entered the clearing, he noticed the door was open. He could hear Holly inside, talking.

To whom?

He set the clothes and cooler down, hiding both behind a tree. Skirting the small clearing, he made his way to the side of the structure and worked his way to the door, staying low and out of sight. Slowly, he peeked around the corner.

The combination of sunset and trees dappled the inside of the structure. He blinked. Holly was kneeling on the floor, a mound of yellow fur in front of her, four legs waving in the air.

Was that a dog? It barked, giving him confirmation.

Kane stepped into the doorway, and Holly looked up. "Can you believe this? Someone abandoned him here."

The dog trotted over, head down and submissive. A yellow lab from the looks of it. Fifty pounds at the most. Kane held out his hand. The dog sniffed him then licked his knuckles, shaking in a full-body tail wag.

Kane rubbed his ears, and the dog dropped to the ground, exposing his belly. "Good boy. Good boy," he murmured, checking for a non-existent collar.

"How long do you think Mr. Wiggles has been here?" Holly asked.

"Mr. Wiggles? Won't all the other dogs make fun of him?"

"Did you see that tail wag?"

It could be worse, he supposed. She might have called the poor dog something with "pants" in it, or "boots." Danielle had done that with her cats, Miss Sassy Pants and Sir Fuzzy Boots.

He held up his hands in surrender. "I'm not making fun of you, I swear. But Mr. Wiggles? You realize this is a male dog, right?"

"That's why I put the 'Mr.' in front of it."

"Can't argue with that logic." Mr. Wiggles it was. He rubbed the dog's belly. "He hasn't been here long. A few days at the most. There isn't any water…" They both knew the rest without him needing to spell it out.

"He could have died."

All righteous anger and fire, Holly crossed her arms and glared at no one in particular. He hadn't seen that in her before, and he liked seeing this side of her—the side that cared.

He understood the fury and couldn't blame her. No animal deserved to be abandoned, but leaving it on a tiny island with no food or water was beyond cruel. It was torture. If they found the owner, someone was getting a punch in the mouth.

For now, Mr. Wiggles needed water. Retrieving their gear while Holly cooed over the canine, he opened the cooler, took out the remaining food, and patted the outside of the plastic. "Come on. Come here."

Mr. Wiggles belly-crawled to him, as if waiting for admonishment. What had the owner done to him? Kane added a few kicks to the payback if he found out who did this.

Mr. Wiggles drank the melted ice water. Kane held up the crackers and cheese. "Do you mind?"

Holly smiled, her eyes crinkling. "Of course not."

She took a few of the crackers and fed Mr. Wiggles. A few minutes later, the food was gone.

The dog plopped on the floor, his back against the bar, shut his eyes, and fell asleep.

"Poor little guy. He's tuckered," she said.

"It was probably a rough few days," Kane said. "It's a good thing we showed up. Remind me to thank Enzo."

"I'll even buy him a drink," she said, scratching the dog's ears. "Right after I smack him for trying to kill us."

"He's a complicated man," he said.

"It's a complicated situation," she responded.

Understatement. Their charge was asleep. Smart dog. Get rest when you can.

"How about a fire?" Holly asked, filling the silence.

The sky had turned hot pink as the sun sank, the air cooled as a breeze blew in over the Atlantic, and he was alone with a barely clad Holly. But the cabin was dry as a bone, and unless they wanted to take turns tending it, a fire was out of the question. "No matches. Even if I could start a fire from nothing. The beach is washed out for a few hours, and if we start one here, I'm afraid we'll burn the place down. And by place, I mean everything on the entire island."

She gave a slow nod. "Then what?"

Their clothes were still damp, but he laid them on the ground. They wouldn't keep the two of them warm, but it beat sleeping on dirty wooden planks. "We manage without and share body heat and the thermal blanket," he said. It sounded sensible. Smart. Their only choice.

The idea of sleeping next to his partner made Kane's palms sweat and his mouth go dry.

• • •

She should not have had the rum.

Holly mentally kicked herself, resisting the urge to snuggle closer to Kane. He'd been right. It wasn't freezing, but it was cold enough to make her shiver. Her back to his chest, he wrapped his arm round her waist, keeping her pressed tight against his skin.

She tensed, but the warmth of his body was irresistible. Relaxing, she snuggled closer, telling herself that it meant nothing. He was asleep. He'd never know. Warming, she closed her eyes, but her mind raced back to a few hours ago when they'd kissed in the bedroom. The taste of his mouth. The feel of his hands on her lower back, working their way under her shirt.

Could it only have been a few hours?

"We're going to have a lot of catching up to do when we get back to the assignment," Kane said, his voice half asleep in her ear.

Dammit. "I know," she replied, embarrassed to be caught snuggling but grateful for anything that took her mind off the fact she was sleeping on the floor. "We're not that far off track, are we?"

"As long as someone picks us up first thing, I think we'll stay on schedule," he replied, his breathing deep. His hand shifted, gliding from her waist to her hip, the tips of his fingers on the hem of her panties. Was he doing that on purpose? Was he even fully awake?

"Bravo will take care of it," she replied.

"Of course he will," Kane said, sounding more awake and a bit annoyed. His hand fell away, letting the chill back in.

She turned in his arms, not wanting to leave the warmth, and as much as she hated to admit, it, she'd liked the closeness they'd developed since they washed up on the island. It was…unexpected.

A part of her was reluctant to let it slip away. "You don't like Bravo, do you?"

Pale silver light from the rising moon spilled in through the cracks in the roof and the dirty windows, offering just enough light for her to make out his face. "I don't dislike him."

"What is it?"

He leaned up on an elbow. "I respect him as an agent. He gets the job done, and he's a good thief. Not as good as you but close."

"Sounds dreamy. So, what's the issue?" she asked, wanting a glimpse inside her partner's mind.

"He isn't someone I would aspire to be."

"His reputation with women?"

His silence told her more than words ever could, confirming that Kane was the guy you took home to the family. Not a man you walked away from once the fun was over. If he thought that of Bravo, what did he think of her? "Do you think less of me for wanting him as my fake fiancé?"

"No. He's the better actor—we both knew that." He wasn't lying or holding back. She sensed it in his words. Heard it in his voice. He didn't know the real reason—that she'd wanted the agent in her bed.

Her head told her there was nothing wrong with lust. This wasn't the middle ages, and she wasn't a prude.

Still, the heat flooded her cheeks. "Thanks for trusting me," she said, making a silent promise that he'd never find out her true motivation for being excited to pair with Bravo.

"I know we don't always see eye-to-eye, but we make a good team—"

"—when we're not fighting."

He chuckled. "Yeah. There is that."

She smiled, surprised to find herself happy to be stranded with Kane. "We're not arguing now."

Silence.

Then his mouth was on hers.

She didn't hesitate but kissed him back, opening her

mouth as his tongue teased the edges of her lips. He tasted like sweat and rum, and she wanted him. With a sigh, she slid her hand up his chest and wrapped her arm around his neck, pulling herself to him as his hand slid from her hip to the small of her back.

With a surprising skill, he rolled her over until she was on top of him, their legs twined together. He kissed a path from her mouth to her throat, biting the sweet spot between neck and shoulder.

Her breath hissed out from between her teeth, and she found herself twisting against him, wanting to strip off the little bits of cloth that kept them apart.

"Holly," he whispered. Winding his hands through her hair, he turned her head and kissed her hard. His mouth almost bruised hers, but it only made her want him more. He might act like the guy you took home, but he kissed like the bad boy on the motorcycle.

Releasing her, his hands lid down her back, under the waist of her panties, his hands squeezing her half-bared bottom.

She groaned at the need that washed over her, and he hardened beneath her.

Who knew all this passion was inside the proper outer shell that Kane presented to the world? A knee on each side of him, she rose, reached behind to unhook her bra…and spotted two glowing eyes watching them.

"What is it?" Kane asked, his voice rough.

"Mr. Wiggles. He's watching us." She let her arms fall, bra still in place. He might be a dog, but she didn't want an audience.

She watched Kane in the moonlight, as he let his head

drop back against the cloth-covered floorboards in sexual frustration, wanting him so much she ached. But she knew that the interruption was for the best.

She'd been involved before with men who weren't from the circus, and when they met her family—her wonderful, large, colorful family—it always ended the same way. They ran.

If she was ever going to have a real relationship, it would be with someone who understood the world she came from—crazy, unpredictable, working class. The exact opposite of the world Kane had been born to, the perfectly mannered, upper-crust world they would head back to when Bravo rescued them. Could you imagine Mr. Rich and Uptight at ease with a crowd that included Alyssa the bearded lady, Fernando the rescue-dog trainer, and the Flying Boreckyi Family? In the meantime, it was best to date slightly left-of-center men who were capable of coping with surprises.

Something she didn't see Kane capable of doing.

"It's for the best," Kane said, as if reading her mind. "We don't want to complicate things."

"Of course not," Holly replied, placing a palm on his well-muscled chest and enjoying it for just a moment, before she used that hand to push back and roll off of him. The last thing she needed was a preppy, upscale, hyper-scheduled boyfriend, but the words still hurt.

Kane patted the space between them, "Come on, Mr. Wiggles. Come here."

Tail thumping, Mr. Wiggles sidled forward and wedged himself between their bodies, panting happily. He was stinky, warm, and seemed to appreciate the attention.

As always, animals were easier to deal with than people.

With a contented chuff, Mr. Wiggles flattened out, and despite the disappointment, Holly smiled at Kane over his prone body.

"I'm glad you like animals," she said, petting Mr. Wiggles.

"Who doesn't?"

"The person who left him here to die."

"Good point."

Silence took over, and it wasn't uncomfortable, but she found she wasn't ready for it. He'd shared a few tidbits of his life with her. Perhaps it was time for her to do the same. "You know, the rumors are true. I grew up in a circus," she said, sinking her fingers in Mr. Wiggles's fur.

"Really?"

She smiled at the surprise in his voice. Growing up in a circus never failed to garner attention. even if the reality ultimately drove many prospective dates away. Telling Kane was probably a sure-fire way to ensure that things between them would go back to being platonic. "Really, but not the kind with elephants or tigers or anything."

"What other kind is there?"

She rubbed Mr. Wiggles's ears, and the dog let out a contented sigh. "Acrobats. Fire-eaters. Some horses and dogs, but that's about it as far as animals go."

"Don't the exotics bring in more money?" Kane asked.

She nodded. "They do, and we kept some at one point but that was years ago. When the owner died, the new ringmaster, Santos, found sanctuaries for all the animals."

"Why?" He propped himself up on one elbow as she spoke. The moonlight created patterns on his muscled body, but shadowed his face, making him difficult to read.

She continued, "Santos said they were too expensive

and controversial, but my mom said that it wasn't the money or the bad press. He thought keeping wild animals in cages for entertainment was bad karma and a dark spot in his soul that would come back to haunt him."

"Even without the tigers and elephants, it sounds like a kid's dream," Kane said.

If he only knew.

But she didn't plan to tell him that without the exotics, the troupe didn't make as much money. That information was private, and while she might not work with the circus anymore, they were her family. Always would be.

He continued, "—and it explains the extraordinary skills."

She disregarded the praise. "Stealing is easier when you've been trained to take calculated risks from the moment you could walk."

"Is that why you fight me when I try to tell you what to do?" he asked, reaching over the now-sleeping dog and tucking a wayward strand of hair behind her ear.

She shivered, but this time, it wasn't the cold. "You don't know what I can do."

He hesitated then gave her a slow nod. "I'm starting to figure that out."

Chapter Seven

"Why are you staring at me?" Holly whispered. The morning light trickled in through the windows, brightening the small room. The dog was gone, and Kane stared at her, sleepy-eyed but curious in the golden glow. It was dreamlike. Unreal.

"Accident," he whispered back.

She didn't buy it. The way his eyes met hers was more than an accidental look. He savored her. Took her in—all of her.

She liked it. "Where's Mr. Wiggles?"

"By the bar," he nodded toward the back wall, then yawned and closed his eyes." I think I kicked too much," he murmured.

She hadn't noticed, but she'd been told that when she slept, it took the equivalent of a grenade to wake her. She slid her arm under her head for a pillow, surprised at the random banter. It was so unlike Kane.

Neither had been themselves since yesterday. "Why are

you whispering?" she asked, half-shutting her own eyes and relaxing into drowsiness.

"You started it."

She laughed, amazed to find that even in the light of day, she was glad to semi-wake up with Kane and not Bravo. The other agent had the reputation with the women, but Kane intrigued her. Before she could think, she reached out and traced his mouth, her fingertips arching up then down to his lower lip, feeling the fullness.

He kissed her finger tips, and her breath caught in her throat. He still looked half-asleep, except for the one corner of his mouth that tipped up in a self-satisfied smile.

She'd stopped him last night. It was for the best. She knew that. She didn't care. Didn't want to care.

She wanted Kane.

She shifted her body a small, almost imperceptible, bit toward him, but it was enough. He pulled her closer, and she let herself fall into the moment. Clasping her hand to his mouth, he kissed a path from her fingertips up her arm and to her neck. Still kissing her, he turned her until her back was to him then stroked her hair aside, biting the back of her neck.

Her breath hissed through her teeth, and he chuckled in response.

Lips followed laughter as he kissed her shoulder blade, moving to her spine. "Morning."

Indeed. She should stop him, but she didn't want to. With the exception of last night, it had been almost a year since a man had touched her, and Kane was anything but a prude when it came to woman's body.

Reaching her lower back, he guided her to her stomach

then straddled her, a knee on each side of her thighs. His hands followed the path his mouth had traced earlier, his fingers rubbing her tense muscles, working out the aches and stiffness that came with sleeping on a wooden floor with only their clothes separating them from the dirt and splinters.

The heels of his hands dug into each side of her spine, and she groaned with pleasure at the unexpected massage.

"Why?" she asked as he worked his way down and then back up. "Why are you doing this?"

"Not sure," he whispered, looking aroused, though slightly bewildered. "I…"

"Am I interrupting something?" a masculine voice asked.

She knew that voice. "Michael Bravo." Funny how everyone either referred to him by his last name or used both names in rapid-fire succession. He was never just "Michael."

Even as she processed the situation, Kane slid off. Holly flipped over and sat up. Their partner stood in the doorway, hands on his hips, the rising sun creating a glowing silhouette.

"Hi, Bravo. Thanks for the rescue," Kane said. "And no, you weren't interrupting."

Just like that, the Kane she'd laughed with, kissed, was gone. Banished. She heard it in his voice. Saw it in his eyes. This was stick-in-the-mud Kane, back from the dead.

She flinched, his change a dash of cold water on her libido.

Bravo strode across the room, helping Holly to her feet. She dusted off her legs, trying to offer a nonchalance that she didn't feel.

In the corner, Mr. Wiggles cowered, whimpering, capturing her attention. His brown eyes on Bravo, he peed on the floor.

Nurturing instincts she didn't know were there roared to life.

Jerk men. Though she knew the anger wasn't all about the dog. It was at herself for thinking that Kane could be different. That *she* might be different.

Approaching slowly as to not scare the canine, Holly managed to get close enough to let him sniff her hand. The Labrador shook his tail in his trademark whole body shake. Holly dropped to her knees and wrapped her arms around his scruffy neck. "Can you two morons back off a bit? Can't you see he's scared?"

Bravo held his hands up, "Sorry. I didn't notice." His eyes skimmed Holly as she soothed the dog. "Have a good night?"

Ass. She'd forgotten she wore nothing but her bra and panties, and her hair was probably a tangled mess. She hated them both.

Kane moved, putting himself between her and Bravo. "We survived. What we'd like now is a vet and a shower. In that order."

"Of course, boss."

Boss. How could she forget?

"What did we miss?" Kane asked.

"Not much. I got in late with no time to reconnaissance, sorry, and found you missing and some idiot named Enzo saying that you both took off so you could fool around. I didn't want to blow your cover, so I pried the truth out of him as soon as I could."

"I hope by 'pry' you meant 'beat,'" Holly said, shaking out her shirt before slipping it on and buttoning it as fast as she could in a futile attempt to regain some semblance of professionalism.

"It only took a little arm twisting."

"Disappointing," Kane replied.

Holly slid on her shorts as Kane finished dressing. They left the crumbling shack, the dog trotting at her side. Once on shore, she spotted another sailboat fifty feet out in the water and safe from the rocky, underwater peninsula. A rowboat waited on the beach. Mr. Wiggles eyed the small craft with suspicion until Bravo opened a cooler and took out a biscuit, bacon, and egg sandwich.

Seconds later, the dog was at his side, treating Bravo as if he were his long-lost best friend.

"Bit of a whore, isn't he?" Kane commented.

"Prostitute. Whores don't get paid," Holly said, trying to be funny, but even she heard the animosity in her voice.

Kane raised a brow at the tone but took up the oars while Bravo kept the dog occupied. Minutes later, they were at the sailboat. Holly watched as the men struggled to get Mr. Wiggles onboard, but once the dog had his paws on the deck, he searched and sniffed the craft as sure-footed as if he'd been raised on the water.

He probably was, Holly realized. After all, he had traveled to the island somehow.

The men readied the sails, and in minutes, they were on their way back to the mainland.

"What happened?" Bravo asked, the wind blowing his dark hair and the blue of the water making his eyes bright. He was as hot as she remembered—

Of course, it helps that he hadn't slept on the floor of a cabin. She ran her hand through her hair, fingers snagging at the multiple snarls.

"About what?" Kane asked.

"I thought I was the fiancé. Why was I made the assistant?"

Holly cringed. Was Kane going to tell about her screw-up in the bedroom? She turned her gaze to the water, not wanting to watch Bravo's reaction and wishing she didn't have to hear.

"Just seemed a better fit," Kane replied. "There were some assumptions made when I arrived with Holly, and we decided to go with it. Does it matter?"

"Nope," Bravo replied. "Like you said, I can spend time searching for the necklace while you keep the rich people occupied."

Holly let go of the breath she hadn't realized she'd been holding. When Kane finally looked her way, she mouthed, *Thank you.*

He smiled in return, and warmth washed over her.

"It shouldn't take too much," Kane said. "With Holly's ability to make people trust her and my knowledge of how their world works, we might even be out of here by tonight."

"You think?" Bravo asked.

"Maybe," Kane said. "She's good. Tells people what they want to hear so they let their guard down. I've seen her in action. If anyone can get someone to slip, it's Holly."

Was that supposed to be a compliment?

Of course it was, her inner voice reminded her.

Something about it rankled her. Did he think she'd played him last night? Could he see when she was being genuine? She didn't know.

Ask him, an inner voice urged.

Did she want the answer?

She peeked through her lashes to watch the men as they kept the sailboat moving and on course. Both were handsome. Fit. But Bravo was the kind of man she needed. The kind she could walk away from. Not that she planned to act on the thought.

Kane was dangerous. If she let him in, he'd break her heart. She just knew it.

So, what did it matter if he thought she was a big phony? There was nothing between them but a few shared confessions and a kiss brought on by too much rum. That didn't make it a budding relationship—especially when balanced with their past encounters.

She needed to focus on what she came here to do. On what she was paid to do.

Get the necklace and get out.

To want anything that involved actual intimacy was foolish and an unacceptable risk when it came to the mission.

• • •

Kane pulled out a chair for Holly at a small table on the edge of the garden where brunch was being served to the other guests.

After they'd moored the boat, Bravo had taken the rescued dog to a local vet while Kane and Holly had retired to their room for showers and a change of clothes. Staying true to character, he'd taken her hand when they left the room, and she didn't shake him off. Instead, she almost snuggled into his side. Like they were meant to be together.

The entire time, she hadn't said a word about the

morning. Or last night. He'd wanted to. There was something unexpected about Holly that made him want to know more.

Work comes first, he reminded himself. It was why HRS put him in charge—he knew his priorities, and acting like an infatuated school boy wasn't on the "to do" list, unless it was part of the act.

A flutter of a hand caught his attention. At the opposite end of the garden and in front of a rose arbor, a blonde woman dressed in a form-fitting, pale green dress came toward them, skirting the tables. He recognized her from the pictures—the trophy wife. Tammi Lynn Burke.

Stopping for only brief hellos, she arrived at their table. "I heard about what happened. I am so sorry. Enzo feels horrible about it. Just horrible."

"I'm sure he does," Kane replied, sure that the mobster felt anything but sorrow.

"I wanted to ask him to leave, but Tim said we should leave it up to you," she said, her voice hushed as she leaned in toward Kane, one hand on the table and the other on his shoulder. "What are your thoughts?"

That Enzo needed to be beaten? Shot?

That would go against mission protocol. His job was to blend, and acting above it all was the best way to do that. Still, he promised himself that once this operation was over, he'd make sure that Enzo would think twice before he messed with anyone from HRS. "An apology is sufficient," he said.

"Thank you," she replied, "I knew you'd be a good sport about it."

"You're welcome," said Holly. "Where is he?"

"He went into town with Rachel. I think he was a tad embarrassed."

"Good," Holly said and went back to her food.

Her attention still on Kane, Tammi Lynn squeezed his shoulder, her hand sliding so her fingertips touched the bare skin of his neck, her nails skimming the flesh.

He jerked back, and Tammi Lynn's hand fell to her side as if nothing had happened.

What the hell? Had Holly seen? She sipped her mimosa, and he realized the hostess' hand was out of her view.

Sneaky. He thought about what Holly said yesterday— that she'd seen Tammi Lynn leaving the bedroom and adjusting her clothes. If this was how she acted with strangers, it wasn't unthinkable that she'd be sleeping around.

He had the urge to scrub his shoulder but resisted.

Tammi Lynn continued. "By-the-by, your assistant called from the vet's. They're going to keep the dog you found for the day. They want to run some tests and give him fluids."

"Of course," Kane said.

"Did they find a microchip?" Holly asked, sipping her drink.

Kane hoped not, but even if they did, he wasn't giving the dog back. On the upside, if there was a chip, they would know who to turn in to the police for animal abuse.

"Not that I know of."

Unfortunate. "Thank you."

"My pleasure," she purred, running a hand along his arm before she headed back to her table at the opposite end of the garden.

"Do you think Enzo will cause trouble?" Holly asked, once they were alone.

"Enzo? He's a coward," Kane replied.

Back at her table, Tammi Lynn clinked a crystal glass

with a spoon, and the group fell silent. Sipping coffee, Kane listened as she made the gratuitous speech about how they appreciated everyone coming.

Boring. He turned his attention to the crowd. Elizabeth Bowler, the girl from yesterday, leaned in toward an older man, his graying hair giving away his age. Normally, he'd say it was her father, but in their crowd, one never knew.

He sipped his drink. Would Tammi Lynn never shut up?

Elizabeth's partner dropped his napkin, his face toward Kane as he reached to retrieve it off the grass.

Lucien Pascua. Enzo's father and a leader in the Corsican mob. Why was Elizabeth with them, and why were they here?

The best answer was that they wanted a politician in their pocket and were here to test the waters. Or perhaps they had already infiltrated the political circle, and this was their way of keeping tabs on their host, Tim Burke.

Or did the necklace factor in? Maybe. Possibly. Or was it just a coincidence that they were all here at the same time? There was no way to tell. If it did, it made it even more imperative that HRS recover it.

"What's wrong?" Holly asked.

"Later," he said, not sure how much he planned to tell his partner. They were here to retrieve a necklace, not take on organized crime.

Should he say anything? Only years of training allowed him to focus his attention back on Tammi Lynn as she continued to talk.

"The game begins right after brunch and ends at four. Any couple not turning in their camera will be disqualified and mocked," she said with a laugh, though he sensed a bit of truth beneath the comment.

There was a collective groan from the group.

"Game?" he whispered. What had he missed?

"We're going on a scavenger hunt," Holly replied, giving him a sideways glance. "We take pictures of whatever we're supposed to find. It's supposed to be fun, though I think it sounds more like an opportunity."

She was right. While everyone was marking pictures off their list, he and Holly could go search for the safe.

Tammi Lynn continued, "The winner will be announced tonight at the auction."

"That gives us just a few hours to find the necklace," Holly said, under her breath.

"We'll still have to take a few pictures," Kane said.

"Why? Let's grab what we came for and leave."

It was tempting, but too risky. If they didn't find the necklace, the Corsicans might wonder why he and Holly weren't participating in the game. He didn't want to draw their attention or anyone else's.

Let them do their thing, and he'd do his. Easy peasy.

Setting the coffee aside, he took a long drink of the mimosa. "We do both," he said, his voice low. "These people live to win—even if it's a token award. If we don't find the necklace then we'll need to show them something besides a shrug."

She shrugged.

He gave her his best, *I'm not amused*, glare, but it didn't seem to faze her. "Can you promise me we'll find it?" he asked.

"No."

She seemed as irked as he did. Why had he dreamed

that a few hours alone would change their basic dynamic of pissing each other off?

Idiot.

He finished the mimosa, and in seconds a waiter filled his glass again. He'd have to pace himself, or he'd be hammered before noon.

"Why are you pissed?" Holly whispered.

"What?"

"You're glaring at your drink like you want it dead. It's champagne and orange juice. It doesn't deserve the animosity."

Slowly, he twirled the crystal stem between his palms. "Just thinking about the person who left Mr. Wiggles to die," he lied.

"Me too," she said. "But more about how I plan to make them pay. It won't be lethal, but it won't be pretty, either."

He couldn't fault her desire for retribution. Most agents saw the world as black and white with very little gray. Not everything was forgivable, and leaving an animal to die a slow death from dehydration and starvation was one of those things. Someone would pay for leaving Mr. Wiggles on the island.

She clinked her glass against his, took a sip, and opened the envelope on their table. Around them, everyone else was already reading the contents.

Inside was a list of objects.

Rooster

Abalone shell

Sunrise

White shoe laces

3 ft. pink ribbon

Left-handed scissors

He folded up the list and crammed it in his pocket, leaving the rest unread. All they had to do was get a few pictures, not the entire list.

Tammi Lynn picked up a small, brass gong and struck it with a matching mallet. "Go!"

. . .

"It seems you have an admirer," Holly said when Kane closed the door behind them. Leaving breakfast with the rest of the group, they'd headed back to their room on the pretext of getting better shoes for Holly, but in reality, they wanted to give everyone the chance to leave so they could search for the necklace.

"You noticed that?"

"I did. It was hard not to. I also couldn't miss the face you made."

He frowned. "A face?"

"Like you tasted something sour." She sat on the bed. "You're lucky that Tammi Lynn paid more attention to your body."

He gave a half-hearted shrug. "What if she did? We're engaged."

"It isn't real," she replied, wishing she could take the words back as soon as she said them.

His jaw tensed, and she didn't miss the subtle flex of muscle as his hands clenched in frustration.

Why couldn't he be more like Bravo? Bravo would see Tammi Lynn's propensity to sleep around as an opportunity to get the necklace. His flexible morality was what she liked about him. Plus, he was a professional thief who did what was needed. Women like Tammi Lynn didn't matter. Even she didn't matter.

Except to Kane. She hated that she cared that he cared.

Knock it off. Just stop it.

This was Kane she was contemplating, and they were working. He'd made that clear from the moment that Bravo walked in on them. She glared at her partner. "She doesn't know this is a fake engagement, Kane. You should remember that."

"Why does it matter?"

How could he not see the opportunity this presented? "Tammi Lynn is predatory when it comes to men. I know her type. Getting a man to break his vows is a way to validate that she is important or beautiful or something equally pathetic. Somewhere in her sad, insecure mind is a little voice saying, 'See. You made him cheat. You are better than his wife.' We can use that to our advantage."

"You want me to sleep with her?" His mouth screwed up, and he gave a visible shudder.

There was that look again, and it helped quell the jealousy rising in her chest. "I'm not saying that, but Bravo would. If we don't find the safe, getting close to her might be the only way to get the necklace."

He shook his head. "I can't."

Holly fell back into the bed. "I know this is out of your realm. You're the guy in the van calling the shots. Disconnected from the action with a microphone and headset, but this is the field, Kane."

"That's not it."

"What is it, then?"

He sat next to her. "I should have been the assistant."

"I agree," she snapped, hating the situation. Hating that she wanted Kane to want her.

Hating herself for being cruel.

She wished she could take back the sharpness in her voice. *He's not the enemy*, she reminded herself. *You brought this on yourself by not listening to him in the first place. If Bravo were the fiancé, you wouldn't even be having this conversation.*

She sat up, hands in her lap. "What's the problem? Did your girlfriend cheat on your or something?"

His breath hitched in his chest.

Dammit. She'd hit the truth with an unintended ferocity. "I am so sorry," she whispered, taking his hand in hers. "I didn't…"

He jerked away. "It's okay."

It wasn't, and they both knew it. She also knew it didn't matter. They were on a mission, and what mattered was getting the necklace. "I know this is painful for you—"

Understatement.

"—but you have to set that aside. This is a job. That's all."

The silence ticked by.

Shit. All this for a trinket? Granted, a trinket worth millions, but she couldn't ask him to do this. "We'll find another way." she said, sliding her hand over his.

"In less than two days?" he replied. The anger and pain she'd seen only seconds ago was gone. Erased as if it were never there. "We have an obligation to the operation, and it's my job to make sure we complete the mission."

She nodded, both frightened and impressed by the speed at which he'd reined in his emotions. "Okay. What's the plan?"

He looked down at their joined hands. "Like you said, we keep Tammi Lynn in play in case we need to use her. For now, we search the house while everyone's gone."

"Where do we start?"

"The master suite."

"Perfect," she tried to rise, and he pulled her back to the bed.

"We need to talk," he said. "There's a wrinkle."

"A wrinkle?" The way he said it told her that he wasn't talking about sleeping with the enemy. Not anymore. This was something more sinister, and only one person who fit that bill. "Is it Enzo?"

"Not anymore. It's his family. His father is here."

"One of the leaders of the Corsican mob?"

Kane nodded.

She wanted to ask how he knew these people, but didn't. "Do you think they'll retaliate?"

"No, I don't think they're here for us." His gray eyes bored into hers. "I think they're here to buy a politician."

"Or for the necklace," she said.

He nodded, not shocked or surprised at the comment, and she knew he'd been considering the same possibility.

Of course he had. He's Kane—the brains behind the thieving. "Which means we have to get to it before they do," she said, rising. This time he didn't stop her.

Chapter Eight

"This would be a lot easier if we could sneak in through the balcony," Holly whispered as they skulked down the hallway. It had taken longer than expected, but the last guest had finally gone outside to start the scavenger hunt, leaving her and Kane to search the house.

He didn't answer because they both knew using the balcony wasn't possible. The master suite was above their room, but its balcony faced the backyard, and while the other guests might be gone, the catering and house staff had swarmed the area immediately surrounding the mansion, prepping an enormous, white tent for the dinner and auction. All it would take was a single glance upward to blow their cover.

It was the hallway or nothing, and this was the best chance they'd ever get. If someone asked what they were doing inside rather than out with the rest of the guests, they'd just pretend they hadn't heard the part about the scavenger items all being located in the small, pretentious part of town just down the road.

Voices echoed up the stairs, followed by the sound of glasses clinking against each other as the staff cleaned up after the Burke's guests, who, from the number of glasses making noise, were a group of lushes.

They kept moving. "Maybe we'll get lucky," she said. "The necklace could be in a jewelry box."

"Or on a silver platter," Kane replied, his smile softening the sarcasm.

The clinking and chatter grew louder, and his arm tightened around her waist. *For the job*, she reminded herself when she caught herself sinking into his touch, memories of their early-morning kiss making her ache for him.

She sighed. For something that was supposed to have been a walk in the park, this op grew more confusing with each passing hour. It wasn't just the kiss. There were all the personal details they'd shared with each other. Bravo. Even the damned necklace. She didn't know what she wanted anymore. Or who.

They reached the stairway to the master suite and went up, keeping to the side where the boards would be less worn and creaky. The noise from downstairs faded as the staff presumably moved to another part of the house.

Holly knocked on the Burke's bedroom door. *Don't be there. Don't be there.* No answer. Another knock. Nothing but silence. "So far, so good," she whispered.

"Careful. You're going to jinx it," he said.

She shot him a surprised look over her shoulder. "Since when did you become superstitious?"

The reply was an arched brow. "Just get us in. Pick the

lock or whatever it is you do."

"Another reason you always stay in the van," she teased.

"What is that supposed to mean?"

Finally, she was going to get to be the know-it-all. It didn't happen often with Kane around, and she'd take what pleasure in it she could. "You forgot the first rule of a good thief."

"Which is?"

"Try the knob." She wrapped her hand around it and twisted, 99 percent sure the door would swing open.

Locked. Okay, that was a little embarrassing.

Kane snickered, and she gave him a half-hearted glare. "It's still a good rule." Extracting a lock-pick kit from the pocket of her shorts, she kneeled down. "Keep watch."

"Of course."

Behind her, his foot tapped the carpet in a nervous staccato. "Knock it off," she whispered. "You're making me lose my concentration, because I want to use these tools to stab whatever is making that infernal noise." She took a moment to give his foot a sharp stare, just in case he missed the point of the comment.

The tapping stopped. "Sorry."

She focused harder on the lock. It might be attached to a bedroom door, but it was high-quality and designed for something sturdier. Which made her wonder what they were hiding.

The tumblers fell into place, and the lock disengaged. "Let's do this," she said.

They entered and then shut the door behind them, locking the deadbolt. There was no going back now. If they were caught, they had no excuse to be in the master suite.

And what a suite. Hazy golden light filtered in through the white lace curtains, making patterns on the butter-yellow walls. A pale yellow silk duvet with matching dust ruffle dressed the king-sized four poster bed.

The smell of a variety of cleaning solutions tickled Holly's nose—housekeeping had been through. That meant no interruptions, not that she planned to let her guard down.

"Let's find the necklace and get out of here," Kane said, striding over to a small nook that served as an office, complete with a fax machine and multi-line phone.

"I couldn't agree more," Holly replied. "The sooner we're out of here, the sooner we can get on with our lives."

Kane paused mid-search. "What's that supposed to mean?"

Dammit. Why was she letting Kane, of all people, get to her?

"Nothing." She started her search. This wasn't the time to argue, discuss, or confess.

"If you have something to say, say it," he said.

Not a chance. She'd bared enough of her soul, he'd done the same, and this was where it got her—questioning the mission and herself. She'd never be having these issues if Bravo were her fake fiancé. He was the partner she needed. Someone fun. Professional. And with no illusions that anything that happened would mean anything.

Kane wasn't that guy. He was the kind of man who required a relationship.

Which would be all well and fine…right up until he met her family. And when it all blew up, because it always did, she'd be left to pick up the pieces of her broken heart.

Exactly what she wanted to avoid.

"I said nothing, and I meant nothing." She scanned the room and, on a hunch, lifted the edge of the area rug at the end of the bed. Just beneath the fringe was a metal box embedded into the floor. "Bingo."

A few minutes to crack the safe and they'd be on their way. She'd be back in L.A. by tomorrow morning. Kane would go to wherever Kane went, and she'd be on her own again.

So, why did the idea make her stomach hurt?

He trotted over. "Is that it?"

"Has to be. Where else would they keep it? On a silver platter?"

He snickered, and she cracked her knuckles for effect. "Just stand back and watch me work."

Voices in the hall caught her attention, and the cramping in her stomach morphed into butterflies that threatened to take over her entire body.

"Again? Seriously?" she half-whispered.

"On the bed," Kane replied.

She wasn't kissing him again. Not now. Not ever. If she did, she wasn't sure she could stop. Besides, they'd used that lie once. Trying it again, and in the master suite, would only get them tossed out. By the time the party ended, Tammi Lynn and Tim would be on their way back to DC, possibly taking the necklace with them. Possibly not. And they couldn't take a chance on the former.

"Under it," she said, sliding beneath and hoping Kane would fit in the cramped space beside her. On the far side, he dropped to the floor and scooted under the dust ruffle as the door opened. Face up, his nose was barely an inch from the slats.

Holly smiled as he turned his head to glare at her.

The door opened, and she held her breath.

"We're going to get caught," a familiar masculine voice said, closing the door as he spoke.

Enzo, Kane mouthed.

Her eyes widened. Crap. If they were discovered, they'd be in trouble with the Burkes *and* the mob. Great.

"We won't. Everyone is out on that half-assed scavenger hunt, and we have the house all to ourselves," a woman replied.

Tammi Lynn, Holly mouthed.

The mobster's chuckle drifted downward. "So, you planned this?"

"I knew from the moment I met you that I had to have you," Tammi Lynn replied.

Liar. If Kane had shown any interest, he'd be here instead. Their hostess was a predator, and whoever was in her bedroom was the weakest in the herd. Nothing more.

"What about your husband?" He sounded unsure again.

"Tim is on a conference call, and the staff is doing the shopping to prep for tonight. We have an hour."

"My wife?"

"Getting a massage."

The sound of something dropping drew Holly's attention from Kane. Holly peered through the space between the floor and the bottom of the dust ruffle. A pair of men's khaki slacks puddled on the hardwood mere inches from her nose, followed by a short-sleeved white shirt and Tammi Lynn's green dress and black lace panties. Tammi Lynn's feet came into view. She kicked off her expensive pumps, shooting one of them under the bed, where it smacked into

Holly's forehead. She bit back a yelp.

Please don't look for your shoe now. Please don't look for your shoe now.

Fortunately, Tammi Lynn and Enzo were too focused on taking care of business to mind the lost Louboutin. The bed creaked as the couple tumbled on to it. Holly flinched, waiting for the weight of the couple to make the mattress sag down and smother her and Kane. But it held.

Good thing Tammi Lynn only believes in buying the best.

The noises the couple soon started emitting were enough to make Holly gag.

Kill me now. She did not want to hear Tammi Lynn and her lover du jour having sex. Especially not Enzo, with his big, close-cropped bowling ball of a head and meaty lips. He looked like the kind of guy who slobbered when he kissed.

She turned her head to focus her attention on Kane once more as the mattress started creaking slightly. Kane's eyes met hers, and to his credit, he remained silent. Stoic.

But his eyes told her that on the inside, he was anything but calm. She glimpsed anger and a pain so deep it seemed tangible. It wasn't about the people above them.

Staying quiet, she slid her hand along the floor until her fingertips touched his.

Sorry, she mouthed.

Above them, the bed creaked and groaned. "Fuck me hard," Tammi Lynn groaned. "Give it to me." *People actually said things like that outside of pornos?*

Kane didn't say a word. He said his girlfriend had cheated on him, but she sensed there was more. Had to be, considering his reaction.

What had he left out of his story?

Above them, the bed began to move in a faster rhythmic motion that told them more than they ever needed, or wanted, to know about their hostess and her guests.

Across from her, Kane stared upward, his face a blank mask. Holly shut her eyes but neither could close their ears.

· · ·

Would it never end? Listening to Tammi Lynn screw Enzo, of all people—not even caring that her husband was in the same house—made Kane sick. Under any other circumstances, he'd make his presence known and leave the room but not before telling the couple exactly what he thought of them.

This wasn't just any circumstance. This was work, and he had a job to do. As much as he didn't want to admit it, what Holly thought of him mattered. If he blew the mission because he let his past get in the way of the present, she would have every reason to call him out.

So, he closed his eyes and focused on Holly. The touch of her hand. The way her fingers wove through his. This scent of her hair. The rhythmic sound of her breathing.

Anything but the memories that worked their way through the wall he'd created to keep them at bay.

Holly sidled closer until her thigh pressed against his, and he thought about this morning. He'd been pissed when Bravo interrupted them. Now, he was grateful.

He didn't want to be like Tammi Lynn and the men she slept with. After Danielle's death, he'd tried to have sex without an emotional connection, but it didn't take him long to realize that meaningless sex wasn't what he wanted.

He wanted more. And while he might not be sure what

"more" meant, he knew it wasn't a series of one-night stands.

Above them, Enzo groaned loudly, and the mattress stilled. Sheets rustled, and a pair of feminine feet landed on the wooden floor inches from his head and headed toward the bathroom.

"Where are you going, babe?"

Tammi Lynn giggled, sounding like a teenager. "I'm going to start getting ready for the party tonight. You can show yourself out."

"What if I want another round?"

"I have to get ready." She walked back over to the bed. There was the distinct sound of a wet kiss. "I'm the hostess. Now go."

The bathroom door slammed, and seconds later, Kane heard the sound of the shower.

As soon as Enzo left, they'd follow, and per their backup plan if Holly ran out of time, Bravo could crack the safe when everyone was at the party.

"Bitch." Enzo muttered, but it wasn't loud enough for Tammi Lynn to hear. He didn't make a move to leave.

Holly tapped Kane with her foot and nodded upward. *What the hell*? She mouthed.

What the hell indeed. They didn't have long before Tammi Lynn finished her shower, and then they'd never be able to leave without blowing their cover. So, it was either expose themselves to the mobster or their hostess. Since they weren't here to take on organized crime, they had only one choice.

Follow my lead, he replied.

She gave him a thumbs up.

Not sure what he'd find, Kane scooted out from under

the bed and peeked over the top of the mattress.

Enzo lay on the bed, the white sheets draped over his hips and his eyes closed.

Thank God for small favors. The last thing he wanted to see was a naked Enzo.

With the sound of the water running providing cover, Kane rose to his feet, leaned over the bed, and clamped his hand over the man's mouth.

Enzo's eyes flew open, wide and shocked.

Good.

He tried to rise, and Kane pushed him back down, knowing he shouldn't enjoy the man's fear, but unable to quell the satisfaction that washed over him.

Holly used the edge of the mattress to pull herself upright next to Kane and waved at Enzo.

Cute. He almost laughed at her sheer joy in intimidating the mobster. She was either the bravest woman he knew or the craziest. Perhaps a bit of both.

Enzo struggled, and Kane went back to the task at hand, knowing their time was limited. "I'm taking my hand off your mouth," he said, "My fiancée and I are leaving. If you make a sound, if you tell *anyone* we were here, if I get a whiff of gossip, I will tell our host and your wife what we heard. Do you understand?"

Enzo's eyes widened, and he nodded, frantic. He might be in organized crime, but even the mobster had the sense to be frightened of Rachel.

Kane removed his hand.

Enzo sat up, eyes narrowed. "What are you doing here?"

"Doesn't matter. We're leaving." He took Holly's hand, grateful that she was with him. She might be a pain in the ass, but right now, she was what he needed. He unlocked the door, eager to get out of the room.

"You don't have evidence," Enzo said. "You tell Rachel, and I'll deny it."

Holly help up her phone. "Yeah, I do."

Enzo paled, and Kane followed his partner into the empty hallway, stopped, and leaned back in. "Remember, not a word," he said.

They slammed the door behind them and walked quickly back to their room.

Pulse pounding with adrenaline, Kane paced to the other side of their bed. That had been close.

Too close, but worse than confronting Enzo was listening to him and Tammi Lynn betray the people who loved them. He ran a hand through his hair, rubbing his scalp and wishing he could scrub his brain with a wire brush. Even if he could, there wasn't enough soap and water to wipe away what he'd heard.

Holly made a snorting sound, and he watched her lean against the wall, head down, shoulders shaking as she burst out in a guffaw and held up her phone. "Can you believe Enzo bought that? What a moron."

Hell, *he'd* bought it.

He could see why HRS hired her. She was quick. Smart. And a helluva actress. "You're amazing."

She gave a what-the-hell grin, slipped the phone back into her pocket, took a deep breath, and gathered herself. "So, we managed to get out of that, but what about the safe?"

Good question, since they were running out of time. "Bravo goes back tonight, during the cocktail party and entertainment."

"We're running out of time. What if the necklace isn't there?" she asked, picking up the camera they were supposed to use in the scavenger hunt. She pointed it at him and took a picture.

"Wing it."

"You're winging it? You?" She took another picture. "Let's make sure we capture that particular moment."

The shutter clicked. "I seem to be picking up bad habits."

She flipped the camera to take a selfie, puckering her lips. "From who?"

Kane added silly to his assessment of her abilities and found he liked the addition. It could be frustrating, but sometimes, like now, it was a good balance to his own, more serious, nature. "No idea."

• • •

"About time you two showed up. Did you get the necklace?"

Holly turned as the door opened, and Bravo walked into the room. He wore the same clothes from this morning, only they were covered in light yellow dog fur.

"How's Mr. Wiggles?" she asked, taking a picture of the agent.

"He's dehydrated, and they wanted to keep him overnight for observation. They mentioned his kidneys."

"He's not going to die or anything, is he?" she pressed.

"They want to be cautious, that's all." He flashed her a smile fit for Hollywood.

A tension in her chest she hadn't realized was there released, and Holly took another picture of Bravo, zooming in on the dog fur covering his shirt. "Thanks."

"Knock it off," Kane said, hand out for the camera.

"What the hell got into you?" she said, handing over the Nikon. Just seconds ago, they'd been laughing. Bantering. He was the Kane she knew from the island and now—

This guy was back.

There was only one explanation, and it stood in front of her—six feet two inches of hotness named Michael Bravo.

Was Kane jealous of the other agent? Granted, Bravo was a woman's fantasy, but Kane was a woman's dream. And she knew the difference—one you slept with and suffered the walk of shame when you left the following morning.

The other made you an omelet and invited you to stay.

Not that it mattered to her, she reminded herself. He likely wouldn't invite a circus freak to stay for breakfast in the real world.

"We didn't get the necklace," Kane said. "But we found the safe. Didn't have time to open it because Tammi Lynn came back to the room."

"So, what's the plan?" Bravo asked, stretching out on their bed, back pressed against the headboard.

"She'll be there all afternoon," Kane replied. "That much makeup and hair that big takes time."

Ouch.

Kane continued, "We wait for dark. Between dinner and the auction, you should have enough time to crack the safe and retrieve the necklace. You can use our room to scale up to their balcony. Or try the hallway. Your call."

"Balcony. It'll be dark, and I stand less chance of running into the staff as they do turn down." Bravo replied. "It's been a while since I've done a residential B&E, but I'll be in and out before you finish the appetizers."

"Don't kid yourself," she said. "The lock on the door is significant, which tells me that the safe is probably high-end."

"Thanks for the heads up," Bravo said. "I got this."

She tossed her best don't-be-an-ass glare his way.

He shrugged it off.

She appreciated that he was cocky—so was she—but this mission became more complicated with each hour, and who knew what the next hour might bring. Besides, she'd seen overconfidence nail more than one performer in the family's troupe. The results varied but almost always included a broken bone of some sort.

"I'd agree under normal circumstances," Kane said. "But we might have other players."

"Who?"

"Corsican mob," he replied.

"Shit." Bravo sat up, all vestiges of carelessness gone in an instant. The transformation took Holly's breath away. He was hot before, but now he had a dangerous edge that she was sure made panties drop worldwide. "What the hell are they doing here?"

"Our guess is that their attendance is an attempt to buy a politician—or ensure that one stays bought, depending on how long ago they got to know Tim Burke," Kane replied. "As long as we stay out of their way, I think we'll be good."

"A little late for that," Holly muttered.

Bravo zeroed in on the comment. "What do you mean?"

Kane explained what happened with Enzo, and Bravo laughed. "Damn, you two have some serious cojones."

Holly blushed at the praise.

"We did what we had to do," Kane snapped. "Now let's

get on with this."

Bravo's brows shot upward. He slid off the bed and headed for the door, footsteps quick and solid. "Works for me. You two work out whatever the hell is going on here. I'm going to take a shower and put on some clean clothes."

The door slammed shut behind him.

Arms crossed, Holly shook her head. "What is wrong with you?"

Chapter Nine

It was a good question—what the hell was he doing? He was the mission leader, and instead of leading, he was acting like a jealous asshole. Camera in hand, Kane headed out of the bedroom and toward the garden. Earlier, he'd seen a ceramic chicken along the path, and they should at least look like they tried to win the scavenger hunt. Holly followed, arms still crossed.

If she were a cartoon, he was sure he'd see steam coming out of her ears.

He couldn't blame her. He'd acted like an ass, and all because of Bravo, who didn't deserve the animosity. It wasn't Bravo's fault that women fell all over themselves when he was around.

Even Holly.

He hadn't missed the way she looked at the other agent.

"Are we going to talk about what happened?" Holly asked while he snapped a picture of the statue. They were in the same garden they'd talked in yesterday before the race. It smelled like a thousand flowers.

There wasn't much to say other than admitting he was jealous, and he wasn't about to confess that to a woman who kissed him and then made googly eyes at another man less than twenty-four hours later. "No."

She grabbed his arm, knocking the camera to the ground. "I don't get you," she said. "One minute we're laughing and joking and getting along, and the next you're the other guy."

What the hell was she talking about? "The other guy?"

"You know, the jerk."

Heat rushed from his chest upward, and he knew his face was reddening, not that it mattered. Holly was on a roll, and he suspected there was no shutting her up until she ran out of breath.

"The guy that told Tempe I was a bad team player. The guy that treats me like I'm a child who doesn't know her job. The guy that doesn't trust me."

The guy that doesn't trust me. There it was, the crux of the issue. Trust. He didn't trust anyone. But he wanted to. To do that, he needed to know the truth. "Did you sleep with him?"

"The guy that—" She stopped mid-sentence. For a long beat, they stared at each other, and he waited for her to speak. He'd already done enough talking.

"What?" she asked.

He forced the words out, dreading the answer. It was the scenario with Danielle all over again, but he seemed unable to stop it from playing out or from asking the questions he really didn't want to know the answers to. "Did you sleep with Bravo?"

She took a deep breath then let it slip out. "Does it matter?"

He looked out toward the marina. It did. He reminded himself that she had a life before this mission. Before he found out how much he wanted her, and he had no right to hold that life against her. He shook his head. "Forget I asked. It's none of my business."

"I did. Once," she confessed, surprising him.

It wasn't the answer he wanted to hear, but there it was— the truth he'd already known. He didn't want to be right. The thought of her sleeping with Bravo was…he wiped the thought away.

She's not Danielle. You have no say in her life. Not now. Not before. Still, his hands clenched into fists at the thought of Holly in Bravo's bed. "The guy's an ass."

"I know."

"So, why?" he asked.

She turned away, but not before he saw the mix of guilt and embarrassment on her face. "We got caught up in the moment. Sometimes things happen in the field."

Things happen in the field.

Danielle had said almost the same thing. She'd sobbed the words, begging forgiveness. He hadn't cared. Couldn't get past the pain of betrayal. So, instead of hashing out the issue, he'd walked out on her, and by the time he was ready to talk to her a few weeks later, she was on to a new operation.

It was never said, but he knew she'd taken the job to get away from the pain they'd caused each other. And under normal circumstances, she'd have been fine. But it hadn't been a normal circumstance, and she hadn't been at her best. She'd entered a drug dealer's compound disguised as a junkie and blown her cover less than twenty-four hours into the mission.

Tempe had broken the news to him and asked him to partner with the DEA to bring her home. He was on the next plane, desperate to save her so they could talk. Maybe they'd work it out. Maybe not. But he owed them both the opportunity to try.

He'd headed the team that breached the building, but when the shooting stopped and all the fires were put out, Danielle had been killed and he had the scar, his constant reminder of what happened when agents got involved with each other.

He rubbed his leg, the scar tissue sensitive beneath the cloth.

"I know," he said, finally responding to her comment. "People get caught up in the moment."

Holly sighed, "I don't plan to revisit my one night with Bravo, if that's what you really need to know."

The tightness in his chest eased a notch, surprising him, and he found it easier to breathe. "Yeah. I guess I do." He rubbed the back of his neck, frustrated with Holly, himself, and the whole damned situation.

A least she admitted the indiscretion and hadn't forced him to pry it out of her or worse—find the evidence.

He managed a grim smile. "And by the way, you're right."

She cocked her head. "I'm right?"

"I don't trust you. I don't trust anyone. So, I appreciate you telling me the answer to a question I had no right to ask."

She sat on the marble bench, her gaze softening. "This would be easier if you stayed a jerk. I can't stay mad when you agree with me."

"You want to stay mad?" He retrieved the camera from

the dirt. Who would choose to stay pissed?

"It sure makes dealing with you a lot easier." Her gaze softened even more, and he found himself stepping into her space, wanting to keep the moment. Camera at his side, he snapped a shot, taking a picture of her.

"What are you doing?" she asked.

"My finger slipped," he lied.

She snorted at his insincerity but didn't seem to care.

"What do you want?" he asked, dreading the answer but needing to know. He knew it wasn't to stay angry. She wasn't an angry person, and it was her optimism that he found both admirable and annoying—depending on the situation.

She took a deep breath. "I want what we had this morning and last night. I want you."

He didn't know what to say. To do. She stared up at him from her spot on the bench, waiting, watching him with those damned liquid eyes.

For the first time in years, he wanted to trust. Needed to put that kind of faith in another person. Perhaps that kind of trust—that truth—would lead nowhere. Maybe he and Holly were meant to just be friends. Colleagues who shared a kiss and nothing more.

Hell, maybe she would talk about him later. Another confession to another agent.

He didn't care.

"Kane?" she finally asked, breaking the silence.

Before he could second-guess himself, he pulled her up to her feet, cupped her face in his hands, and kissed her.

• • •

Holly slid her fingers into Kane's hair, the strands falling through her grasp like thick silk. He sat on the garden bench and pulled her into his lap, straddling him.

His hands on her hips, he pulled her against him, and she felt his erection and gasped. The first time they'd had a moment together, she'd stopped them. The second time, Bravo had.

She wasn't giving Kane a chance to make it a third. As crazy as it felt, she wanted him. He was damaged. A pain in her ass.

And she couldn't get enough of his hands on her body.

"You realize this is a really bad idea," Kane whispered, nuzzling her neck before baring her shoulder.

Her breath hissed through her teeth as his hands slid from her hips to her bottom, lifting her. "I don't care," she replied.

"You might."

"I won't." She pressed her mouth to his to shut him up.

He pulled her away. "If you're having second thoughts, you need to tell me. Now."

Holly smiled. Bravo had taken her to bed without hesitation. *Bravo was an ass.*

Bravo had also left her without hesitation, although she'd expected it, so it hadn't really bothered her. And now here was Kame, offering her an out. *Idiot.* She didn't want an out. She wanted him. And if he didn't shut up, either one might come to their senses. "What I'm thinking is that you need to stop talking."

He clasped her hand and kissed her palm. "We should find someplace more private."

Good point. What she planned to do was not something

for public consumption.

She looked over his shoulder and spotted the tops of the sailboats over the bushes. It was close, but with everyone on the scavenger hunt in town, odds were that it would be deserted.

"The marina," she whispered. Putting her on her feet, he took her hand in his and they ran for the dock. Holly found herself laughing at the urgency. The need.

They reached the wharf, and there was nothing to see but boats and nothing to hear but the cry of the gulls and the sounds of the small waves as they lapped at the hull of the vessels. Kane stopped and pulled her against him. She could feel him, already hard, with wanting for her.

Then, they were in motion again. Seconds later, their feet pounded on the dock, wood slats bending under their weight.

They tried the first boat. The cabin door was locked.

Holly flashed him a wide smile. "I have an idea," and she grabbed his hand, pulling him along. She stopped in front of the *Glory*, Enzo's boat.

Kane's brows shot up. "Probably not a good plan."

She stepped over the rail. The boat rocked beneath her feet, but she found she didn't mind it nearly as much as before. She gave the cabin door a pull. It opened. "Are you kidding? It's a perfect idea," she countered, hands on her hips, daring Kane to disagree. "He almost killed us and we had to listen to him and Tammi Lynn. He owes us."

Kane shook his head. "You're a helluva lot of trouble."

"Worth. It," she said, punctuating each word with a shake of her hips.

He hesitated then stepped over the railing. "Sold."

His hand in hers, he led her down the steps into the cabin. A table folded out from the wall. A single sink. A refrigerator that barely qualified as anything more than a cooler.

And a wide, padded bench that probably folded out into a bed.

Kane sat and dragged her onto his lap, so she straddled him. She buried her head in his neck, inhaling him. He smelled like shampoo and soap—a definite improvement from their time stranded on the island.

She flicked her tongue against his ear, and he groaned. She did it again for the sheer pleasure of listening to his breath deepen as he tried to control himself.

His hands glided under her shirt and up her back, tracing paths on bared skin while she clutched him with her legs, rocking back and forth, both desperate to remove her clothes and not wanting the anticipation to end.

He grabbed her hips. "You need to stop, or this is going to be over a lot sooner than either of us will like," he said, his words somewhere between a moan and coherent speech.

She laughed and gave a small wriggle. "You can take it."

He held her close until she was unable to move no matter how hard she tried to break the strength of his grasp.

"You never listen," he said. "Always have to do things your way."

Classic Kane, but she heard the laughter in his voice. "You never trust me to know what I'm doing," she challenged, but in this case, she knew he was right, since he pressed hard between her legs, throbbing. If she didn't slow down, he'd be finished before either were naked.

She wasn't going to have that.

She bit his ear. "You win. After all, you're the boss."

"I'm the boss?" He wound his fingers through her hair, and their eyes met.

His gray eyes were darker than flint. Dangerous and thrilling. She shivered. This was the Kane she wanted—a man in control of the fire within...but barely.

"Can you say that again?" he teased. "I think I heard wrong."

She stuck her tongue out at him in reply.

He laughed, lifting her and flipping her onto her back on the bench. "For that, you're going to pay."

She doubted that she was going to mind. "Do your worst. I can take it."

"You say that now." Slowly, he unbuttoned her shorts then slid them down her hips, leaving her panties on. His breath washed over her stomach, hot and so close, she squirmed.

He traced a path with his tongue, stopping when he reached her sternum.

She closed her eyes as he unbuttoned her shirt and un-clasped the front hook of her bra.

Come on. Come on. Please.

As if reading her mind, he took a nipple into his mouth, biting and licking until streaks of pleasure made her toes curl and her breath came in gasps. How could she have ever thought he was a stick in the mud?

She'd never been more wrong about a man.

He tweaked her other breast with skilled fingers, and she arched into him.

"Ready to cry mercy?" he asked, kissing his way back down her body, pausing at her stomach. She shifted toward him, showing him what she wanted. He ignored the silent pleas, and instead, ran a thumb under the waist of her panties, teasing and taunting her with possibilities.

"Not a chance," she said, although surrender was starting to sound appealing.

He slid his fingers farther under the waistband, brushing against her and making her gasp and squirm, eager for more tension. A little more. Just a little.

So close.

He laughed. "You sure?"

Smart-ass. She'd never been more positive of anything in her life. "Do your worst."

He slid her panties off with a flourish and knelt between her thighs, his mouth replacing his hand, his tongue sliding down. Teasing. Tasting.

There. "Oh God." Her climax tumbled over her like a rogue wave. She groaned as the world disappeared. His mouth moved, extending the pleasure until she whimpered and tears wet her cheeks.

He let her pause, and the world returned, hazy and glowing.

"I told you," he said.

She glanced at him through her lashes. He kneeled between her thighs, and she wondered when he'd stripped and where he had found a condom. Trust Kane to be the Boy Scout and have one handy.

He slid inside her, and she didn't care about anything other than the man in her arms.

Her muscles, still tense and tingling, clamped down, and she squeezed, both pushing herself back toward the edge of orgasm and making him gasp at the same time. "I told you, I'm an acrobat," she whispered. "I have superb muscle control. Everywhere."

"Worth it," he replied, but his eyes rolled back in his head when she did it again.

She shivered in his arms, her bare body sliding along his, the rough scar on his thigh a sharp contrast to his otherwise unmarred skin. All coherent thought faded as he slid inside her from tip to base, each stroke bringing her closer.

His breath in her ear, he grew harder, thicker, and she knew he was close. She wrapped her knees around his hips, wanting the friction.

So close.

He increased his pace, his face buried in her hair, and she pressed against him, not wanting the moment to end but knowing there was no stopping it. Not now.

"Holly," he groaned her name, arms stiffened as his hips pressed into her, and she felt him shudder as orgasm took him.

She clenched her muscles one more time and joined him.

• • •

How long had they slept, half-naked and coiled around each other on the too-small bench? Holly wondered.

Ten minutes? Ten hours?

Not long, she realized. The sun hadn't set yet. They still had time before the auction, so no hurry.

She didn't want to rush. She was satisfied. Happy. More content than she'd been in a long time. Kane might be a pill on occasion, but all that focus and diligence paid off when it came to sexy time.

"You're amazing." He nuzzled her ear then kissed the tip of her nose. "That was worth the wait. You're worth the wait."

She grinned, knowing she probably looked like an idiot but not caring.

"You too," she said, gliding her nails down his back, his thighs, and tracing the scar she'd first seen in the locker room just days ago.

He tensed.

She kissed his mouth. "Does it hurt?"

He shook his head, his eyes hardening for a flicker before he blinked the ache away. "Not anymore."

She imagined it did at one time. She'd seen scars on other agents and most wore them like badges of honor. But she'd never heard chatter about what happened to create something so wide and ragged on Kane's perfect body.

"Are you going to ask how I got it?" Kane asked.

She wanted to, but she knew how he felt about prying, and she didn't want to end this moment. Not yet. That would come soon enough. "You'll tell me if you want to," she replied.

His eyes widened. "I'm shocked. When do you not try to steal information?"

She stuck her tongue out again.

"Such a child," he admonished.

He brought it out in her, that much was true. She liked that she could act like an idiot, and he didn't think less of her.

He continued, "When this mission is over, we should try this on a real bed." He cupped her cheek in his hand.

A sliver of panic intruded into the happy warmth. What did he mean by that? "You want to see me after the mission is over?"

"Is that such a bad thing?"

Mentally, she kicked herself for letting her libido and her emotions make her decisions. This was why she'd wanted Bravo. With a man like Bravo, she'd never have to have this conversation or introduce him to her mother and the rest of her motley circus family. And watch his expression grow stonier and colder, until he made his excuses and left—for good.

He kissed the tip of her nose. "You okay?"

Commitment. Intimacy. She swallowed hard. She'd avoided both since she was a teenager. *With Kane, it might be worth the risk*, a small, quiet voice in her head, suggested. *It would be so easy. Just open up. Let him see the real you.*

What if he hated the real her? What then?

Right now, he gazed into the eyes of a thief. An acrobat. A tightrope walker. All of that made her seem exotic and thrilling, and people wanted to share in that excitement. She knew that and used it to open doors to places she might not normally be welcome.

Once in a great while, she dropped her guard and let a potential boyfriend move past the facade. When they met the real her, they realized that she was a packaged deal that included a bearded lady, knife thrower, clowns, and a psychic mother. Overwhelmed, they always ran screaming for the hills.

She didn't want to see that kind of shock in Kane's expression. Not now. Not ever.

She squelched the urge to open up before it could gain hold. "I'm fine. Better than fine. But we should talk."

For more than a few heart beats, the only sound was the water lapping against the side of the boat. "You're running away, aren't you?" he asked when the silence grew to almost painful proportions.

"I'm not running away," she said, trying to make a joke and failing. "Where would I go? We're on a mission."

"Don't play dumb."

Could she be a bigger jerk? "Sorry." Untangling herself from his arms, she sat up, grabbed her panties and slid them on, needing the movement and the distance. "Please don't make this harder than it needs to be."

"I won't," he said, retrieving his clothes.

That was it? He wasn't even going to try? A part of her ached even as she told herself this was what she wanted. Freedom from responsibility. No boyfriend. No Kane.

"Thanks," she whispered, the words like sawdust in her mouth. "Look, I didn't—"

She was interrupted by the thudding of footsteps on the dock, and she clamped her mouth shut.

Her eyes met Kane's, and he put a finger to his mouth. This might be nothing and no one, but she appreciated that it was best to find out before announcing their presence.

"Here. This should be far enough," someone said. She knew that voice. *Enzo.* From the comment, he wasn't alone.

Shit.

Kane grabbed her arm. "Move," he whispered.

Scooping up the rest of their clothes, he pushed her into the bathroom built for one. Standing on the toilet lid, she moved as far back as she could, giving Kane enough room to join her.

The thudding stopped. The boat rocked. Hell. They were coming on board.

Her heart pounded hard, and she was sure Enzo and his

friend could hear it smacking into her sternum.

There was scuffling and the squeal of a metal hinge when someone opened a cupboard then slammed it closed. "Got it. Happy now?" Enzo asked.

Enzo must have left something behind.

"Not quite," and unknown man said. "What the hell happened?"

"That's Lucien, Enzo's father," Kane whispered, his mouth against her ear and his voice so low, she barely heard it. "The one I told you about."

Awesome. A mob leader was outside the door, searching for who-knew-what, and she was barely dressed.

She didn't want to die wearing nothing but yellow satin panties with butterflies embroidered on the butt.

"I did as you asked," Enzo said. "I fucked the bitch, and when she went to the shower, I searched the room."

Her heart sped up again, and she was sure she was going to have a heart attack as they waited to hear if Enzo was going to tell Lucien about their part in the story.

"So, where is it?' Lucien asked.

"No idea. She wasn't wearing it. It wasn't in her dresser. There's a safe in the floor. I'm guessing she stashed it inside."

Holly took a long, silent inhale then let it out in relief. Apparently, Enzo didn't want to let anyone know about his fuck up—not that she blamed him. She doubted that the head of the mob was tolerant when it came to mistakes.

"You sure you didn't miss it?" Lucien asked, the depth of anger in his voice made her shiver, and she counted herself glad to not be on the receiving end of his wrath.

"It's a fucking gaudy turtle necklace. Trust me, if it was there, I'd know it. I'm not a fucking moron."

The hairs on the back of her neck rose, and she glanced down to Kane. His mouth was pressed tight. Whatever the Corsicans were doing here had nothing to do with gaining a foothold in the political arena. They were after the same necklace HRS had been hired to retrieve.

"What do we do?" Enzo asked.

"Send Rachel to get it during the auction," was the reply. "Everyone will be occupied. If someone asks, tell them she has girl trouble or something."

Rachel? A thief?

Great. What else had they missed?

Chapter Ten

The two men left, the weight of their shifting bodies making the boat rock hard enough that Kane had to brace himself against the wall of the bathroom. He signaled for Holly to wait. They weren't safe. Not yet.

She nodded, more compliant than usual, and he wasn't sure if he liked the change. The upside was that her silence meant they weren't arguing, and right now, he needed the reprieve.

He needed to think. To process and deal with what had happened, but it was hard to ignore the anger bubbling inside. He glanced at his partner, her hands pressed against the walls for balance. It wasn't her beauty that drew him in. She was fascinating and always kept him guessing, and something told him that what they had was special.

But he'd had been wrong before, which made her decision to bail all the more painful. He wasn't sure what pissed him off more—his misjudgment of Holly, that Mira Burke withheld some obviously critical information about the necklace, or himself for giving in to lust.

"I think we can go," Holly whispered. "We should get to Bravo."

Her words brought back some of the clarity that had fled, and the heat in his chest dropped to bearable levels. Answers could wait. He knew his priority—the mission.

He wasn't going to forget it again.

He cracked the door open. The cabin and cockpit were empty. Climbing the short ladder, he watched the men disappear off the dock and into the gardens as they headed toward the house.

"They're gone," he said. "We need to do the same." It would be dark soon—time for the auction—and they'd lost valuable time on the boat. At least they now knew about Rachel and could neutralize her so Bravo didn't run into her in the master suite.

And then there was Enzo. Was he going to be an issue? It was doubtful the mobster would take a chance on confronting Kane, Holly, or their "assistant." But Enzo had left them out of his story to Lucien, so that meant he was afraid of what would happen if his father knew he'd been caught.

Fear made men do stupid things—like killing the people they were scared of. Killing was something HRS agents didn't do unless they had no other choice.

The scar on his leg itched at the memory of almost losing his life, but it wasn't so much the near-death experience that bothered him, it was the fact he had lost a fellow agent.

As far as he was concerned, death shouldn't be categorized under "trivial things," so he'd left the volatile world of retrieving kidnap victims and turned to running item retrieval ops for HRS instead. Trinkets, files, and photos didn't die. With the exception of working with Holly, it wasn't as exciting, but his conscience was clear, and at the end of the day, he went home. He liked it that way.

"Any idea why they want the necklace?" Holly said as he helped her off the boat and onto the dock, her hand warm in his.

He wished he knew. It was his job as mission leader to know everything—even what the client wanted to remain secret. He'd poured over the files before they left but didn't see any red flags besides the usual. Just a divorcee wanting her property. Of course it wasn't because she cared about it. He'd known that much was a lie, but had assumed her reason was to hurt the trophy wife.

An obvious motivation. Too obvious, it seemed.

He had missed something. But what? "No, but we'll find out."

They headed toward the house in silence, passing back through the garden where they'd kissed.

"Do you want to talk about what happened?" Holly asked, her attention on the bench.

"No." There wasn't anything to say. Though, if he knew his partner, she wasn't going to let the conversation drop. She was tenacious as hell—one of the things he liked about her.

They reached the edge of the grass that surrounded the luxury home. Caterers carried in trays of food. Designers strung lights and flowers over and through the tent, until it looked like something out of a fairy tale.

"You know you're going to have to talk about it some-time," Holly said when he grabbed her hand to maintain the illusion of coupledom.

"I've been here before, and I know how it ends," he said. She'd made it plain how she felt, and he had no plans to beg her to stay. There was only moving on.

"You dated an agent?" she asked.

Great, he'd piqued her curiosity. He shrugged, sorry he'd let his frustration with the situation get the best of him. "It was a long time ago."

"Oh," Holly said. "That doesn't mean we shouldn't talk about what happened back on the boat. On the couch."

She just couldn't let it go.

So much like Danielle.

He stopped mid-step. This was going to end here and now, before someone got hurt. Or worse. "We fucked. That's it. End of story."

Despite the clattering and noise, he heard her sharp intake of break. Like she'd been punched, and he hated the petty sense of satisfaction that came with winning the argument.

She yanked her hand from his, and he didn't bother to take it back. Let the other guests think they were arguing. Couples did it all the time, and in this crowd, they'd stand out more if they didn't submit to the occasional public bickering session.

"Do you have an alternate plan to get the necklace, now that we know Rachel is a thief?" she asked, her voice tight.

Good. Back to what was important. "We're on limited time. There may not be an alternative."

"We could let this go. We both know there's more happening here than Mira let on."

He wished he could, but even though Mira withheld information, this was about more than the necklace. If the Corsicans wanted it, it wasn't just a tacky piece of jewelry, which meant they couldn't walk away, despite Mira's deception. "We'll find out what she left out as soon as we finish this job."

Holly stopped mid-step and crossed her arms over her chest. "What about Bravo? He could get killed."

"That's why we're hurrying. To try and mitigate the danger."

"There's no guarantee," she countered.

"I know." Was that where her emotions rested—with Bravo? He put a hand on her shoulder. The show was over, and they needed to discuss this in private. "Let's go."

She jerked out of his grasp. "Are you going to continue acting like an ass because of what happened today? Because you're jealous?"

"Do you think I'm that petty? That small?" he said when he found his voice. She may be blind to what was happening between them and call him a stick-in-the-mud behind his back, but did she think he was such a jerk that he'd sacrifice another agent—out of jealousy?

A bright blush spread up her neck and to her face. "No. No... Of course not."

She'd suffered enough, but he didn't know what to say to fix it. Not anymore. Life was a helluva lot easier when she'd been a pain in the ass and nothing more. He headed toward the front door. "We have to talk to Bravo and get dressed for the auction."

• • •

"You sure they said it was the same necklace?" Bravo asked. Wearing black slacks, a black formal shirt, tuxedo jacket, and black shoes, their "assistant" paced the floor, waiting for

Tammi Lynn and Tim to vacate their room.

As soon as they'd entered the house, they'd give him the new information that stealing the necklace might not be as simple as they thought, now that there were other players in the mix. "Positive," Kane replied. "Unless she owns another ugly diamond necklace shaped like a turtle."

"Doubt it," Bravo replied, slowing his stride and taking a seat to open a bottle of wine.

Kane continued, "Besides, it makes sense. It's why the client wanted us here this weekend—she knew the mob was going for it. The question is, why?"

"I wish we knew," Bravo said.

"The real question is, how are we going to get it before they do?" Holly said, frustrated at listening to the men talk as if time was on their side. "We're sitting around here yapping, when Bravo should be in the room cracking the safe."

"Tammi Lynn is nowhere to be found. That means she is still in the room," Kane said. "Which means we wait."

They'd done a quick search when they'd arrived, and their hostess was nowhere to be found—not even the kitchen, though no surprise there. Tammi Lynn wasn't the type to get her hands messy.

Holly took the offered glass of wine from Bravo and stepped outside. The trees only partially obscured their view of the tent, making observation difficult but possible. So far, there was no sign of Tammi Lynn or Tim, which meant that even though the party—cocktails, hors d'oeuvres, and a string quartet—was only minutes away, no one would dare step on the lawn until their hosts arrived. Anything else would be rude.

She glanced up to the balcony of the master suite just

above her head and their room. *Their room.*

Taking a large gulp of the pinot noir, she reminded herself that she could not let Kane into her head. If she did, she'd blow the mission, and while she'd made mistakes before, it was never because of a man.

Slowly, she took in her surroundings, gauging the chance she could take care of this herself while Kane and Bravo went on and on, discussing ramifications, scenarios, and whatever else they could come up with.

She expected this kind of detail from Kane but was surprised that Bravo seemed as determined to go through the options. She'd thought he was more spontaneous like her, and that was another reason she'd wanted to get closer to him.

It seemed she was wrong. He was as annoyingly regimented as her partner. She hated them both. Or wanted to. Instead, she found herself watching Kane. Replaying their hours in the boat in her head and wishing that things had been different. That she was different.

"Stop it, you idiot," she muttered to herself. There was no going back from turning him down. She reminded herself that she didn't need or want a relationship. Certainly not with Kane. That was inviting trouble.

She gulped down the rest of the wine and forced herself to address the current situation.

None of the balconies were lit, and the large trees filtered out the lights below, leaving the back of the house shaded. It would be fully dark soon, providing even more coverage. She wasn't sure that even mattered. If someone did wander out, their attention would be on the impending festivities below.

No one ever looked up. It would be so easy to scale the

wall and sneak into the room. If she did this right, she'd have the necklace before Tammi Lynn could say "bless her heart."

But as long as either of the Burkes were in the room, that idea was too risky.

She took another sip of her wine, and as if on cue, the downstairs patio door slid open beneath them, and Tammi Lynn and Tim Burke appeared, starting to walk across the yard. *Speak of the devil.* She watched as the Southern belle began ordering the servants, rearranging the rainbow of gerbera daisies and greenery that made up the centerpieces, and fretting over the other decorations—an arbor, some strategically placed lights, damask chair covers with tasteful bows tied at the back. Tim took a seat at one of the tables and began drinking, as the other guests filtered out now that their hosts had arrived.

She spotted Enzo stomping toward a table. Alone.

A ripple of tension raced through Holly. It was time to steal the necklace and get the hell out of here. She stepped back inside. "Tammi Lynn and Tim are outside. I don't know what you two are planning, but I think we need to take advantage of the situation and get the necklace. Now."

"Any sign of Rachel?" Kane asked.

"Just Enzo." Which, under other circumstances, might be normal. Under these, it mean only one thing.

"She'll probably make her move any minute," Kane said, finishing her train of thought. "Holly, I want you to go to her room and stall her."

"And how do you propose I do that?" she asked. There was nothing she could say that wouldn't either make her look obvious or sound like a lunatic.

"Tell her you heard she wasn't feeling well. She won't be

able to leave," Kane said, but his jaw was tight and his stance anything but relaxed. "Not while you're in the room."

They were overthinking it—probably trying to keep her safe. Sweet but unnecessary. She faced them down. "I have a better idea. Send Bravo to distract Rachel."

"He's our assistant and out of her league."

Holly waved off his worry with a flick of her wrist. "Trust me, she's not going to care. He's seduced waitresses and even a royal or two. It's what he does."

"She's right. I'm good at it,' Bravo said. "As your assistant, I can chat her up. Tell her that you want to share a table or something." He straightened his tie, looking pleased with himself. "Once I have her alone, you'll have all the time in the world."

What an ego.

"It's settled," Holly said, heading for the door. "Now if you can grab Bravo's grappling hook from his room, I'll get dressed, steal the necklace, and we can get the hell out of here."

. . .

Kane slammed the door behind him, grappling hook and rope tucked under his jacket. Holly had already slipped into a pair of black leggings and a long-sleeved black T-shirt.

Not an outfit for the weekend but one for robbing, "Did you know you'd be doing this?" he asked as she pulled a pair of black leather gloves from a zippered compartment in her suitcase.

"I always assume I might have to," she replied, not bothering to hide her smile.

He should have known. Add Holly to a mission, and it was going to go sideways. It was bad enough that he had to deal with the Corsican mob, but an agent who had her own agenda was beyond frustrating.

"Let's do this," she said, taking the hook and rope from his arms and slipping it over her shoulder.

Let's not, but he kept the thought to himself.

Opening the door to the balcony, Kane took a final survey at the scenario on the other side of the lawn. It was dark, making the event at the tent difficult to see, but as far as he could tell, there was no sign of Rachel.

Kane took a deep breath. "Let's get this over with."

Using his shoulder to steady herself. Holly stepped up onto the three-inch-wide, wooden rail that outlined the wraparound balcony, and Kane's stomach did a summersault. "Aren't you using the hook?" he asked.

"Yes, but that railing juts out an additional foot. I need you to hold my legs so I can lean out just a little bit and get a good swing of the rope."

Ask him to shoot a bad guy or hack a computer system, and he was all for it. But holding Holly's life in his hands as she dangled in the air tweaked his nerves in a way he hadn't known was possible.

"Okay, what do I do?"

"Hold my thighs and don't let go," she said.

Dammit, she was enjoying this. But he grabbed her legs, wrapping his arms around them.

She leaned backward at the waist, more flexible than anyone had the right to be. Arms out for balance, she kept her eye on her target—the floor above her. She let the grapple hang a few feet from the end of the rope, and he watched her mouth. *One*. She took a deep breath. *Two*. She exhaled. *Three*.

He held her tighter, and she tossed the hook upward. There was a clink of metal on stone. She pulled. It held.

Success.

She grabbed the rope, and he let go. "Back in a jiff," she said and climbed upward Seconds later, she disappeared, and he heard the click of the door as she entered the bedroom above them.

Time to wait.

He rubbed his forehead. She was fearless, which he loved. And loathed. Danielle had been as daring, and it had served her well. Until her luck ran out and her "I can do anything and survive" attitude got her killed.

Leaning on the rail, he caught a glimpse through the leaves of the hostess running around as if this party were the most important thing in the world. Did Tim know his bride slept around?

He suspected it didn't matter as long as she looked good standing at his side. For the thousandth time, he was grateful he'd left that life behind. He'd lost a lot of people, but at least he could sleep at night.

"Look what you did!"

Kane zeroed in on the screaming. Seconds later, Tammi Lynn strode across the backyard with what looked like red wine staining the front of her cream-colored dress. A server dressed in classic black and white and her hair tied back in a ponytail, followed her, apologizing.

Tammi Lynn stopped, and began to berate the young girl, screaming that she's ruined the dress.

Which meant she was going to change clothes.

Shit.

"Holly?!" He stage whispered her name.

No reply.

"Holly," he called again.

No answer.

Below him, Tammi continued her rant.

Racing through the room, he ran out to the hall and bounded up the stairway to the master bedroom. "Holly," he whispered, tapping on the door. "Holly. Dammit. Open the door."

No answer. But he didn't dare knock louder. The sound of footsteps stomping up the stairs heralded Tammi Lynn's arrival. Kane leaned against the wall and tried to channel Michael Bravo's ability to fade into the woodwork.

Tammi Lynn came into view. Petite. Perfect hair. Narrowed eyes and mouth tight with anger.

Then she met his gaze, and her mouth softened into a smile. She reached the landing. "Kane, what brings you here?" she asked, her voice so low it was almost a purr.

He did the one thing he knew would work, he crooked a finger at her. Two steps later, and she was in his arms. Soft and lush as any woman he had ever touched.

And married.

He cringed on the inside. He'd done many things for the agency, but never this. The bile in his stomach rose. He thought of Danielle and her infidelity. Their last fight. The guilt on all sides.

And how he never wanted to be a part of any scenario like that again.

But he also didn't want Holly found out. If it were just Tammi Lynn, he might risk it. They'd lose the chance to steal the necklace, but he carried loyalty to HRS only so far.

But with the mob involved, who knew what might happen, and he wasn't taking a chance that she might get hurt.

Or worse.

Holly owed him.

Tammi Lynn's tongue ticked his lips then slid into his mouth. She tasted like the red wine she'd been drinking. "We should get inside," she whispered, opening the door. "We'll have to make this quick."

Kane placed his hands on her hips, and stopped the door from opening more than a crack. As Tammi Lynn started to kiss his neck and run her hands through his hair, he looked past her and spotted Holly kneeling at the safe. She'd shoved the rug into an accordion pile on the side. Had she retrieved the necklace? He tried to mentally telegraph the question, bugging out his eyes and pursing his lips.

She gritted her teeth at him and winced, looking younger than he'd ever seen her without her trademark confidence in place.

This mission wasn't going to fail, if he could help it. He had a duty—not as an HRS agent but as a human being—to make sure Lucian Pascua didn't get what he was after.

All he needed to do was buy her a few more seconds, and she'd be out of the room. And he could get rid of the woman who insisted on shoving her tongue down his throat.

"What about your husband?" he asked Tammi Lynn.

"He's outside," she replied with a small laugh. "We don't have long, but I'm sure it will be long enough." She cupped his crotch, caressing him through his slacks.

The bile in his stomach rose a little higher. He put all he had into looking like he was enjoying himself and not about to projectile vomit. "Excellent," he said, tilting her chin upward and kissing her again to give Holly the time she needed to escape.

Tammi Lynn's fingers clutched his shirt, and she pulled him into the room. *Please be gone.*

Other than themselves, the bedroom was empty, the rug back in place. There was no way to know if his partner had gone out the balcony or was under the bed. He hoped for the former, but knowing Holly, anything was possible.

Either way, he'd done what he could, and it was time to extricate himself from the situation. The question was, how?

Tammi Lynn reached behind her, the distinct sound of a zipper being undone caught his attention, and her dress slipped down her shoulders, revealing a trashy red Frederick's of Hollywood bra. Holly would have looked amazing in it. On Tammi Lynn, it screamed low-rent. "Lock the door."

Hand on the knob and debating the ramifications of bolting, he heard a familiar voice.

"Kane? Honey? Where the heck did you run off to?"

Holly.

From the faraway sound of her voice, he guessed that she stood at the bottom of the stairs. He looked at Tammi Lynn over his shoulder, working hard to keep the relief from his face and voice. "I have to go."

Tammi Lynn's thin mouth flattened into an angry line. "You owe me," she said.

She wasn't scared of getting caught, he realized, but she sure as hell was pissed at being denied.

"Of course," he replied with what he hoped was a convincing look of contrition, as he closed the door behind him and breathed a sigh of relief.

Chapter Eleven

"I knew that was a bad idea," Kane said, pacing back and forth in their room, clutching his cell phone like he wanted to squeeze it to death.

Sitting on the bed, Holly tried not to fidget as Kane loosened his grip on the mobile and texted Bravo, telling him what happened. "It was a good idea, just bad luck," she said. "How was I to know that our hostess would douse herself in wine and need a change of clothes?"

He continued as if she hadn't spoken, "You could have been caught."

Holly glared at Kane. She didn't let her mother talk to her like this. She sure wasn't going to let him. "There is nothing she could have done to me if she caught me. And I don't need or want a lecture. Let me know when you're finished being a giant nag, and we can get back to work and figure out our next move."

"I am not a nag. I am leading this operation." Kane

snapped.

"Let it go, Kane." Bravo interrupted.

Holly turned. The other agent stood in the doorway.

Kane stopped mid-step. "Excuse me?"

"Let it go. She took a shot, and it didn't work. If Tammi Lynn hadn't spilled wine all over herself, Holly would have succeeded. So, let it go. Things happen in the field, you know that." He finished his wine. "Now if you two don't get downstairs, people will start to talk, so I suggest we get on with the job. As far as I can tell, there's no reason we can't keep to the original plan. No harm done. Just get to Rachel, and I'll give it a shot."

No harm unless she counted putting Kane in the position of kissing a married woman. He tried to act as if nothing happened, but she'd noticed the smudge of fuchsia lipstick on his shirt as soon as they were in the room. Even if there wasn't the telltale lipstick, the nauseated expression told her that he'd done something he hadn't wanted to.

Add it all together, and it meant he'd kissed Tammi Lynn in order to save her.

The combination of sacrifice and guilt was the only reason she'd let him berate her for more than thirty seconds.

She glanced at Bravo. *Thanks*, she mouthed.

He toasted her with the empty glass.

Kane ran a hand through his hair, the simple gesture seeming to help him rein in his anger. "As you said, no harm done. I think we can proceed as planned."

He walked over to the French doors and cast a glance outside. "Our hostess is back at the tent. Bravo, I'll text you the all clear." He held up his phone. "Holly and I will head to the party and make sure that Rachel doesn't get a chance to interfere."

"This would be a hell of a lot easier if we went to her room," Holly said, knowing they couldn't without giving away the fact they overheard Enzo's conversation.

"If it was easy, we wouldn't be here," Kane shot back.

"On that note, I'm outta here," Bravo said.

"Where to?" Holly asked.

"A little privacy. You can't go like that," he nodded toward Holly, still dressed in her leggings and black T-shirt.

"Wouldn't want to disappoint," she snipped.

Bravo paused at the door, as serious as only a thief could be before a job. "As soon as you text, I'll start my run."

"Good luck," Kane said.

He was gone, and she was left alone with Kane.

He didn't say a word but grabbed a suit from the closet and retreated into the bathroom.

"Awkward," she said to no one. But it was her own fault, she knew that much.

She rose from the bed and headed to the closet, unwrapping the pale blue mini-dress from its box. Simple but expensive, the dress's halter-top neckline was attached to a thick silver chain that fastened around her neck. The hemline was higher than she'd normally wear, but the sales lady had convinced her it was appropriate for such an occasion.

Seeing the more prim and proper women at brunch earlier made her wonder if she'd made a bad choice.

On the upside, her flashy, super-short dress was bound to command attention, making it a bit less unlikely that anyone would spare the main house a single glance. Even if they did, darkness would hide anything that Bravo might do, even if he wasn't a skilled thief.

Leaving her leggings on the floor, she slid the dress over her head. No bra tonight, and while she sometimes wished she were better endowed, at times like this, she was glad she had a minimal bust. Anything more and she'd be jiggling. Painfully.

Sitting at the vanity, she opened up her makeup case. There wasn't time for the full face. A little mascara, lipstick, and eyeliner would have to be enough.

She was finishing applying her mascara when Kane walked out.

Wearing a dark charcoal gray suit with a blue shirt to match her dress and a darker blue tie, he looked every inch the businessman. But it was more than the suit. It was the way he carried himself—as if he belonged.

She realized he wasn't acting. The wealthy were his people. He was born and raised in a place like this, and he knew this echelon even as he seemed to try to pretend that wasn't the case.

"You look nice," she said, rising and gathering her silver sandals from the bottom of the closet.

He didn't respond. *Great. Still pissed.*

With a barely repressed sigh of exasperation, she sat on her bed to put on her shoes.

"You look amazing," Kane said, his voice rough.

She stopped with one sandal halfway on and looked up. She wasn't sure what was going on in his head—there were too many conflicting expressions racing across his features. Guilt. Sorrow. Jealousy. Passion.

Desire. For her.

She swallowed hard, not sure what was the best move and fought the urge to do the one thing that came to mind:

kissing Kane and asking for forgiveness. But if she kissed him, she knew where it would lead—whether now or later. She wasn't sure she could make love with him again and walk away with an unscathed heart.

"Thanks," she whispered and went back to putting on her footwear. "Do you think we can do this?"

"If I didn't, I'd cancel the mission," he responded. "We have no allegiance to Mira. She lied to us."

He was the guy who took care of his team no matter what. She liked that about him.

Mostly.

• • •

The party was in full swing when they arrived, Holly's arm laced through Kane's. He was still quieter than usual, but from the way he looked at the crowd—minute indications of dread breaking through the facade—she realized he didn't like these people. Any of them. At all.

She spotted Tammi Lynn. Her back to them, she wore a fitted red dress that showed off her curves. Their hostess was the least of their worries. They had to deal with Rachel and keep her from making a run for the necklace.

Piece of cake.

Elizabeth waved to her, threading her way through the crowd with Lucien Pascua in tow.

"That's Lucien," Kane said.

The one from the boat. "What do you think Elizabeth is doing with him?"

"Sugar Daddy?" Kane offered.

She hoped not.

"Holly. Kane. How are you? I heard what happened," Elizabeth kissed her on the cheek.

"What are you talking about?" Holly asked.

"Yesterday. The wreck," she replied. "Enzo can be such an ass sometimes, not that Daddy cares," she finished, giving the older man slight glare.

Ah, her father. How did a sweet girl like Elizabeth come from a mob family? It boggled the mind.

"No argument from me," Kane replied, taking Holly's hand in his and kissing her knuckles. "But it wasn't all bad." His eyes met hers, and she saw the truth in them.

He wanted her.

Heat began in the pit of her stomach and worked its way outward. She wanted him, too.

But now wasn't the time. Steadying her smile, she put her hand out toward the head of the Corsican mob. "Hi, I'm Holly, and this is my fiancé, Kane."

Lucien's grip was solid. "Lucien Pascua. And despite what my daughter thinks, I am appalled at my son's actions. He seems to think everything is a challenge to be beaten." He patted Elizabeth on the cheek. "My daughter is much sweeter. My angel.

"Judge me by her. Not Enzo," he said with a chuckle.

Elizabeth seemed like the light to Enzo's dark. She could only imagine what their childhood was like. How did Elizabeth survive living with a sociopath?

No sign of Rachel, though. "Where are Enzo and Rachel?" she asked, "I just want to let them know there are no hard feelings." She smiled to show her sincerity.

Lucien stiffened and gave her a pointed stare.

She let her smile reach her eyes. His shoulders relaxed,

and he gestured with his glass. "Enzo is over there. I don't know where Rachel disappeared to."

She knew where. *Go*, Kane mouthed, running a hand over his hair to hide the order.

"Thanks, I'll be right back," Holly said and headed toward Enzo, surprised that Kane trusted her to do this alone after what happened upstairs.

Snatching a glass of champagne from a passing waiter, she made her way to her target where he held a young couple in thrall. When she was close enough, she heard him going on about Rome, art—

Blah. Blah. Blah.

He was a bad man, and she could only imagine why he was in Rome, and it wasn't the art—unless he planned to steal it. She sidled up next to him, flipping her hair. "Hi, Enzo. Where's Rachel?"

He stopped mid-sentence, his dark gaze taking in her short dress. There wasn't a shred of remorse in his predatory stare.

Ass.

"Why?" he asked when his eyes reached her face. His tongue flicked out, an unconscious gesture, but it made her queasy. She took a sip of champagne and forced herself to relax.

Do the job.

"I don't trust you to tell the truth, but I am hoping she'll tell me if you meant to wreck us," she said, though she was sure that the answer was a resounding "yes".

The young couple he'd been talking to gave each other an uncomfortable glance and side-stepped away, making a beeline for a waiters and a tray of canapés.

"Why does it matter? You lived," he replied.

And so it began. The dance of lies. Luckily, he didn't know she was leading. "That's not the point. Where's Rachel?"

"In the room. You know. Girl trouble."

She took a quick drink. "Well, I have some lovely drugs for that. Let me pop up to the room, and I can drop them off. She'll be feeling better in no time, and then we can have that chat."

Enzo's hands clenched around his glass for a brief second as annoyance overrode interest in her legs. "That's not necessary. She prefers to be left alone."

Nice try.

"Of course it's necessary," Holly insisted. "We girls have to stick together. It won't take but a minute." Patting his arm, she left before he could protest any further.

Suck on that.

In seconds, she was back at Kane's side.

"That was quick," he said.

"It didn't take much. Watch," Holly replied. As if on cue, Enzo retrieved his phone from his jacket pocket and stepped behind a tree. "He's calling her right now. Let's get this done."

"Give it five," Kane replied.

It only took three minutes for Rachel to walk out the back door, adjusting her dress, and obviously pissed that her attempt to steal the necklace was thwarted. For now.

Kane hit send on his phone.

She squinted, watching the balcony for Bravo. A few moments later, a dark form crossed the master balcony and went inside.

Kane's phone buzzed, and he glanced down. "He's in."

She sipped her champagne. This was going better than expected. The mission would be over in a few minutes, and she'd go home. Alone.

Impending reality seemed less thrilling than normal. She knew why. Kane. He'd sneaked past her defenses, and as much as she wanted to ignore what had happened, it wasn't going away.

He wasn't going away.

"We make a good team." Kane fingers curled around hers and reinforced her feelings.

"We do. All of us," she agreed as the desire to flee, to be free, paced alongside her need to lean into Kane. Carefully, she pulled her hand from his.

His face darkened, but he nodded. "Agreed."

Dammit. What was she doing? Antagonizing him one moment then wanting to kiss him the next.

"Are you all right?" Kane asked.

She'd been shredding a cocktail napkin without realizing it. She waded the paper mass up and set it on a table. "Why did you let me go talk to Enzo alone?" she asked, turning the conversation. "I was a bit surprised."

"Pretending to be something you're not is what you're good at. And I thought that both of us going might make Enzo feel ambushed. I'm not sure how he'd react to that, and since we're running low on time, I didn't want to find out."

"Thanks for trusting me," she replied, knowing the confession wasn't easy for him. "It's not easy, blending. When I approach someone like that, it's a bit unnerving."

He looked surprised. "Really?"

"Yeah. Really. When I'm undercover, all I want to do is fit in. Public confrontations take that away." She took a final sip of champagne, unsettled that she'd revealed so much. It had to be the alcohol. She set the half-empty glass on a side table. Out of the corner of her eye, she caught a glimpse of Rachel. Holly waved, and Rachel glared at her. Holly waved again.

"Should you go talk to her?" Kane asked. "Keep up the facade and keep her here?"

"Attention, everyone. The auction is about to begin." Tim Burke called over the crowd from where he stood at a podium at the far end of the tent. His cheeks were flushed from alcohol, but he sounded sober enough.

"Don't have to," Holly said, "She can't leave now. It would be much too obvious." She took Kane's arm. "Don't you just love it when a plan comes together?"

"Are you trying to jinx this?" Kane said under his breath as he escorted her to an empty chair at the back of the tent. Holly took a deep breath. Just a little longer and this would be over. She'd be home. Back to her apartment. Her life.

And no Kane unless work brought them together again. Likely months from now.

She closed her eyes, but it didn't matter. Once the mission was complete, he was gone.

At the front, Tim continued, once everyone was seated. "My lovely wife, Tammi Lynn, will present the first item."

Their hostess walked up to the podium, a large crystal vase in her hand—

And the turtle necklace around her neck.

• • •

Kane spied the necklace on Tammi Lynn but wasn't surprised.

They were not catching any breaks on this mission. The race. The wreck. Enzo. And Tammi Lynn—the memory of kissing her still made him nauseous.

The one thing that had made the trip worth taking was Holly. Her hand in his, he stroked her skin with his thumb, telling himself that it was to maintain their cover, but he knew better. There was something about her that touched him, and he wanted to maintain it, even though he knew that couldn't last.

"What next?" Holly asked, her eyes glued to Tammi Lynn's neckline.

There it was. The thief beneath the fancy dress and soft skin. Illusion over. "First thing's first," he said. Taking the phone from his pocket, he texted Bravo.

Abort Mission. T.L. is wearing necklace.

"And now?" Holly asked. "What's the plan?"

The plan? "Good question."

There weren't many that came to mind. Everyone was leaving tomorrow morning, so the window to steal the necklace from the safe was gone unless they wanted to try and retrieve it while the Burkes were sleeping.

That might work. Might not.

There was a better alternative—all he had to do was get Tammi Lynn alone for a few minutes. It wasn't what he wanted to do, but it was the easiest, and he knew she'd agree.

"What's wrong?" Holly asked.

"What?"

"That face. You're making it again." She leaned in, staring into his eyes as if she could will herself to see what he was thinking.

"What face is that?"

"The same one from earlier." Holly's big blue eyes stared into him, searching and then widened with realization. "You're going to seduce her, aren't you?"

She knew him better than he wanted to admit. "She's willing, and it's our best option." It wasn't something he looked forward to, but he'd deal.

Her lips pressed tight. "It isn't right."

"It's not her first time."

Her hands tightened into fists as if fighting with herself. "I'm talking about you, you ass."

She was angry at him? That was unexpected. He wasn't sure what to think of it. "What did I do?"

Her spine stiffened. "I can't believe you'd compromise yourself. With *her*."

"Are you jealous?" His own anger welled upward.

She cast him a sideways glance. Her eyes were glassy, and he realized he'd misjudged. It wasn't anger.

It was worry. For him. She was trying not to cry.

"Holly?"

She shook him off. "I'm not going let you do this. I saw your face when you came out of her room, and I am not going to see you like that again." She rose, kissing him on the cheek. "Tell Bravo to meet us out front with our car keys and plane tickets in four minutes."

"What are you doing?"

"What I always do." She paused. "Whatever I want."

Pushing through the chairs, she approached Tammi Lynn as she auctioned off the next item—a weekend for two at Martha's Vineyard.

Their hostess frowned at the interruption. "Miss Kennedy, please take your seat. We'll be done in a minute."

Holly moved faster, her acrobat body tensed but limber. Her feet hit the small, wooden dance floor with a solid thunk.

What the hell was she going to do?

Tammi Lynn glared. "I said—"

She was cut off abruptly when Holly shoved the podium aside and tackled her, knocking her to the ground.

The crowd jumped to its collective feet, watching in horror as the two women rolled across the ground. Tammi Lynn tried to scramble away. Holly grabbed her by the back of the head and yanked her back. "Try to seduce my fiancé? You whore!"

Kane stared at the unfolding scene, shocked. She'd just said that fitting in was how she did what she did. To some, the conversation might be shop talk, but he'd seen the insecurity in her eyes as she spoke. There was more to what she'd said. It wasn't just about work. It was about her life.

To change that now. For him...

Tammi Lynn screamed as Holly came away with a handful of hair, refocusing him on the situation. They ended up in one of the flower beds, and Kane watched with the rest of the crowd unsure of what to do but for different reasons. Did his partner have the necklace?

The fight continued, and he caught a glimpse of Tammi Lynn's cleavage.

The necklace was gone.

Holly wasn't stopping.

She straddled Tammi Lynn and shook her. "You need a lesson."

Slap. "In manners."

Shake. "No one tries to seduce my man but me. No one."

Slap. Their hostess's head rocked to the side with the force of the last hit, and even Kane felt sorry for her. A public pummeling was going to be impossible to sweep under the radar, even more so when the reason for it was infidelity—everyone loved good gossip.

"I'm sorry," Tammi Lynn cried, trying to cover her face as Holly shook her. Hair disheveled and her blue dress riding up her thighs to show her pink panties, Holly didn't seem inclined to stop punching her adversary, and no one in the crowd seemed inclined to get involved.

Finally, security stepped in to pull the women apart.

Kane joined them. "She's had enough, slugger," he said, lifting Holly off of her victim.

"She tried to seduce you," Holly screeched, kicking the air.

Damn, she was a good actress. "I know. But she didn't." He tilted her face up. Her eyes glimmered with tears, and her mascara ran down her face.

Was it an act? Or was it real?

"I'll sue you," Tammi Lynn screamed as she struggled to her feet, dress torn and bits of grass and dirt in her blonde hair, several strands of which had come straggling out of her hot-rollered updo. "I'll sue you for slander."

"Good luck with that," Holly shot back, grabbing her arm, and landing a final slap as Kane hustled both himself and his partner toward the front of the house.

Chapter Twelve

"You got it, right?" Kane asked as they took a path to the front of the house, a motion-operated light flaring to life when they reached the front of the driveway.

"Of course," Holly said, knowing she looked like the cat that ate the big-haired canary and not caring. She'd done some extreme things for her job before — tightrope walking between buildings, impersonating a French diplomat, and even BASE jumping off an office building, but this was her first physical fight. It felt satisfying to know she could get into a tussle and win.

Even better that it was against someone like Tammi Lynn.

Her smile broadened despite her attempts to stop it, and she held out the necklace. It glittered in her palm.

"I have to admit, as far as thieving goes, that was amazing," Kane said, taking the necklace and shoving it into his breast pocket. "How did you do that during a fight? And how did no one notice?"

"Diversion. Just like a magician," she explained. "They were too busy wanting me to yank out her hair with this hand," she held up the right one, "to see me yank off the necklace with this one," and she held up the left. "My dress riding all the way up to my ass probably helped."

Kane chuckled and stroked her cheek with his thumb. "You're a surprise. Each and every day."

Warmth spread through her with his touch, and she leaned into it. No man had ever tempted her like Kane. Sure, they tempted her into their bed. To dinner. And she willingly accepted. Even instigated.

But unlike any other man she let into her bed or her life, he'd made her consider a relationship. In two days.

That was a first, and a gamble she knew she wasn't ready for. She took a step back, and he caressed a strand of hair from her cheek, tucking it back into place before he let his hand drop to his side.

"Where's Bravo?" he said, more rhetorical than a question, as he surveyed the circular drive.

"Here," Bravo said, coming around the corner, two sets of keys dangling from his hands. "And we need to get moving. I heard two of the servers whispering that a necklace is missing. I take it that was you?" Bravo asked, addressing Holly.

"None other."

"Kudos."

"Move it," Kane snapped, and the three broke into a trot, heading toward the cars parked at the far end of the driveway.

"We take both cars," Kane said as they ran. "If anyone suspects us—"

"They will," Holly interjected.

"—they can't be sure who to follow. We'll meet at the airport."

"What about the police?" Bravo asked.

"Tammi Lynn isn't supposed to have the necklace," Kane said. "She can't call. Not without admitting guilt. She's not the one I'm worried about."

The hairs rose on the back of Holly's neck. The Corsicans were not people she wanted to tangle with.

They arrived at the cars. "She goes with you," Kane said, guiding Holly toward Bravo. "Keep her safe."

She glared at him. He was not getting rid of her that easily. "I'm with you," she said.

He gripped her shoulders. "For once, stop arguing with me. I'm trying to do you a favor."

Did he think she still wanted the other man? What an idiot. He'd had never been more than a dalliance. Kane was her partner. He'd said so himself, and she wasn't going to abandon him. "We're a team," she said, breaking his grip. "I stay with you, and we're wasting time."

He shook his head. "Dear God, you are so annoying. You *never* listen."

Reaching into his pocket, he retrieved the necklace and tossed it to Bravo. "You take this. They'll be searching for a couple."

The other agent snatched the trinket midair. "See you at the airport." And disappeared into the dark. Seconds later, a car engine overturned, and Bravo raced out of the driveway, headlights off until he reached the road.

"What are we waiting for?" Holly asked. Anxious to get the hell out before the Corsicans tracked them down.

"That," Kane said, gesturing in the direction that the other agent had gone. "Bravo's out of sight. Time to go."

The sound of gravel crunching under foot echoed through the night. The Corsicans were coming. "Let's go," Kane said as he opened her door and ran to the other side.

She slid into the seat and slammed the door shut, her heart pounding. "We have to make sure they follow us and not Bravo."

"They will," Kane said, revving the engine.

There as a knock on the window. Outside stood Enzo, gun out and aimed at her head.

Kane killed the engine.

The mobster was faster than they'd thought. Or more motivated. Either way, they weren't leaving yet.

"Stay quiet," Kane said. "Admit nothing."

"I know how to do my job," Holly replied as Enzo opened her door.

Lucien appeared at the border of the light. "Where is it?"

"Where's what?" Kane asked, stepping out of the car. "Who the hell do you think you are, pointing a gun at my fiancée?"

"Where's the necklace?" Lucien asked, impatience making his voice tight.

"What necklace?" Holly asked.

"You know what necklace," Enzo said, grabbing her arm and yanking her from the car. His fingers dug into her flesh, and she winced before she could stop herself. "That ugly piece of crap you stole during the fight."

Holly put on her best "outraged" face. "Excuse me?"

"You heard me," Lucien snapped. "Hand over the

necklace. Now."

She spread her arms wide. "Where is it? In my underwear? It's not like this dress has pockets." Tugging on her dress, she gave a little jump. "See. Nothing."

"Get in the car, Holly," Kane said, sounding like the annoyed, exasperated agent she was used to. The sound of chatter coming from the house and getting closer caught her attention. People were coming. Unfortunately, they were not hurrying.

Witnesses. They just needed to buy another minute.

Lucien pulled a gun from his jacket. "Do as your fiancé said. Get in the car."

Time's up. Hell.

• • •

"We're not going anywhere with you," Kane said. "Search me and the Audi, and you'll see we don't have it."

"Oh, I plan on it, but not here."

"I'm not going," Holly said, her jaw set.

So pigheaded.

This was why he hated field work. Enzo had pushed them into this scenario, and they weren't walking away from it alive. Not if the mobsters had their way. He didn't plan on letting them win, but with Enzo's gun pointed at his partner's head, he couldn't make a move. Not yet. "Get in the car, Holly."

Her eyes met his over the roof of the vehicle, and he gave her a slight nod. She slid into the passenger seat as he took the driver's. "No seat belt," he whispered as the mobsters took the backseat, guns out and pointed at their backs.

There would be no more conversation.

She gave a long, slow blink in reply, and he hoped to hell she understood what he planned to do. It wasn't much—bail out of the moving car.

Would she even do it?

The laughable thought came, then left as fast as it appeared. Holly lived for the dare. She'd do it and without hesitation.

He started the car but kept it in park. "Where to?"

"Follow the car that just left," Lucien said.

They might not know Bravo had the necklace, but they suspected. Wonderful. "You're the boss." He headed down the drive. The longer they were in the car, the more likely someone would be shot. They'd have to jump as soon as possible.

Reaching across the seat, he took Holly's hand in his and squeezed. She squeezed back.

"Why do you want the necklace?" Kane asked as he drove.

"Why do you?" Lucien replied.

"We don't."

That earned him a snort of disbelief.

He continued, "Did you ever think that it came off in the fight, and someone else picked it up?" He watched Lucien in the rearview mirror. The mobster didn't look convinced— not that Kane expected he would. "How about Enzo?"

Lucien chuckled. "He's my son. I trust him a hell of a lot more than I trust you."

"Yeah? Did he tell you that we were in the room when he was banging Tammi Lynn?" Holly asked.

"Shut up," Enzo snapped.

"That we caught him and threatened him with exposure?" Holly continued. "He cowered like a bitch."

Kane tried not to smile. She was laying it on thick, but it was working. The men were getting wound up. The trick was not to push them too far. He wanted them careless—not shooting.

"I said, knock it off," Enzo smacked the back of Holly's head with the gun. The headrest prevented a full-force connection, but it was enough to make her cry out.

Kane's hand tightened on the wheel, and he chanced a look at his partner. Her eyes were wet with tears, but she didn't cry.

Good. Don't give them the satisfaction.

"Is this true?" Lucien asked.

Using the mirror, he watched Lucien. His attention was on his son.

No time like the present.

He squeezed Holly's hand. Once. Twice. He caught her attention and gave an almost imperceptible nod toward the door handle.

She squeezed back, which seemed to be short code that she understood, and he prayed they were having the same conversation.

On the steering wheel, he uncurled a finger. *One.* He slowed the car. Not much but enough to give them a better chance at survival.

Her attention zeroed in on his hand.

Another finger. *Two.* He edged the car closer to the side of the road so she'd land on dirt and not pavement.

Three.

He let her go, released the door handle and fell out of

the car, tucking into a tumble as soon as he hit the road. The asphalt tore at his suit as he rolled. The world was a jumble of darkness, pain, and adrenaline. He stopped after a few feet and sat up. The car had continued on but was already slowing.

They had seconds to escape. "Holly!"

"Over here."

Stumbling to his feet, he ran toward her voice. She sat in the dirt, filthy, dazed, and her clothes torn.

But she lived. "Anything broken?"

"No," she said, wincing as she tried to rise. "Just had the wind knocked out of me."

He hauled her to her feet. She groaned but stayed upright. The car came to a stop, and even at a few hundred feet down the road, he heard the doors slam.

They weren't going to hurt her. He wasn't going to let that happen. Not now. Not ever. He was going to protect her no matter what. "Can you run?"

• • •

Holly held her side as they ran through the brush and the trees, heading farther into the interior of the island. She said a grateful prayer that she'd worn flat sandals. Sneakers would have been better, but at least she wasn't in heels.

Each breath ached. She didn't think her ribs were broken, but they were bruised. A day or so and she'd be fine. Until then, she'd cope, since a single moment of rest might mean death. She tripped over a tree, and a grunt of pain escaped before she could stop herself.

"Are you hurt?" Kane asked.

"Fine," she lied, glad that the darkness hid the grimace that she was sure distorted her features each time she inhaled.

"You suck at lying right now," Kane said. "What's broken?"

She did not suck at lying, but even a skilled manipulator had a hard time staying in character when running with an injury.

"Nothing," she said, forcing herself to smile. He might not be able to see it, but she knew it would translate into sound, making her seem more convincing.

"I can't help you if you lie."

Dammit. She sighed in surrender. "I landed hard. I think I hit a rock or something. Nothing's broken, but breathing is a bitch."

"Which side?"

"The right."

Moving to her left side, he put her arm over his shoulder. Maybe it was a placebo effect, but his physical support made her ribs ache less. "It helps."

"Just hold on," he said. "I'll take care of it."

She didn't doubt him. Since she'd seen his scar in the locker room, she'd suspected there was more to Kane. He'd seen action. Possibly death.

She was so grateful he was at her side and not Bravo. The other thief was handsome and skilled, but Kane... He was an enigma. Beneath the stick in the mud was a warrior.

She tripped over a rock, and Kane caught her as she stumbled. "This is ridiculous," he said, swinging her into his arms.

Her breath hitched at the sudden pain, but then she relaxed, and the ache ebbed back to tolerable. "Let me know if I get too heavy," she said.

"Please. I've had groceries that weighed more than you."

She snickered. "Thanks."

"You know what I meant."

She did, but right now, she hurt too much to argue or correct. She leaned her head on his shoulder and let him take over. The world became darkness, his heartbeat against her ear, and the sensation of being cared for.

But the fear was as strong. Fear of allowing him to care.

Fear of being caught. Hurt. Of Kane risking his life for her. Of being helpless. Of his leaving. So much fear.

Behind them, branches cracked as Lucien and Enzo took up the pursuit. She might be petite, but Kane could only carry her so far, and soon, they'd have nowhere to run.

"We need to hide," she said.

"We need to get to safety."

"Not mutually exclusive ideas," she countered. "If they catch us, we're dead. We have to stop them. Be proactive."

"Shit."

There was nothing around them. Just trees damp ground and the chase. "Just hide," she insisted. "Hide."

He stopped. "You're right. We can't keep running. I have no fucking idea where I am." Carefully, he set her down at the base of a large oak.

"What are you doing?"

"Wait here. I'll be back." He kissed her, his mouth bruising and rough. She gripped the back of his head, keeping him close, savoring the taste and touch. Finally, he broke away. "Be quiet. Wait. I'll be back."

He disappeared, branches breaking as he led the men away from her.

Ribs aching, Holly took a deep breath, trying to collect

her thoughts. What the hell was happening? She was a thief—not an operative who got into actual danger. This was insane.

When they got out of this situation, she was going to a have a few words with Mira Burke.

Pressing one hand against the bark of the tree for leverage, she stood and took a cautious breath.

Better. Good. That meant nothing was broken.

Leaves rustled. Branches snapped. Twenty feet. Ten. They were on her.

Holly flattened out against the tree. Her pulse beat in her ears. She held her breath. *I'm vapor. Air. Invisible.*

They moved past her, dark figures just a shade darker than the shadows, pursuing Kane, disappearing into the night. In the distance she heard Kane swear. He had to be doing it on purpose. To lure them away from her.

What an ass. A brave, little bit-crazy, ass.

Supporting her aching ribs, she followed the sound of Lucien and Enzo. *Stay calm. Stay quiet.*

The sound of a car backfiring broke the silence. Not a car. A gun. Her heart slammed against her sternum, and she gasped. If Kane died. If he never knew how she felt—

Knock it off. She snapped back to the present. Getting morose was not going to fix the situation, but action might.

She broke into a careful trot, following the mobsters and Kane's general direction.

Shouting echoed back to her, then a cry of pain. There was no way to tell who screamed. Faster. Faster. Bushes raked at her bare skin as she plowed forward. The ground squished beneath her feet, sucking at her sandals.

Movement ahead of her made her slow. If Kane was in

trouble, she'd need to help, and getting caught didn't factor into the scenario.

There were only two men in sight. Moonlight poured down through the leaves and into a clearing. Two men struggled. She squinted, finally seeing a flash of paler hair. A glimpse of broad shoulders. *Kane.*

The relief at seeing him alive almost knocked her over, but her heart didn't slow its racing beat. Her partner fought Enzo. So where was Lucien? She scanned the edge of the clearing, watching for movement. A silhouette. Anything that didn't belong.

He had to be here somewhere. Probably waiting to see who won the battle. If it were Kane, she knew he'd shoot her partner before he could escape.

Her partner took a hit to the gut that made him double over, but he recovered, snapping upward, and landing an uppercut to Enzo's jaw.

Slowly, she melted back into the trees and began circling the open space.

She'd only gone one third of the way around when she spotted Lucien. Crouched down next to a tree, he hid in the shadows like the monster she knew him to be. Just beyond him, Kane and Enzo continued to battle.

Enzo landed a jab to Kane's jaw, making his head snap back. Holly flinched but kept quiet, waiting for the outcome. Kane returned the punch with one of his own, and Enzo stumbled sideways with the force of the blow. Her partner kept on him, and Enzo tried to block hit after hit, but Kane was relentless in his attack.

Enzo wavered on his feet, and Holly held her breath, still edging toward Lucien, being careful not to attract attention.

Her partner took a step backward and landed a roundhouse kick to the side of Enzo's head. Enzo swayed on his feet and then fell over. The battle was finished with Kane as the victor. Lucien raised his weapon.

"Get down," Holly screamed at Kane as she crashed through the remaining brush toward the mobster, tackling him to the ground. The gun went off, a deafening boom next to her ear.

Lucien might be her senior, but he was strong and toughened by his line of work. Before she could land a punch, Holly found herself on her back, Lucien straddling her, his fist raised. Her ribs screamed at the weight of his body.

She covered her face with her forearm to help deflect the blow.

There was the familiar sound of flesh hitting flesh.

Then nothing.

Chapter Thirteen

Why is the floor moving?

Holly tried to force her consciousness to return, but her head ached and her brain felt like it was wrapped in layers of wool. She grabbed bits of reality and clung to them, refusing to slip back into nothingness.

She blinked, but wherever she was, it was too dark to make out anything.

She only knew that she was on her side, and...

"Holly?"

Kane. The evening's event came flooding back. The necklace. The desperate dive from the car. The fight in the clearing. Lucien. "I'm here," she said, relieved to know he was still alive. Trying to sit up, she realized her hands were tied behind her back as she lost balance and tumbled back to the floor with a thud. Holly groaned, her ribs aching.

"You okay?" Kane asked.

"Fine." she replied, though her ribs begged to differ.

"What's going on?"

"Lucien knocked you out," he explained. "By the time I got him under control and to you, Enzo recovered the gun, and we ended up here."

"Where's here?"

"The Glory."

Enzo's boat? She shuddered. That explained why the ground kept moving beneath her. Between the movement and her aching head, she wanted to barf. "Are we at the dock?" she asked, sure she knew the answer but hoping she was wrong.

"No," was Kane's brief reply.

Wonderful. She tried to sit up again, this time making sure she took her time. Her head continued to clear now that she was upright. She leaned against the wall, grateful they left her ankles free, but then, where was she going to run?

"Do you know that they have planned?" she asked.

"No, but I'm fairly sure it doesn't involve cookies and crumpets."

She managed a weak laugh, wishing she could see him but the dark was absolute. "You think?"

The door to the cockpit opened, and Holly looked up to see Enzo standing at the top of the stairs. Behind him, the night sky was bright with stars.

He flicked on a light, and she blinked at the sudden brightness. Kane sat across from her—both his wrists and ankles bound with zip ties.

"I see you're awake," Enzo said, the steps creaking as he walked down into the berthing area. "That's good. Because we need to talk."

"About what?" Kane asked.

"Not you," Enzo said, his full attention on Holly. "Her."

He took a seat across from her, his gaze traveling from her feet to her legs where he lingered. "Tell me what you know about the necklace." He said, still looking at the spot where her dress hiked up to show a generous amount of thigh.

She swallowed hard, not sure what to do. She had training on what to do if caught, but it had never actually happened. "It's expensive?" she offered.

"Wrong answer," Enzo said. Pulling a gun from the back of his waistband, he pointed it at Kane, his gaze still on Holly.

"What do you know about the necklace?"

She glanced at Kane, and he shook his head.

"Uh, I don't know what you mean. Can you be more specific?"

Enzo cocked the gun, and finally, he tore his gaze from her legs. When his eyes met hers, there was no pity in them. No remorse.

It was like looking into the eyes of a shark.

"One more lie, and I'm sure you can figure out the next move," he said.

Her gaze narrowed in on the gun, then back to Kane. He shook his head again. Was he insane? Did he want to die?

"Well?" Enzo pushed.

She knew what she had to do. They may not know what was so important about the necklace, but it wasn't worth dying for. "Nothing, but we know it's not just a necklace."

Enzo hesitated, seemed to come to a decision, uncocked the gun, and laid it on his lap. "Finally, some truth."

Holly's racing pulse slowed a notch, but she seemed

incapable of taking her attention off of the weapon.

"Where is it now?" Enzo asked. "We know it's not in the car."

"Our partner took it." Holly replied. There was no point in lying. There was no way he could get to Bravo. Too much time had passed, and by now, the other agent was either on his way to the Atlanta airport or had already arrived.

"Don't tell him anything else," Kane snapped.

Enzo turned, glaring at Kane. "She saved your life. You might want to shut the fuck up."

"You tell him more, and he'll kill us anyway," Kane said, glaring at Holly.

With a sigh, Enzo rose and grabbed a roll of duct tape from underneath the sink. "That's enough of you," he said putting a generous slice over Kane's mouth.

He took his seat again. "Now, where did your partner go?"

"Los Angeles."

Enzo gave a thoughtful nod. Holly cocked her head, surprised. He seemed so calm—not at all like the angry monster that wrecked their boat just yesterday. What was different? Was it his father?

"And who sent you?" Enzo asked. "How did you know about the necklace?"

"Mira Burke."

He rubbed a large hand over his scruffy face. "Dad will not be pleased," he said.

Bingo. He wanted to impress Daddy, so he behaved. That was good to know.

His mouth pressed into a tight line, he patted her knee, taking a moment to slide his hand up her thigh. Holly clamped her legs shut. "No."

He pulled his hand away. "You wait here. We're not done yet," Enzo said, grinning.

There's the monster I remember.

And he went back to the cockpit and shut the door, leaving them alone.

She looked at Kane and shrugged. Even with the groping, she'd expected more questions. More intimidation. More *something*.

Then again, he'd asked the important questions. The *Who*. The *What*. The *Where*. Maybe it was all he and his father needed.

On the other side of the cabin, Kane stared at her, but his expression was unreadable. Was he angry that she'd divulged the information or upset that Enzo touched her? Perhaps a bit of both? One way to find out.

Holly staggered to her feet and made her way over to Kane. "Hang on," she said. "Give me a minute and you can go back to yelling at me," Dropping to her knees with her back facing him, she searched for the duct tape with her fingers and ripped it off.

"Damn," he said.

"Sorry," she replied, letting herself fall sideways so she could sit on the floor.

"I swear, I am going to kill him," Kane said, his voice low.

She'd never seen him so angry, but she didn't need angry Kane. He was irrational. She needed the guy that knew how to make a plan. "I'm okay," she assured him. "And I believe you, but the killing will have to wait. Right now, we need to escape."

Her words seemed to reach him, and he took a deep breath. "You're right," he said.

Finally, the Boy Scout had returned.

Kane continued, "The first order of business is to free ourselves. Once we do that, we can make a swim for it."

Holly straightened. Swim? As in the ocean? The thought of drowning—like her dad—made her heart race. What would her mom do if she died like that? She might never recover.

There had to be another way. "We don't even know where we are," she countered. "Wouldn't it be easier to push them overboard?"

Kane shook his head. "If they didn't have guns, sure. But they do, so we're going to take our chances in the ocean."

Dammit. She'd kept so much from him, and it hadn't seem to matter. Why this? Why now? "We can't," Holly said, dreading the path the conversation had to take.

"We don't have a choice," Kane insisted.

She bit the metaphorical bullet, feeling like a landbound doofus. "I can't swim."

• • •

Holly couldn't swim?

That explained a lot. He'd thought her overreaction to the wreck was the shock at being tossed overboard. He'd guessed wrong.

He took a minute, absorbing the information. "You can scale walls. Walk a tightrope. Break into uncrackable safes. But you can't swim?" When one thought about all that Holly was capable of, her pronouncement seemed like a joke.

She shook her head, eyes downcast "Nope. Not a stroke."

"How did that happen?"

She turned away from him. "My dad died drowning, so my mother thought it was a sign and never let me near the water."

Kane could only shake his head. She had to be telling the truth. But the reason didn't really matter. Somehow, they'd have to get around her inability to swim because as it stood, it seemed to be their best option at survival, and even that was sketchy.

That left him with one option. "Can you not panic if you're in the water?"

"Why?" she asked, looking at him like a wary animal.

"If we can get clear of the boat, I can tow you."

She stared at him, eyes wide. "That's insane," she finally said. "Where are you going to tow me to? We don't even know where we are."

He wasn't the one unconscious. "We haven't been underway that long, and there's a ton of little islands around here. Once we're in the water, I'll head toward the closest one, and we can flag down someone tomorrow morning. Maybe the next day."

He hesitated "But before we do any of that, we need to get out of these," and he nodded at his bound ankles.

Holly sighed. "Are you sold on this insanity?"

"I am. Unless you think you can talk him into letting us go." *And good luck with that.*

She shook her head. "Not a chance." Another sigh. "Just give me a minute. I have an idea."

Unable to move, he watched as she shifted on the floor, edging her bound hands closer to her bottom and then under it. Wincing, she bent her knees, then pulled her legs through her arms, leaving her bound hands in front of her.

If they got out of this, he was going to have to see just how flexible she really was. "Impressive. Considering you probably broke a rib."

She rose. "Not to Wanda."

"Wanda?"

"Our contortionist."

"Point taken," he said, watching as she rummaged through a drawer. After a second, she pulled out a lighter.

Not as good as a knife but fine for zip-ties. Fumbling, she flicked it on and managed to get the flame near the plastic. Her breath hissed through her teeth, and he had no doubt that she was burning skin as well. After a few seconds, she pulled, snapping the plastic.

She was amazing.

She dropped to his feet, and in seconds they were free, followed by his hands. Kane rubbed his wrists in an effort to get the blood back into his veins. Enzo was a vindictive son of a bitch, there was no doubt there.

"What next?" Holly asked, rocking back on her heels. "You're the plan guy."

It wasn't much, but it would have to do. "We exit the forward hatch," he said, pointing toward the ceiling access that led to the desk. "We'll have to take a chance and turn off the light so it doesn't spill out when we open it. But as long as that works, and we move fast, we should be good. They're running dark, so that should help."

"Once we're on deck, keep low, and get to the sides. I'll jump first, and then you jump to me. If we have to go under, go limp and just hold your breath until we surface."

She glanced at him, and for the first time since he met her, he saw doubt. But it wasn't in him or his half-assed plan. It was in herself.

It was almost unbearable and right now—lethal. He took her hand in his. She was shaking. "You can do this," he assured her.

"I wish I was as sure."

He wished he had more time to encourage her, but Enzo had already been gone longer than expected, and he couldn't count on their luck to last. "I'll be sure enough for both of us. Now let's get out of here before Enzo comes back."

He squeezed her hands and walked her to the hatch. "I'll get the lights. If they notice, don't bother being subtle. Just open it and get out. I'll be right behind you."

"Promise?"

"Promise."

He wasn't going to let her die. Not when he could save her.

Adrenaline surged through him as he went to the steps and turned off the light.

• • •

Holly held her breath, waiting for all hell to break loose.

Silence. They hadn't noticed.

Then a shout.

Reaching up, she unlatched the forward hatch and pulled herself upward and onto the deck, sliding across the teak boards to keep her profile as flat as possible.

Beneath her, she heard a scuffle and a grunt. A pair of large hands gripped the edge of the forward hatch, and

Kane's head popped up. "Go," he shouted.

She nodded and crawled to the front of the boat.

"Hey, bitch!"

Lucien. She turned, the moon giving her ample light to see the elder mobster making his way forward, gripping the top of the cabin with one hand and clutching a gun in the other.

Kane struggled with the tight fit of the hatch and his large body.

Oh God, if Lucien got any closer, he'd see Kane.

And there was only one outcome in that scenario. One too awful to consider.

She knew what she had to do. Slowly, she stood on shaky legs and staggered to the other side of the boat. "You want me? Then come get me," she said, drawing his attention.

Out of the corner of her eyes, Kane popped free.

Finally.

But what now?

Lucien raised a gun, and she held her breath. She knew what she had to do.

Step off the boat. Step off the boat. But her legs refused to move.

She squeezed her eyes shut.

And something hit her in the chest, and she was flying through the air.

She hit the water, screaming.

"I got you!" Kane screamed back. "Now hold your breath." And he pulled her under.

Her mouth filled with salty water and her limbs flailed, as Holly fought to stay afloat. A few seconds later, something shook her.

Kane.

And his touch cut through the panic, giving her the clarity she needed to push it down. Despite the fear, she remembered what he told her and went limp, holding what little breathe she had left.

Slowly, Kane towed her under the water, her ribs aching at the motion, until she struggled, the need to breathe stronger than the fear of being shot or even the possibility of sharks.

He pulled her upward, and she broke the surface, sucking in air. The boat was only twenty feet away but moving in the opposite direction.

"Again," Kane said, pulling her back under. Like a kitten carried by the back of its neck, she went limp again, trying to decide if the sounds she heard were bullets hitting the water or her imagination.

Kane dragged her deeper, farther, and when they surfaced again, the boat was over a hundred feet away. He didn't tell her again. Instead, he wrapped his arm around her torso, placing her on her back.

"I got you," he said, as she struggled to remain afloat. "Just relax and let me tow you."

It took every ounce of willpower not to thrash. She'd never felt so helpless. Never.

But this was Kane, and he was a Boy Scout. A planner.

And he'd never let her die.

Holly forced herself to relax, trusting Kane to keep her alive. Using a sidestroke, he dragged her through the water, and she kept her eye on the Glory.

The mobsters' voices carried over the water—Lucien was screaming at Enzo for letting himself be jumped.

Maybe Lucien would shoot his son instead. Not likely, but

it was possible. She allowed herself a small smile at the dark thought. After a few minutes, she heard the sound of an engine, and the sails on the Glory dropped to the deck.

"Kane," she whispered.

"Got it," he said, and for the final time, he dragged her under, though this time, there was no swimming. Just waiting as the sound of the engine echoed through the water, growing closer.

Then it was over them and going away. They were safe.

They surfaced and once again, Kane held her in his arms, keeping her afloat.

Chapter Fourteen

Kane sat in Tempe's office, with Holly next to him. Bravo waited at the window, his white shirt washed orange and red by the rising sun.

Just over twenty-four hours ago, after crawling ashore on one of the islands, they'd spotted an early morning fishing crew and had managed to flag them down and convince them to take them to the mainland.

After that, it was a quick collect call to Tempe for help, a message left on the vet's answering machine saying they would send someone for Mr. Wiggles in a few days, and then waiting for a car to take them to the airport where Bravo and the company jet stood by.

The flight home was wonderfully uneventful but what troubled Kane was that Holly had barely said two words the entire time. He talked to Bravo, but she didn't join in, and when he tried to speak to her, the answers were monosyllabic and forced.

He'd thought it might be her ribs, but once she rested, she seemed fine. She'd even refused ibuprofen.

Whatever was bothering her, she wasn't sharing.

Behind him, the door opened, and Tempe entered the room with Mira at her side.

Kane rose. It was time to end the charade and find out why the hell he and his team had risked their lives.

Lagging behind the client, Tempe motioned for him to sit down. She had a plan, as Tempe always did.

He sat back in his seat, and Bravo moved to lean against the wall, as relaxed and nonchalant as if he were at home. It was a good skill, and one Kane knew he'd never possess.

Not that he wanted to. Bravo was a good thief and always welcome on any mission Kane led, but he was missing something crucial.

Heart. Nothing mattered to the other agent. It was what made him an excellent seducer. He could walk away from anyone.

But how had he walked away from Holly? One weekend with her, and Kane was hooked. It wasn't the sex. The laughter. The defiance. Or the way she lied through her teeth or offered the truth like a gift.

It was the whole package. She was playful, mysterious, and he could only wonder why she didn't have an actual fiancé instead of the imposter he had played.

"Did you get the necklace?" Mira asked, her nearly frantic eyes meeting each of theirs in turn, not sure who to address.

"Please, take a seat," Tempe said.

Bravo retrieved a chair from the meeting table, placed it on the other side of Kane, and returned to his stance against the wall.

Mira sat. "You didn't get it, did you?"

"We did," Tempe said.

"Thank God. Where is it?" She sounded as relieved as if they'd told her they'd saved her child from a kidnapper.

Tempe continued, "We have some questions."

Mira wasn't listening. She rummaged through her purse and pulled out a credit card. "This should take care of the balance," she said, waving the black plastic at no one in particular.

Tempe took the card, and next to him, Holly snickered. Mira might have conned them and put the team in danger, but Tempe always got paid. Kane flashed a quick, knowing look at Holly, and for a moment, the connection he'd felt on the op was back. If he reached across the space between them, would she take his hand or act as if he were still the same Kane she knew from a few days ago?

Then her face tightened, and the connection disappeared as if it had never existed, giving him his answer. Whatever it was he had done, or not done, she wasn't ready to forgive him for it. Of course, it would help if he knew what that something actually was.

Tempe finished running the card and handed it back to the client. Now that the money portion was complete, he could focus on finding out what she was hiding.

"Where's my necklace?" Mira asked.

Tempe opened a drawer, took out a small box and pushed it across the desk. "Here."

Mira opened it, and her breath caught in her throat. Carefully, she held the necklace up by its chain, letting it sparkle in the morning light. Then the joy on her face died.

"There's a stone missing."

He hadn't noticed, but then again, he'd only held it for a few seconds. Bravo had served as the courier for the trip back to L.A.

"Not our problem," Tempe said, casting a quick glance at the team. *Wait for it.*

Mira's mouthed twisted. "It is your problem. I paid for you to get the necklace. All of it."

Tempe folded her hands on her desk, her shoulders rigid, her hair perfect, and her suit as pressed as if she'd picked it up from the cleaners minutes earlier. The epitome of calm. "You lied. You're lucky I'm not charging you double."

Mira dropped the necklace back into the box. "I don't understand."

Tempe cocked her head. "Yes, you do."

Mira glared at the petite redhead, and her hands shook as they tightened around the box. "You have it, don't you? You took the chip," she said, her voice trembling with rage.

Chip? The energy in the room shifted.

"What chip?" Tempe asked.

The fury that had caused the slip was gone. Mira surveyed the room, looking down her nose. He knew that expression. They were beneath her. The moronic masses as far as she was concerned. She didn't have to tell them anything, and she wouldn't.

Unless threatened.

"The Corsican mob was after the necklace," Kane said. "We almost died because you didn't tell us everything."

"The mob?" Mira shrugged, as if the mob was on par with kittens when it came to her mental list of "things to worry about." "Tim always ran with a rough crowd. I'm not surprised that the guest list included a few thugs."

"They wanted the necklace," Holly interrupted. "Not to socialize."

Mira rose, confident. "Thank you for returning my property," she said. "But I'm not going to stay here and be insulted by the people I hired to help me."

Tempe rose, the flats of her hands pressed onto the table top. "Sit down. Now. Or I will leak the information that the necklace was returned to you intact. I imagine that the Corsicans would be thrilled to find out that bit of news."

"Do what you have to do." Mira jutted her chin out.

Mistake. Tempe wasn't the kind of person who caved when it came to a test of wills.

"I'll make sure Lucien knows you have the chip," Holly said, finding her voice and interrupting Tempe. "He tried to kill us to get it, and he'll come for you, too."

"He can try."

Holly crossed the few feet between them, confronting Mira head on. "Do you think any amount of security will keep you safe? It might be at brunch. During a pedicure. Perhaps attending some bogus charity ball, but he will come for whatever it is he thinks you have."

She stepped closer, breaching Mira's personal space. The client didn't move away. Didn't flinch. Instead she remained as still as stone, mesmerized by Holly's voice. "Don't kid yourself. He will torture you. You'll tell the truth, that you don't have the chip. He won't believe you, and there will be nothing you can do about it except scream for mercy."

Holly leaned closer, until her mouth was inches from Mira's ear. "You'll beg for death. Beg. You know the worst part?"

"No," Mira whispered, her skin tone fading to a greenish gray.

"Your money won't matter. The only thing that can save you is the chip, and it's the one thing you don't have."

The room remained silent as Mira took her seat again. "What do you want to know?"

An almost imperceptible smile curved upward on their client's mouth for a fraction of a second, and Kane realized that the sudden meekness was nothing more than an act. Did she think she could still lie her way out of the situation?

Fool. She didn't know HRS, Tempe, or his team. Mira Burke wasn't leaving until she told them everything.

"What's on the stone?" Tempe asked.

Mira smoothed her hair back with a manicured hand. "Insurance."

Tempe rounded the desk. "Quit fucking around. I don't have time for your lies. Tell me exactly what it is, or I'll call Lucien myself."

The client flinched at confronting Tempe's fury. She might be petite, but she walked like she towered over the room. Mira waved Tempe off. "The stone is an optical memory chip. My ex-husband wanted to keep it secret, which means it's important. But don't worry. Even if they have it, they can't read what's on it without this." She pulled out her car keys.

"Excuse me?" Tempe said.

Mira pushed a button on the fob, and a laser shot out and hit the wall, creating a blue dot. "They need this to access the chip."

Tempe sighed. "Is that the only laser that will work?"

"Yes. Well, there's one other, but I think the Pentagon has

it. They work by combining light with sound or something."
She shrugged. "I don't really understand the specifics, but I
know it's special, and that's good enough for me."

Tempe snatched the keys from her hand. "What's on the
chip? What am I dealing with?"

Mira stared at her car keys, her finger's twitching. "I
don't know."

Tempe moved in closer, eyes narrowed. "Tell me, and maybe I won't turn you in to the government when this is over."

Mira bit her lip. "Tim was the head of an oversight com-
mittee for military research development. They created
a new missile. It isn't just a bunker buster. It can destroy
entire cities from a continent away. The stone carried the
schematics."

• • •

"Can I get a lift? My car's still at the airport," Bravo asked
as he followed Holly down the hallway away from Tempe's
office and toward the bay of elevators. Kane was still with
the V.P., and she'd been speculating on the reason he'd been
asked to stay. Did Tempe know that Holly and Kane had
slept together? If so, did she even care?

Company policy didn't allow two agents to have a relationship, but from what she'd seen and heard, it wasn't en-
forced unless it interfered with field work.

It had to be something else. She hoped it was a plan to
retrieve the necklace. But why exclude herself and Bravo?

Jerks.

"So, can I?" Bravo asked again when she didn't respond.

"Sure," she replied, but if he thought he was getting her

into his bed, he was mistaken. It was a drop-off at the curb and nothing else.

They left the building in silence, and he followed her to her sea-foam green Miata at the far end of the lot and slid into the passenger seat.

Holly gunned the engine as she merged into traffic. It was early, but in Los Angeles, traffic was already grid-locked. As much as she loved L.A., sitting on the 405 at nine in the morning, choking on the exhaust in the air, and wedged between a Hummer and semi made her wish she lived in a small town.

Someplace where it didn't take twenty minutes to get to the grocery store.

"You want to talk about it?" Bravo asked as they inched their way along the highway.

"About what?"

"Whatever it is that has a stick up your ass," Bravo said.

She cast him a sharp glance. "Excuse me?"

He chuckled. "There's the girl I remember."

She refocused on the road. "I'm doing you a favor. Could you not act like an ass?"

He chuckled. "I like you better when you're pissed. Or happy. Or horny. Anything but this pensive thing you've been doing since we stepped onto the plane." He patted her knee. "If this is what you being in love is like, I think you need to walk away."

She almost hit the brakes. "What the hell are you talking about?"

He shook his head. "You. Kane. Puppy eyes at each other when you're not arguing. Frankly, it's nauseating. And exhausting."

"You're out of your mind," she snapped and turned on the radio, cranking it up to drown him out.

She wasn't in love. She'd only been on those few missions with Kane. Most lasted only hours and ended with them yelling at each other. This weekend was by far the longest time they'd spent in each other's company, but three days was not enough to fall in love. Lust? Sure. But love took time. Getting to know each other. Wanting to make the other person happy.

A whole myriad of emotions and experiences that she didn't associate with Kane.

What she felt for him was nothing but desire combined with the occasional urge to kick his ass.

That wasn't love.

Who the hell did Bravo think he was? One didn't accuse someone of being in love without evidence. She flipped off the radio. "What makes you say that?"

Bravo shut his eyes and leaned back into the seat. "I know it when I see it."

"You?" She tried not to laugh at the idea that the biggest player at HRS considered himself an expert on love.

He cracked open one eye. "I'm wrong?"

"I think you're trying to get me into your bed," Holly replied. "Been there. Done that."

He shook his head. "I'm not, and for the record, if I wanted you in my bed, you'd be there. Willing and waiting."

"Like hell," Holly said, changing lanes and regretting that she agreed to give him a ride home. She should have made him take a company car.

"Sure you would," Bravo replied. "I remember you enjoying yourself last time."

She blushed at the memory, but kept her anger closer. "Tell yourself whatever you want, but I'll never be in your bed again."

"Why not?"

Because she loved Kane.

No.

She didn't love him. It was something Bravo stuck in her head to mess with her. Nothing more.

"Because I'm tired, and I want to go home," she replied, the lie sounding lame even to herself.

Bravo chuckled and shut his eyes again. "Whatever helps you sleep at night."

"Shut up." Jerk. He'd done that on purpose.

She took the next exit and dodged cars as she drove over the speed limit in her hurry to be rid of him. In five minutes, he'd be out of her life, and she could forget this weekend happened. Let Kane and Tempe sort out what to do. She wanted to go to bed, yank the covers over her head, and sleep.

"Can I give you some advice?" Bravo asked as she turned on to the road that led to his condo.

"Can I stop you?" she asked, knowing that when people asked if they could give advice it was code for "I'm going to give you advice whether you like it or not."

"No," he said with a chuckle. Twisting in the seat, he took her hand from the wheel and held it. "I think he feels the same. So, if you love him, don't ignore it. Don't walk away. We only get so many chances at love, and when they're gone, that's it. Don't blow it because you're scared."

He sounded sincere and something else. Broken. Guilty. She looked at him again. The way he held her hand. There wasn't anything sexual about his touch. Just concern.

"I'm not scared," she lied. Maybe she was missing out, but she wasn't ready for love. And she sure as hell wasn't ready for loving someone like Kane. He was intense. Serious. Everything she wasn't.

She stopped at the curb and popped the trunk. Bravo placed her hand back on the wheel. "You're a good agent. A great thief. But there's more to life than the job."

A funny statement coming from a man who was never home. "You're one to talk," she said. "That's all you do. You're always working. Traveling."

"I know." He opened the door and hesitated. "But ask yourself why."

• • •

He's running away from his past. That's what Bravo was telling her. That he used the job to keep his brain occupied.

She wouldn't become him, she told herself. She wasn't Bravo. She wasn't going to use the job to run away. Besides, if she wanted to do that, she could always go back to the circus. She smiled to herself at the idea. Most people ran away to the circus. She'd run away from it.

She did always like to be different.

"I wasn't sure you'd come home."

Holly jumped. Kane stood at the top of the stairs. She'd been so preoccupied she hadn't seen him waiting. Now, her heart beat hard. She wanted to hate him. Needed the anger and the animosity if she wanted to stay out of his arms and his bed.

He leaned against the wall, wearing jeans and a plain

dark blue T-shirt. His hair still damp and his expression both unsure and expectant—a mix of emotions that reflected her own.

I will not let him get to me. She hardened her heart. "What do you mean?" she asked, digging out her keys from her pocket as she slid past him.

"You. Bravo." The words hung in the air.

How could he think so little of her? That she'd jump from man to man without hesitation? "Do you think I'm that easy to get into bed?"

She opened the door. The apartment was empty. Her roommate Eva had to be out with Quinn, her boyfriend. Ever since she'd returned from her last business trip, she'd been practically living with the man.

"I don't think any such thing," Kane said, as he followed her inside and shut the door behind him.

Holly whirled to face him. "What are you doing? I didn't ask you in."

He nodded. "I know, but we need to talk."

The talk. She knew it.

"If it's about the mission, let's hear it." she said as she went into the kitchen, opened the fridge, pulled out a bottle of pinot noir, and poured herself a glass.

Kane raised a brow. She knew it was early but didn't care. She'd been awake all night, and as far as she was concerned, she'd earned it and a few glasses more.

She didn't offer one to Kane—intruders who were about to deliver "the talk" didn't get wine.

He took a seat on the couch. "Okay, we can discuss the mission. What do you want to know?"

"Oh," she said, surprised at her disappointment. Then

again, it solidified her argument that Bravo was wrong—he didn't have feelings for her beyond respect as a colleague and perhaps a bit of lust. The disappointment inside grew deeper. Stronger. "What's the scoop? Are we going after the chip?"

"I am."

She wasn't? Great. Today was one big frustration after another. She sucked down half the glass.

"But Tempe did say I could pick my team," he said, looking much too satisfied with himself.

For a beat, she stared at him. "What. An. Ass," she said once she was able to talk.

He laughed. "You seem to think I'm a predictable stick in the mud, so I thought I'd mix it up."

She took a seat on the puffy chair across from him and set the glass down on the coffee table between them. "You think you're so smart."

"No. I don't," he replied, his arms crossed.

He's always been a pain and occasionally a jerk, but he'd never been deliberately cruel. "Then why torture me?"

He leaned across the table, so close that his mouth was inches from hers.

She held her breath.

"I'm not trying to torture you," he whispered.

"Then what?" she whispered back, not daring to raise her voice. Not sure what to do. Or what she wanted. Except that it involved the man staring at her from across the table.

She leaned across the table, meeting him halfway. He brushed his lips against hers, and she shut her eyes. Sinking into the sensation, she breathed him in as Bravo's words came back to her. *We only get so many chances at love, and*

*when they're gone, that's it. Don't blow it because you're
scared.*

She was well and truly terrified.

"What do you want?" she asked, the words soft against
his mouth.

He kissed the tip of her nose in reply.

The air between them shifted as he rose. She opened her
eyes, and he stood in front of her, right hand outstretched.
Offering.

She placed her hand in his and let him help her to her
feet. Wrapping her arms around his neck, she rose onto the
tip of her toes and kissed him before she could stop herself.
Her tongue slid past his lips to taste him. Take him in. Make
him hers.

Kane groaned against her mouth and lifted her up and
against him. Her ribs protested but didn't make her flinch.

He was already hard as she wrapped her legs around his
waist, and her body responded, making her catch her breath.

Maybe it was love. Maybe it was lust. Perhaps both.

Whatever she felt, she wanted more of it. "Down the
hall. First room on the left," she said.

He walked them down the hall as she bit his ear. One
hand holding her, he opened the door to her bedroom. Once
inside, he kicked it shut and tossed her onto the bed.

She winced as she bounced on the mattress.

"Shit. Sorry."

She laughed, patting the space next to her. "I was raised
in the circus. Trust me, I've had worse. A lot worse. But if you
want to show me how sorry you are…"

He dove toward her, and she rolled out of the way,
laughing. "You'll have to do better than that."

He straddled her—she noticed he was careful to keep his weight off of her—pressing her wrists into the pillow. "Like this?" he asked, biting her neck before blowing a raspberry on her bare skin, tickling her.

She half-laughed, half-shrieked, and tried to get away.

Kane was having none of it. He blew another raspberry on her neck, making her scream. Pulling up her shirt, he un-hooked her bra then took a nipple into his mouth. Then the other. Alternating until she squirmed beneath him, eager to be naked and in his arms.

"Say Uncle," he laughed, sitting up and cupping her face with a free hand.

She reached up and mirrored him, his skin rough with stubble beneath her palm. Life was a hell of a lot easier when she loathed him.

"Say it," he said, staring down at her, his eyes eager. Begging. Wanting her so much that she knew she could ask for anything and everything, and he would give it to her.

There was only one thing she wanted.

She kissed his palm. "Uncle." She bit him. Hard.

Chapter Fifteen

Kane clenched his teeth as Holly sunk her incisors into the padded flesh below his thumb. It wasn't painful but served as a sharp reminder of who he was dealing with.

Holly Milano.

A woman that did what she wanted, whether it was in bed or on a mission. Both infuriating and intriguing, he was starting to wonder how he had ever lived without her.

But was forever an option? The strengths that drew him were also her greatest weaknesses. He'd learned that the hard way with Danielle.

Plus, Holly made it clear she didn't want a relationship. She wanted her freedom. She wanted no strings attached.

Asking for more than she was willing to give would only get him hurt.

So, he wouldn't ask, he vowed, as he kissed her inner wrist. He'd take whatever she was willing to give, whether it was her body, her humor, her mind, or even her heart.

Not that he had illusions on the latter. He hesitated, knowing he was a fool.

She kissed his palm where she had bit it only seconds earlier then licked the tip of his index finger before she slipped it into her mouth and sucked on it. He groaned at the obvious innuendo. "If you don't stop that, this is going to be over much too soon."

She laughed and released him. "We wouldn't want that."

This time it was Holly who straddled him, her long blond hair pulled to one side and over her shoulder. The ends tickled him as she leaned over to scrape a hard nipple against his mouth. He flicked his tongue out once. Twice. Three times. Each time her breath caught in her throat making him smile.

He wasn't going to walk away from her. It wasn't the sex. It was the way she smiled. Her laugh. How she defied him. Argued. How much she cared.

Still leaning over him, Holly pushed his shirt up and kissed her way down his body. When she reached his jeans, there was no hesitation. She wasn't a shy, inexperienced girl playing a game or acting as if this were her first time.

She was confident and playful, and it was one more thing to love.

"Take your clothes off," he said after she'd stripped him bare.

She stood and started to pull her shirt over her head.

"Stop."

She hesitated, staring at his wide blue eyes. "Is there a problem?"

Time was the problem. There was never enough. "Slow," he whispered. "Take your time. I want to enjoy this."

She blew him a kiss then turned her back to him. Her

arms crossed, she gripped the hem of her shirt. Slowly, she inched the material up her back, exposing her skin an inch at a time. Glancing at him over her shoulder, she flashed him a wicked grin, yanked the material over her head, and tossed it to the floor.

Still facing the wall, she unbuttoned her jeans but didn't pull them down. Instead, she leaned over, her bottom so close he could touch her if he reached out...

Holly slapped his hand. "No. Just watch."

It was difficult, but he pulled his hand back to his side. He'd asked for slow, and it seemed she wasn't going to let him change his mind.

Worth it.

Her hips swayed from side to side, making the occasional figure eight, as she teased him with her body.

Finally, she inched her jeans over her curves, taunting him with a peek of her panties. Pulling her jeans back up. Then inching them down again.

"You're killing me," Kane said, falling back with a groan. He was starting to regret his request that she go slow.

She laughed, and when he looked again, her jeans were in a puddle at her feet, and she wore nothing but a black bra and white panties with black polka dots.

Both sexy and sweet, she stood at the end of the bed, running her hands down her sides, over her hips and between her legs. No shame. No coyness. Just a woman confident in her body and what she wanted.

It took all of Kane's willpower to not cross the space between them and pull her onto the bed.

She reached up to unhook her bra. It fell to the floor to join the rest of her clothes.

There wasn't much left other than her panties, and he counted himself lucky that Holly didn't believe in layering. He wanted her to turn around but knew if he asked, she'd only tell him no.

She hooked her thumb under the waistband of her panties and pulled them down an inch. She stopped.

"Brat," he said.

She gave a wiggle of her hips to show she didn't care what he thought. She pulled the panties down another inch then did the same with the other side.

"Are you sure you're ready for this?" she asked.

"For you? Always."

She let her panties fall to her feet, and with a flourish, she picked them up and tossed them at his head. He batted them away. "Like I said, brat," he teased.

She responded by crawling toward him from the foot of the bed. Lithe as a cat, she stalked him. Made him wait. Dared him to touch her.

He wasn't sure he wanted her to win this test of wills. This was Holly—who knew what the penalty might be. Probably something he'd like, he realized.

I can live with that.

He forced himself to wait for her to come to him. Not touch. Not kiss. Just. Wait. Then she was on top of him. Thigh against thigh. Chest against chest. Skin against skin. She stared into his eyes, and the energy between them shifted. Time slowed.

"Tell me how you feel," she whispered.

Under the circumstances, he knew what she expected. Something erotic. Sexy. But how he felt about her encompassed more than the physical. She hadn't just aroused his body, she'd brought his heart back to life.

And now, he was going to give her the chance to break it.

He stroked her cheek. "I don't want this to be a one-night-stand. I want you now. Tomorrow. Next week and the week after."

"Can't we just have this and not worry about the future?" She leaned into his touch, her blue eyes staring into him, pleading with him to understand.

Not what he wanted, but he couldn't walk away if he tried, not from Holly Milano. He pulled her closer and kissed her forehead. "Worth it," he said, planting tiny kisses along her cheeks, her nose, and the line of her jaw until he found her mouth.

He brushed his lips against hers, savoring their softness. She groaned against him and he kissed her again.

She hesitated as the energy shifted back to erotic, and she returned the kiss, eager and ready.

He wasn't going to wait any longer. "I want you," he said, hands on her hips as he pressed against her.

"Condoms are in the side table," she said. "Top drawer."

Still kissing her, he reached for the table, pulled the drawer open and felt around until the found a square packet. He tore it open. He'd waited long enough.

"Let me," Holly said, taking the plastic packet from him, she removed the condom and slid it over him. Her touch made him shudder. Shiver.

So close.

He gritted his teeth and clenched the sheets in his fists, desperate to maintain control.

She shifted, and he was inside her. She was as warm and

wet as he remembered, and it took all of his willpower to not lose himself. She rocked against him, and he knew he had to slow her down.

Holding her against him and careful to not crush her ribs, he sat up so she was in his lap. "Wrap your legs around me."

She did, surprising him with the easy compliance.

"Make me yours," she whispered, wrapping her arms around his neck as she ground her pelvis against him. "Just for today."

There was no stopping. No hesitation. Kane held her as he pulled out then thrust into her. She followed his lead, and the world around them fell away as he lost himself in the touch of her hands and the scent of her hair.

She buried her head in his neck and whimpered, her nails digging into his shoulder. She tightened around him. So close. He gritted his teeth.

Her nails dug deeper, and she arched backward, crying out and shaking in his arms.

He wanted to wait. To freeze the moment.

Even as the desire crossed his thoughts, he let himself join her.

· · ·

"Are you going to tell me what this team you get to pick is going to do?" Holly traced the jagged skin that ran from his thigh to his hip. After the love, the morning had been relaxed and lingering, but thirty minutes ago, she'd made coffee, and the caffeine was taking hold.

"Not much to tell," Kane said, his voice muffled by the

pillow.

He didn't drink coffee. A defect in character as far as she was concerned, but one she could overlook.

She bit his left butt cheek to wake him up. He flinched but remained face down. "We can talk later. I'll get a briefing together and everything, if you let me take a nap."

"Nope. Now," she insisted, pushing his shoulder in an attempt to force him onto his back. Most people slept after sex. She wanted to run a marathon or clean the house. Anything to burn her excess energy.

He didn't budge. "You weigh a ton."

"Liar."

With a sigh of resignation, he turned over, hands under his head. "You win. What do you want to know?"

"What's the plan?"

He closed his eyes. "Fairly straightforward. We talk to Mira again, and she's thinks that Tammi Lynn has the stone."

"What makes her so sure?"

"She had the necklace, and according to Mira, she isn't as dumb as she looks." Holly knew all too well that things, and people, weren't always as they seemed.

"How do we make her hand it over?" She ran a nail down his sternum down to his bellybutton and back up again.

"Tempe called her, told her we had the laser, and offered to partner up. She hopped on the first plane to L.A. Once she arrives, we force her to hand it over. Assuming this isn't all a giant scam." He grabbed her hand. "Stop that. It tickles."

"What happens when we get the chip?" she asked, yanking her hand away and not stopping.

"Give it back to the government."

"If she refuses?"

"Turn everyone involved into the authorities. Either scenario seems to work for Tempe."

Easy enough. She snuggled against his side and drew expanding circles on his skin, starting at his hip and stopping when she got to the point where the massive scar began.

"How did you get this?" she asked.

"The field. You know how that can be."

She didn't but wasn't going to correct him. Being a thief involved its share of taking chances, but it was more controlled than being in the field and retrieving kidnapped victims. Being in "the field" was exotic. Dangerous. And paid a hell of a lot more than breaking into buildings and vaults.

There was also a larger chance of getting killed. Plus, she'd be out of contact with her family for months at a time, and as much as she loved adventure, she loved her family more, and her mother would have a conniption if she couldn't reach her daughter for more than a week.

"Where were you?" she asked, raking a nail down his thighs. "South America? The Middle East?"

He caught her hand and kissed it. "Chicago."

She gave a nod and tweaked a nipple, making his breath hiss between his teeth. "Sensitive?" she asked, feigning innocence.

His right brow shot up, seeing through the weak subterfuge.

She returned to the scar. "Sounds exciting. You know, windy city and what not."

He hesitated, and she snuck a glance. His mouth wasn't turned up in laughter. Instead, his lips were pressed tight.

She'd struck a nerve. Unintentional, but a nerve all the same. Whatever had happened in Chicago wasn't something he wanted to discuss. She reached up and touched his mouth, trying to smooth the tension. "I'm sorry. Just ignore me."

Instead, he pulled her into his arms and held her. She rested her head against his chest and listened to his heartbeat.

"You have nothing to be sorry for," he said.

She didn't meet his gaze again. There wasn't any need. The pain in his voice told her everything she needed to know. "Did you lose the client?"

"No." He stroked her hair. "Not the client."

An agent then. She squeezed him. "Sorry."

"Me too," he kissed the top of her head. "She saved my life. Saved my leg. And was killed for her trouble." He swallowed hard, and she knew there was more, and whatever it was, she wasn't going to like it.

Kane continued, "She was also my lover."

The confession didn't take her breath away—it opened a Pandora's box of questions. She centered on the one that seemed to matter most. "Did you love her?"

He nodded, his gray eyes dark with the memories of a love gone wrong. "I did. And I thought she loved me, but I found out she slept with another agent."

"Like me and Bravo," Holly whispered, dreading where the conversation was headed.

"No. Not like that." He stroked her hair. "Who you slept with, who you loved before me is just that—before me. It doesn't matter."

She believed him. His eyes were still angry, but his mouth smiled at her, and it wasn't superficial. She let herself relax in his arms. He didn't care. "Do you want to tell me what happened?"

"There isn't much to say. We were both angry and not thinking straight. She accepted a job she had no business taking and got caught. I found out and tried to save her and failed."

She kissed his bare skin. "I'm sorry for that, but I'm not sorry you're here. Not at all. And I wish I could thank her for saving you."

"Me, too."

She couldn't imagine the guilt that came with losing a friend and teammate. And lover.

Worse, there was nothing she could do about it. No way to fix the scars he carried on his skin or in his thoughts. "Kane? I—"

The theme song to *Mission Impossible* emerged from his pocket.

"That's Tempe," Kane said, reaching for his pants in a heap on the floor. Digging out his phone, he held up a finger for silence.

She reached out to tickle him, but he waved her away. One didn't need to be a psychic to know something was wrong.

She waited, listening to the one sided-monosyllabic conversation.

After what felt like hours, he rose. "On my way," he said. Grabbing Holly's jeans, he handed them to her.

"The Pascuas have kidnapped Mira Burke."

She grabbed a shirt and slipped it on. "How? Wasn't someone watching her?"

"Only from the street. It's a big damned house, and apparently, she wouldn't let our people in."

There was no fixing stupid, Holly thought with a sigh. "What is wrong with her? Doesn't she realize her life is in danger?"

Kane's phone buzzed, and he turned it on. He frowned and handed it to Holly. The text was open. Tempe had sent them a photo. It was grainy but legible. It showed two men had Mira by the arms, leading her to a car.

The man on the left was unknown. The one on the right was Enzo.

"I think she does now," Kane replied.

• • •

"Do they really think that kidnapping is the way to go?" Holly asked, taking a seat in Tempe's office.

Kane had briefed her on what little Tempe had told him on the drive over. Instead of handing over the chip to Tempe, Tammi Lynn had sold it to the Corsicans, but they needed the laser and were willing to trade Mira for it.

"They're the mob," Tempe said. "I'm fairly sure they think they can do whatever they want."

"Do you think she's still alive?" Holly asked.

Tempe's grip tightened on the key fob. "She better be if they want to make the exchange."

Holly hoped the V.P. was right. She was rarely wrong, but she'd never seen her this agitated.

"There was no way you could have prevented this," Kane said. "If Mira had the laser, the Corsicans would have both items, and we'd all be screwed. You saved lives by taking it."

Tempe didn't stop moving. "I know. I don't like being caught unawares." She stopped long enough to glare at the pen in her hand then restarted her stride across the room and back again. "What the hell is on that chip?"

"Whatever it is, we can't let them have it," Kane said. He was all business now, and Holly appreciated the distinct line between his modes. Granted, working Kane was a bit of a bore, but he knew his job—and that kept her alive and out of jail.

"Agreed," Tempe said, taking a seat at her desk.

"So, what's next?" Holly asked.

Tempe continued. "The good news is that I was able to talk them into meeting in a public space."

Better than in a dark alley, Holly supposed.

Tempe leaned back. "The bad news is we're dealing with the mob. I think we're all aware of how *serious* they can be."

Kidnapping Mira. Trying to kill her and Kane.

Oh yeah, they knew how serious the Corsicans were, as long as by serious Tempe meant lethal and psychopathic. "When does the exchange happen?" Holly asked, hoping they'd at least have time to come up with some kind of plan.

"Three hours."

Kane straightened at the news. "Three hours? You can't be serious."

That gave them little to no time to make a plan, free Mira, and steal back the chip. It seemed that the Corsicans weren't idiots—contrary to what the movies would have one believe.

"Not much choice."

Kane shook his head. "That's not enough time. Can we stall? Tell them we don't have the laser but that we can get it?"

Tempe gave him a sympathetic look. "We can wait, but they threatened to start cutting off her fingers, and I don't think that's something we can live with."

"Dammit." Kane groaned and rubbed his chin. "At least tell me you picked a place we can control."

"Control?" Her mouth thinned as exasperation replaced

sympathy. "There is no control. Just be glad I refused to meet them at the mall."

"Understood," Kane replied.

"Small favors," Holly said. The mall was a maze of stores and places to hide. She didn't want to have to check racks of clothes for a sniper while they bargained for Mira. "So, where is the exchange being made?"

Tempe tapped a remote, activating the overhead projector connected to her computer. Holly swiveled the chair around. A satellite view of L.A. shone on the wall.

She followed Tempe's pointer as it made its way across the screen. Over the reservoir. Past the infamous Hollywood sign and Griffith Park.

It stopped on Griffith Observatory.

Her stomach dropped. It was more than public. It was a historic landmark that brought in millions of people a year to use the public telescopes, stargaze, and even take sunset nature walks.

People that would be put in danger if the Corsicans didn't behave.

"You can't be serious," Kane said.

From the incredulous look on his face, his thoughts were on the same track as hers.

"I am," Tempe said. Coming around the desk, she walked to the screen and tapped an icon on the bottom. The picture flipped sideways, giving them a 3D view of the structure and surrounding landscape.

Holly's worry deepened. Set on top of a mountain, the observatory dominated the site. The sheer walls were scalable, but unless it was dark, there was no way she could blend with the white stucco sides.

"It's a weekday, so it will have fewer people—"

"Still, civilians," Kane said." Lots of them."

"—and I have a diversion planned." Tempe finished. "They're not stupid. They're not going to shoot me when there's hundreds of tourists around."

"Let's say this works," Kane countered. "That we get Mira, and they take the laser. Can we afford to let them have access to that kind of information?"

"No," Tempe tapped her pencil on the desk. "That's why Holly is going to go to their hotel and rob them while I make the exchange. Once we recover the crystal and give it back to the government, their laser won't matter anymore."

Holly straightened. B&E was exciting, she'd been looking forward to giving Lucien and Enzo a little payback. "What makes you think they'll have the chip in the room? Why not bring it with them to verify that it works?"

"I don't think that they will," Tempe said. "But if they are foolish enough to put both together in my presence, I'll take them down. Still, we have to cover both scenarios. If this chip contains what Mira said it does, we can't let them have it." She faced Holly, hands clasped in front of her on the desk. "Which is why I need you to do what you do best— breaking and entering."

There was no arguing that it was her primary skillset. It was a pity she wouldn't get to see Lucien's expression when he returned to an empty safe, but it would be almost as good to know she'd thwarted him and his son. Almost. "Do we know where they're staying?"

"The L.A. Live, Marriott side. Chairman Suite. Plus the rooms next door."

"How about above or below?" Holly asked.

Tempe raised a brow. "Nothing useful below. The only thing above them is the roof."

"Not as prepared as they thought, are they?" Holly said with a snicker. No one ever thought that someone might be crazy enough to try and break into a penthouse from the outside.

"This is the mob," Kane cautioned her. "Not some mark that has no clue we're going to break in. It doesn't matter that it's in a hotel. It's going to be guarded, and they will be waiting for you. For us. And while it might be sunset, it will still be light enough for anyone to see you. Including anyone waiting in the room."

He was the best kind of Boy Scout—the kind that could do anything from make a fire to prepare and execute the robbery of a guarded penthouse suite.

But she had diversion plans of her own. "They won't see me," Holly said. "No one will. They'll be too busy."

"Doing what?"

She smiled. "Watching their very own circus, of course."

Chapter Sixteen

"Are you sure you don't mind?"

Kane drove while Holly talked to her mother on her cell, multitasking, since time was running out. With L.A. traffic, it could take them over an hour to get to the downtown hotel. Kane could cut that down by half.

"I appreciate it. Nothing fancy. I need people to be watching you," she said into the phone, her free hand tracing absentminded circles on his thigh as she spoke.

She hesitated. "You don't want to know. Trust me," and hung up. "They'll be poolside in an hour."

"Can they get there that fast?"

"You've never seen my mom drive. Or the rest of the family. Santos is a maniac on wheels, and the Boreckyis drive their minivan like it's a Porsche."

"What do they all do?"

"Acrobats. Fire-eaters. Contortionists. A little bit of everything. Dog tricks. They don't even need equipment." She leaned her head back against the seat and closed her eyes, her fingers splayed wide on his leg.

He envied how Holly's mother took her daughter's word with no questions asked. In Holly's case, that might not always be a good thing, but he appreciated the trust behind it.

It only took dodging a few more cars before he pulled into the parking garage of the hotel. It was crowded but it was downtown L.A.—which meant it was never quiet.

"Let's do this," Holly said, shaking with excitement as she opened the door.

A part of him knew this was what she was—a daredevil. The kid that climbed to the tiptop of a tree and laughed while it swayed.

Fearless.

It was something he would never want to change, but while he loved her boldness, it also scared the hell out of him since it echoed back to memories of Danielle and her risk-taking nature.

Two women. Both agents. Both pushing the limits of safety. And he'd slept with both. Who knew he had a type? Of course, life would be a helluva lot easier if his "type" was the kind of woman who preferred making cookies as opposed to rappeling off of high-rises. "Wait."

She stilled, and her inner excitement didn't diminish, but she focused on him. "What?"

He didn't know what to say. That he wanted her to be careful? To not die? Any and all of that would only make her hesitate, and hesitation might get her killed. So he settled for pulling her close. Breathing her in, he brushed his lips against hers. There was no rush like the morning lovemaking. No teasing. No biting.

Just the taste of her mouth and the warmth of her breath. A gentle moan as he savored her. To tell her that he worried and to let her know that she was important. Not just to her family. But to him.

He wove his hands through her hair, savoring the feel of the strands. The roughness of her skin—a thief's palms calloused by years of climbing ropes, rappeling, and who knew what else—when she cupped his face.

"I'll be careful," she said, when he released her.

Trust her to know what he meant, even when he couldn't find the words. "I know," he said, "But when you're not careful"—

She stuck her tongue out. Such a Holly reaction. It made him both want to laugh and cry. The scar on his leg throbbed.

—"I'll have your back," he finished.

She put in her earpiece, opened the car door the rest of the way, and hesitated. Her eyes met his, but she didn't look *at* him. She looked *into* him.

Tempe had said Holly was the best when it came to reading people. So he didn't even try to disguise his emotions. What he wanted.

She took a deep breath and turned away. "I'm counting on it."

. . .

Holly closed the hotel service door behind her as she reached the roof of the hotel. L.A. glowed in the sunset, the mirrored building reflecting red and orange of the clouds and the millions of city lights. Beneath her was the penthouse and her target.

"Beautiful," she said, hands on her hips.

"Are you on the roof?" Kane asked in her ear. "Don't forget your check points. It's the only way I know what's going on."

Stick in the mud. The unkind words floated through her thoughts, and she blushed that she'd ever considered him anything less than an amazing combination of boss and lover.

"Checking in," she said. "It won't happen again."

He didn't say a word, but she thought he breathed disbelief.

Let him think what he wants. She'd prove she could do as asked. He deserved her trust. She continued, "I'm in place. Prepping for the run."

Shedding her jeans and T-shirt until she wore nothing but a black unitard, she jammed the clothes in her gym bag and pulled out her climbing gear. The sunset deepened. She gazed over the edge of the roof.

Thirty feet or three hundred, it'll all kill you, Mrs. Trieu had told her when she learned to walk the tightrope.

Still. It was a hell of a long way.

Don't. She shut down the insecurity. She'd never listened to it, and five minutes before she hung her ass in the air wasn't the time to start. She turned away from the edge and slipped the harness over the lycra suit, adjusting it until it rested snug against her body. Looping a webbed belt around her waist, she attached a smaller version of her gear bag then wound the rest of the rigging and rope over one shoulder, took out her binoculars, and focused her attention on the pool area.

One person stood out. She carried a parasol. An ankle-length batik skirt peeked out from beneath it. That could only be one person.

Madam Sarah, a.k.a. Mom.

If she was here, then so was everyone else.

Holly glanced at her watch. Tempe should be making the exchange soon, and she needed to be in and out before that happened. "Kane?"

"I'm here." She scanned the parking structure on the other side of the wide road and found him at the top. She waved. He waved back. From his vantage, he could watch Lucien's suites and direct her.

"What's the situation?" she asked.

"One man in the middle room."

"Enzo?"

"No. Someone new. The bedrooms are empty. So are the other suites."

"Slackers," she said, hoping she sounded more amused than she felt. It stood to reason that the guard had a gun so one in the room was plenty.

"Let's hope. Go about thirty feet to your right. That will put you in the smaller bedroom on the corner of the building. As long as he stays in the main room, you'll be out of sight line even if the bedroom door is open."

This was so much easier having a set of eyes to tell her where the danger waited. They made a great team. She blew a kiss.

"I'll hang on to that," he said with a chuckle. "Now get moving."

"You got it, boss." She pulled out her cell phone and dialed her mother.

The woman holding the parasol dug something out of her purse. "Hi, Cookie."

"Hi, Mom."

"Ready to give these people a taste of the circus life?" Sarah asked.

Ready to put those you love in danger? was what Holly heard. She shut the voices down. They weren't the ones in trouble. Lucien was at the Observatory, and no one in their right mind would take on a troupe of acrobats—not unless they wanted their asses kicked for ruining the show.

She stared down at the crowd. Her family blending in among them. *Be careful.* "Do it," she replied.

Slipping on her leather gloves, she hooked her rope around a large metal pipe, secured it with a carabineer—checked it twice like she'd been taught—and jumped over the edge of the building.

She halted, and for few seconds, she let herself hang over the abyss—reveling in the adrenaline that rushed through her, the sense of mortality, and the thrill of accomplishment.

"Are you okay?"

She held up her hand, making the forefinger and thumb in the "okay" symbol.

"I don't know how you do it," Kane said. "You have some massive balls."

"If I had massive balls, I couldn't wear this harness," she shot back, hoping he heard the smile in her voice and know she was teasing. "Now, what's the guard doing?"

"Watching the show from the window."

She lowered herself a few more feet until she was level with the bedroom window Kane had told her to use. "This would be much easier if they had a balcony," she muttered, reaching into her side bag to retrieve the high-tech glass-cutter — an industrial suction cup that sported an adjustable cable with a laser at the end, it could cut through almost anything. Taking on a glass window — even one made to withstand winds and earthquake — would be like slicing through hot butter.

"If it were that easy, I'd be doing the thieving and not you." Kane said.

"Everyone's a smartass," she said. Setting the suction cup on the window, she put the laser to glass. "This is going to weigh a ton," she said, drawing a circle just big enough for her to slip through.

The glass came loose, the weight making her swing in the harness.

"Don't drop it," Kane said, sounding rattled.

She caught the now open window with her foot to stop the sway. "You think?" Slowly, she slid her feet through until she stood on her toes. With her free hand, she let go of more rope until her feet were flat on the floor, and she hung out of the opening from the waist up.

Her biceps screamed with the weight of the glass. Letting out the rest of the rope, she pulled herself into the room, fitting the glass through the opening and placing it on the floor — not wanting to alert the man in the next room by creating a thudding noise.

Kane breathed a sigh of relief. "Like I said. Giant, badass balls."

She didn't say a word but retrieved a tranquilizer gun from her side bag and made her way to the door that led into the main living space. It was closed. *Dammit*. She didn't need any movement to catch the target's attention. Still, not much to be done about it now.

In the other room, the phone rang.

She held her breath. She'd stolen a lot of items, but she'd never shot someone. It wasn't like he was going to die, but still, it was more unnerving than stepping off the roof of the high-rise.

The ringing stopped. She pressed an ear against the door. *One.*

"No. This isn't Enzo's room," the man said from the other side of the door. He had the same accent as Enzo, but his voice was deeper.

Two.

"I'm sure."

Three.

"No, I don't know who they are. You need to call the front desk."

It had to be Kane. Helping her even when she didn't ask for it. Slowly, she cracked open the door, leaned out, and sighted the target. His back was to her, giving her a view of his broad shoulders and dark hair.

It's only twenty feet. She raised the weapon. *You can do this.* She prayed one tranq dart was enough. He wasn't just broad and tall. He was heavy. Two-fifty. Maybe two-seventy.

She pulled the trigger, and he leaned over to slam down the phone.

The dart hit the wall.

Time halted. She watched as he tracked the dart in the drywall. Turned. Spotted her. Time sped up again as he barreled toward her, murder in his eyes.

She fired again. The second dart pieced the fabric of his blue silk shirt. Dashing back into the bedroom, she slammed the door shut, locked it, and braced herself against it. She'd had the training, dammit. How the hell had she missed that shot?

He slammed the entire force of his big body into the door.

"Hang tight," Kane said in her ear. "I'm already on my way."

Great, he'd seen her screw up. She was sure to get a lecture later and about a thousand hours of training on how to fire a weapon and hit something only twenty feet away. "Hurry."

The door vibrated as the thug tried to break it down. "Open up," he shouted from the other side. "Or you're dead."

If she opened it, she would be dead. There was no doubt. He might not toss her off the roof, but something would happen, and it wouldn't be pretty. "Thanks. I'll stay here," she replied.

He slammed into the door again, and the wood splintered. It wasn't going to take much more. A few hits at the most. She was screwed. "Hurry, Kane," she whispered, bracing her feet against the floor.

No answer.

He was probably in an elevator or something. She needed to hear his voice. To know he had a plan. That he could figure out a way to get her out of this and get the chip.

"I'm going to kill you," the man screamed as he hit the door again.

Holly braced herself, ready to run past him when he broke through. A thud sounded on the other side. Then nothing.

Did he have a heart attack? Or was it a trick?

She stood, silent. The thud of footsteps caught her attention. These were lighter. Too light to belong to the man who'd tried to kill her.

Carefully, she opened the door. On the floor in front of the threshold, the man lay sprawled on the carpet, his shirt stained red. A hole in his chest.

There wasn't time to feel sorry or queasy or even relieved he wasn't going to kill her. Past him stood a Southern belle she knew all too well.

"Come in," the blonde said, aiming her gun—equipped with a silencer—at Holly's head.

Raising her hands, Holly walked into the room. "Hi, Tammi Lynn."

. . .

"Tammi Lynn? That's unexpected," Kane said in her ear.

Relief washed over Holly that he was back. She'd need the back up now more than ever. She'd never been caught while trying to steal something before, and other than trying to stay alive, she wasn't sure what to do.

"You didn't have to kill him," Holly said. "I drugged him. He was going to pass out any second."

Tammi Lynn clenched her mouth tighter. "Drop your weapon."

Holly had forgotten she had it. She set it on the carpet.

"Thanks for the heads up," Kane said to Holly through the earpiece. "I didn't think she had it in her to be a killer. She's full of surprises. Don't be one of them."

The sound of traffic sounded through over the earpiece, giving her information as to how close he was. A car honked near him. He was outside. His breathing was heavy in her ear as he ran.

He continued, "Do what she says. Stall for time. I'll be

there in less than five minutes."

"What's the plan?" Holly asked. "You didn't come here to save me, that's for sure."

Tammi Lynn cocked her head. "I imagine we're here for the same thing. The chip. That's what you were after when you took the necklace, wasn't it?"

"You got me."

"Good. Then you can open the safe." She motioned for Holly toward the high-end safe in the closet.

Shuffling her feet, Holly headed to the built-in vault. Better quality than average, it was something found in an upscale home, not a hotel room. Holly nodded. Nice. It seemed the people who paid for the penthouse suite did get the best of everything.

"Please don't try anything," Tammi Lynn said. "I don't want to kill you."

But you will. As soon as Tammi Lynn had what she wanted, Holly was dead weight and a witness.

Great.

"So, did they steal it from you?" Holly asked, eye-balling the safe. The original plan was to crack the safe, get the chip, and run. Right now, she needed to buy time until Kane arrived. "Is that why you're pissed?"

"I'm not pissed," Tammi Lynn said. "Focus, please. Can you open it?"

"Stall," Kane said, still breathing heavy. "I'm in the lobby."

"I don't think I can crack this," Holly lied. "It's pretty high end."

The chill of metal behind her ear brought her up short. "If you can't open it, you're useless to me," said Tammi Lynn.

"On the other hand, I could be wrong," Holly said,

putting her ear to the safe, she turned the dial.

"Hurry."

Holly glared at her. "This is a TL-30. Its six-inches of metal with individual bolts designed to keep out both fire and people like me. You don't just crack it open. This isn't a movie."

"I don't care. Just get on with it," Tammi Lynn said, shifting from foot to foot, agitated. "Lucien isn't going to stay gone forever. I'd like to be well away from here when he returns."

"Considering you killed his man, I'd say it's a good idea," Holly muttered, turning her attention back to the task.

The familiar "ding" of an elevator sounded in her ear. Kane would be here soon. Of course, getting into the room to help her was another matter. She'd need to distract Tammi Lynn.

And the best way to escape was by letting her think she'd won. She reached for her gear bag, "Just getting my tools," she said and pulled out the laser she'd used to cut the window.

"What's that?"

"A laser."

"*The* laser?" Tammi Lynn's voice rose an octave in her excitement, and her finger tightened on the trigger of the gun.

Holly's gaze zeroed in on Tammi Lynn's slight movement, but she refused to let the fear grab hold. "Of course not. So you might want to hold off shooting me in the head," she said, with a bravado she didn't feel, now that she'd all but confirmed that Tammi Lynn planned to kill her once the safe was open.

She continued, "This one is specialized for cutting metal. With this baby," she patted it with a combination of respect and admiration, "it should only take a few minutes to get the safe open," Turning it on, she pointed the thin blue light at the seam where the bolts went from the frame to the door.

Like hot butter.

Tammi Lynn leaned over her shoulder, the gun resting behind Holly's ear again. "Why didn't you use it earlier on him? If you had, you would have been out of here before I arrived."

A good point, but since she wasn't a sociopath, it was also a moot point. Holly tilted her head away from the weapon. "Does it matter?"

"I suppose not. Now get it done."

Holly focused her attention on the task, being careful to not rush. She didn't want to be shot, but at the end of the day, HRS also needed to retrieve the contents of the safe. If she failed in that, it wasn't just herself who would be screwed, it could be entire populations.

"What's on the chip?" Holly asked, trying to distract Tammi Lynn, looking for an opportunity to get the gun.

"Shut up."

"Fine, don't tell me," she said, as she worked her way down a seam. *I already know, anyway.* "Want to tell me why you're stealing something you sold?"

Tammi Lynn sighed, "You've never been involved in politics, have you?"

More than once, she'd listened to people argue as each tried to change the other's mind, and what she found was people believed what they wanted and only presented evidence to support their own ideas. "I try to avoid any and all political discussions whenever possible," Holly replied, sneaking a glance at the woman behind her.

Tammi Lynn shook her head as if Holly were the biggest idiot she'd ever met. "Well, I can tell you this. If you want to survive, to succeed, you need both secrets and insurance. This will give me both."

"Don't forget the money," Holly said. She was at the sixth, and last, bolt. "That's why you sold it."

"There's nothing wrong with a nest egg."

Unless you kill to get it. Or sell out your country. She didn't say the words. There was a fine line between keeping the woman with the gun occupied and pissing her off.

"I'm here," Kane said in her ear. "Can you get her attention so I can break in?"

"Of course," she replied.

"What?" Tammi Lynn said.

"It's done," Holly said. Opening the safe. Tammi Lynn's eyes turned to the movement, and Holly flicked the laser back on and pointed it at her captor's foot.

Chapter Seventeen

Kane stood outside the door, listening, waiting for a signal or a word that he could break the door down without getting Holly killed. On the other side, a woman screamed, but it wasn't in the heat of anger. It was a shriek of pain.

Holly. Kane kicked in the door and rushed inside, weapon raised. He stopped mid-step. Tammi Lynn was on the ground, clutching her foot. A gun was on the ground next to her. Holly stood over her, laser in hand.

"You wanted a distraction," she said, voice shaking.

He crossed the space, kicking Tammi Lynn's gun under the couch as he went, then wrapped his arms around a shivering Holly. "It's okay. You did great."

Her skin felt cool to the touch. Her breathing was fast and shallow. She was going into shock.

"She cut off my toes,' Tammi Lynn howled.

"I've never hurt anyone before," Holly whispered. "Not like that."

"You did what you had to," he said. He should never have let Tempe put her into this situation. She was a thief, not a field agent. Escorting her to a nearby chair, he sat her down and pushed her head between her knees.

"Check on her," Holly said, her voice muffled. "I don't want her to lose her foot."

The Southern belle wasn't going to lose anything but her freedom when he turned her over to the police for murder, but for Holly, he'd do as asked. He kissed her hair. "I'll be right back."

Kneeling in front of Tammi Lynn, he held out his hand, palm up "Let's see it."

She whimpered as she moved her hands, then screamed when he touched the seared flesh.

It was more of a hole than an actual cut. She'd need stitches when this was over, but she'd survive. "You'll be fine," he said. "You're toes are intact. All of them."

She screamed again when he let her limb drop to the floor. "You need to shut up," he said. "Or someone is going to call security."

Her blue eyes filled with tears. "Let them come."

"Do you want to explain the dead guy on the floor? You're the one with gun powder on her hands and fingerprints on the weapon, not me. It sure as hell isn't Holly."

She snapped her mouth closed. "Fine. What are you going to do?"

Finish the job, and get Holly out of here before either the cops or hotel security arrived. "We're getting what we came for and we're leaving."

He checked the safe. It was empty except for a small velvet box. Inside was a diamond solitaire more appropriate for an engagement ring than subterfuge. "This the chip?" he asked, holding it out for Tammi Lynn to see.

"Yes," she said with a sigh of exasperation. "That's it."

He pocketed the stone but quashed the sense of satisfaction that came with acquiring their target. They were still in enemy territory, and all it took was one wrong move for this entire situation to go south.

With one eye on Tammi Lynn and the other on Holly, he called Tempe. She picked up on the first ring. "It's done," he said.

"We have Mira," Tempe responded. "Get out and back to the office before they return." In the background, a woman sobbed.

Mira.

"Can you shut her up?" Tempe said, talking to someone else.

The V.P. sounded pissed. He couldn't blame her. Mira wasn't their normal client. Generally, their rescue victims were just that—victims. People taken for their knowledge, their bank account, or revenge. There were a myriad of reasons.

Mira was none of those things. She was a blackmailer, and Tempe did not like having to put her neck out for someone who basically deserved to be kidnapped by the mob. Almost. "How much time do we have?" he asked.

"Traffic sucks, so a while. But that doesn't mean you should hang out. Why?"

"We ran into a snag," he said, glaring at Tammi Lynn.

"What kind of snag?" Tempe asked.

"The dead body kind."

Holly rose at the sentence. The color was back in her

cheeks, and she didn't look like she was going to pass out or puke.

"Do not tell me you shot someone," Tempe said.

"Of course not. It was Tammi Lynn."

"Tammi Lynn?" In the background, Mira shrieked, screaming obscenities about Tammi Lynn. Kane caught "whore," "home-wrecker," and even "strumpet." He held the phone away from his ear until the screaming stopped.

"What's the plan?" Tempe said when it grew quiet again.

He handed Holly the laser. "Watch her," and headed to the side room. He didn't need Tammi Lynn to hear what he was going to say. "The plan is to tie up Tammi Lynn, along with a note and the gun. Call the cops."

Tempe laughed. "Sounds like something out of a super-hero movie."

Kane smiled. "Or Tarantino."

"If it were Tarantino, you'd take her head off."

"Holly shot a hole through her foot with the laser. Does that count?"

"I can't wait to hear the rest." Tempe didn't laugh again, but he knew she was smiling. "Do what you have to and get out. Now."

"On it boss, and—"

"What happened to Marco?" A woman's voice in the living area cut through his conversation. Kane flattened against the wall. Someone was here. Someone unexpected. "Tempe, we have a situation. I'll call back."

He hung up the phone and slid it into his pocket, retrieving his weapon at the same time. It seemed the mobsters that were supposed to be in the other two rooms had returned. As much as he wanted to rush in and be the hero, he knew it was wiser to hang back and wait.

Holly was safe. For now.

Still, his finger twitched on the trigger, eager to take out the enemy. He held back, promising himself that he wasn't going to let Holly die. He'd seen someone die for him before and he'd be damned if it were going to happen again.

. . .

"Elizabeth?" Holly tried not to stare at the woman walking toward her, gun in her hand. She knew the girl's father was capable of murder, and her brother had been certifiable, but Elizabeth?

She'd seemed so normal. Still did. The same sweet girl Holly had met in South Carolina.

Except for the weapon.

"Hi, Holly. I wish I could say I was sorry about this, but you kind of brought this on yourself," the younger girl replied, her hand steady. Much like the dead man, she wore a suit, only hers sported a skirt instead of slacks.

"You can't be serious?" This was her fault?

"I am, and now it seems that Marco is dead." She shook her head at the body on the floor, but seemed more annoyed than heartbroken. She tightened her finger on the trigger. "Daddy is going to be upset. Marco is a first cousin. Aunt Athena is going to be beside herself."

Holly swallowed down her rising fear and the self-recrimination at not seeing the true Elizabeth beneath the facade. There was no time for either. She wasn't going to let anyone else get hurt. Not even Tammi Lynn, though she knew the woman didn't deserve mercy.

That didn't mean Holly wouldn't try to help her. Right now, she needed to distract Elizabeth. To stall and stay alive, and keep Tammi Lynn breathing until Kane could make a move.

She hoped it didn't come down to them or the girl with the gun. She'd seen enough of death and blood in the last ten minutes to last a lifetime. She knew Kane wouldn't kill unless he was forced. He'd had enough of killing.

She focused her attention on Elizabeth. "He was like that when we arrived," Holly said, rising. Hands in the air, she circled around to try and put the girl's back to the door Kane had walked through.

"What are you doing?" She cocked her gun.

Holly's heart thumped hard in her chest. "Just getting my phone."

Elizabeth wasn't listening anymore. She'd seen the safe. She refocused the gun on Tammi Lynn. "Talk."

Tammi Lynn's eyes darted from the barrel of the weapon to Holly. "She did it. She broke in and killed him. I was trying to stop her. I sold Lucien the chip. Why would I take it?" she lied.

"Where's the chip?" Elizabeth insisted, glancing into the now-empty safe.

"Gone," Holly said, glaring at Tammi Lynn and daring her to give Kane's location away. She hoped to hell the Southern belle was smart enough to know if she did, they were all dead.

Tammi Lynn swallowed hard but didn't say anything.

Good. She'd grown a brain.

"She doesn't know," Holly said. "Kane took it with him. Kill me and you'll never find it."

"Then, why are you where?"

"To finish the job." She nodded at Tammi Lynn. "She was supposed to sell the chip to my employer," Holly improvised. "He doesn't like losing."

Elizabeth gave her a thoughtful look. "Interesting. Who do you work for?"

Holly took another step sideways, then stopped as the gun swung back in her direction. "Just let me get my phone," she said. "I can call my boss. This is business, that's all. I'm sure something can be arranged as far as compensating you for your troubles."

Elizabeth frowned "The only thing you need to arrange is to bring the chip back. If my Dad finds out we lost it, he'll be furious. He'll never trust me again. Never." Her hands shook, but Holly sensed it was more a fear of her father's wrath than the situation.

Pathetic.

"Of course." Another step and Elizabeth followed her, turning until her back was to the room where Kane hid.

Finally. "I am sure Kane will be happy to do what he can," she said.

Behind the mobster, Kane peered out of the doorway and gave a nod of understanding. Slowly, he crept into the room.

Holly dug around in her gear bag, making as much noise as possible and taking her time. "I'm sure it's here somewhere," she muttered.

Kane reached the mobster and pressed his gun into her back. "Hi. I'm Kane. Remember me?"

Elizabeth stilled as Kane reached around him and took her weapon. Tucking it into the back of his jeans, he brought the butt-end of his gun down on her head. The young girl hit the ground with a thud.

Holly's stomach did a slow flip at the sound. "Will she be okay?"

"She'll feel like hell when he wakes up, but yes, she'll wake up," Kane said.

Relief washed over her. No more death. No more blood. "What about her?" If Tammi Lynn were still here when Lucien returned, she'd be killed.

"We'll let the cops take care of her," Kane said.

"You can't," Tammi Lynn said. "I'll tell them about you."

Holly took a deep breath to try and contain the sudden anger bubbling up. What was wrong with that woman? She'd killed a man. Slept with anyone and everyone. An all-around bad person who seemed to think it was her right to do as she pleased and damn the consequences.

And now she had the gall to say she'd try to hurt Holly and those she loved.

Righteous rage won over, and she stalked over to Tammi Lynn, kneeling down so she could talk to her, face to face. "You won't mention us at all. In fact, if I ever hear my name pass your lips, I'll do everything in my power to make sure you're convicted of treason. I know people. And some of them owe me favors. You think life in prison is bad? Try death for betraying your country."

Tammi Lynn's face went pale. "Fine."

Scared. But not upset.

Because she's going to get out of this. Holly realized. She had money. A politician husband. She might go to jail, but it would be for manslaughter, and she'd be out in a few years.

The reality tasted like ash in her mouth.

At least when it was done, she'd have done some time,

and she wouldn't have the chip. It was a small consolation, but Holly clung to it.

Kane took her arm and pulled her to her feet. "We have to get out of here. If she's here, it's a safe bet others are on their way."

"You mean like me?" a deep voice answered.

She knew that voice. A shiver raced up her spine.

Enzo.

"Run," Kane shouted as gun shots filled the air. Her hand still in his, he dragged her into the room she'd entered when she broke in and slammed the door shut.

They wouldn't have long, not with Enzo willing to shoot.

Putting himself between her and the door, Kane scanned the room. There was an adjoining door to the suite next door. A bathroom.

"What are you doing?"

In the other room, Tammi Lynn begged. Pleaded. Time slowed to a crawl. Holly's stomach rolled again, this time making the full turn. She swallowed the rising bile.

"Please. Talk to Lucien," Tammi Lynn sounded panicked. Frightened.

She knows, Holly realized. She knows she's going to die.

I left her on the floor. Hurt her so she couldn't run. Couldn't even try to save herself.

"Please."

There was the snick of a silencer-equipped gun being fired.

Silence.

Tammi Lynn had paid for her sins.

• • •

"Oh God," Kane turned at hearing Holly's whisper.

Her skin was pale again. Her eyes wide. Empty. It wasn't shock. Not this time. He knew that look. For months after Danielle's death, he'd seen it when he caught a glimpse of himself in the mirror.

Guilt.

Her eyes met his. "We have to get out of this hotel. Someone else is going to get killed."

Someone like Holly, if he didn't keep it together. "Working on it," and he kicked in the adjoining door. He'd have preferred to leave a false trail, to buy them even thirty seconds, but no time for finesse. He pushed Holly through and followed. She moved on autopilot as they sprinted to the main door and into the hallway. "Elevator," he said.

They ran now, pelting down the hallway. Behind them, a door slammed, followed by the sound of running feet.

They'd never make the elevator. Kane headed toward the exit sign. "Here." He pulled her into the stairwell and down the stairs, taking two at time. His pulse beat hard, and the only sound he heard was Holly's labored breath.

The sound of Enzo's footsteps as he drew closer.

Kane needed to lose their pursuer. "Out." The twentieth floor. He held the door, making sure it didn't slam.

They ran down another hallway. "What are you doing? Aren't we supposed to go to the first floor?" Holly asked.

"He was too far back. He won't know which floor we're on. It'll buy us some time when he has to check." Unless he's smart and goes to the lobby. Not that he planned to mention that to Holly. She was already in shock.

It pained him to see the remorse in her beautiful face. All he wanted to do was hold her and tell her that it wasn't her fault until she believed it.

Comfort would have to wait. Right now, his priority was keeping her alive.

They reached the elevators.

Kane pushed the down button. A few second later, the elevator arrived. A man. Woman. A little boy. The woman wore a robe while the man and boy wore T-shirts, board shorts, and had towels draped over their shoulders.

The little boy's eyes widened as they approached. He realized Holly was wearing her unitard.

He tightened his hold on her hand as the little boy gawked, until his mother pulled him close, as if Holly might hurt him.

He wondered what the kid thought. No doubt the mother saw the black spandex, harness, and leather gloves and thought Holly was a hooker, dominatrix, or both.

So what did that make him? Her client?

The elevator stopped at the pool level. He placed his hand on the gun in his pocket and held his breath. Would Enzo be waiting for them? Would the little family be caught in the line of fire?

No Enzo. No anyone. The family left and the elevator continued downward. There was no relief, though. There would be no relaxing until Holly was safe and Enzo was either dead or behind bars.

They entered the crowded lobby and he scanned faces. Enzo could be anywhere, in this crowd, and difficult to find.

"Where to?" Holly asked.

The one place they'd be safe. "Back to the office per orders. We can't take the chance that Enzo could catch us and get the chip."

"We can't. He'll get away." He thought she might cry.

He didn't like the idea of letting Enzo escape any more than she did, but he wasn't risking her life. And he wasn't going to get into a gunfight in a crowd.

Behind them, a man swore at someone.

The hair on Kane's neck rose even as he turned to confirm what he already knew. Only twenty feet away, Enzo shoved his way through the crowd.

Kane pulled Holly behind a pillar and held her close.

"If we go to the office, he's going to kill someone," Holly whispered. "We need to get him away from anyone and everyone. We need to stop him. Tonight."

Kane's mouth pressed tight. "I'm not putting you at risk."

"Please." She wrapped her arms around his neck, pressed her head to his chest. He sympathized with the desperation in her touch. The need to fix the situation. The overwhelming guilt.

As much as he wanted to keep her safe, he knew deep down that stopping Enzo was the only way to help her.

Or at least a good first step.

Tempe was going to be pissed.

He kissed her, quick and hard. "Okay. You win, but for once, you do what I say."

"I promise."

Enzo walked past them, and Kane slid to the far side of the pillar, taking Holly with him. Counting to three, he peered around the edge. Their stalker went outside, turned left. He counted to three again. Then followed, keeping twenty paces behind their quarry.

"I'm open to suggestions on where to lead him" Kane said. There were few unpopulated places in L.A. A parking garage was their best bet, but even that was going to have people passing through.

"I have the perfect place," she said, staying close to his side. "My family has a training area outside the city."

Outside the city? "How do you propose we get him to follow us there?"

Ahead of them, a group of young men wearing leather and looking too young to even drive were parking their motorcycles. "There," she said, nodding toward the closest biker.

Damn. The parking garage would have been easier. Kane let go of her as he punched the kid in the jaw, knocking him to the ground, dazed.

The rest of the group stared at him in shock as he straddled the bike, but he was more interested in Enzo.

The thug turned at hearing the scuffle. Their eyes met. There was no guilt in the man's face. Just rage. Anger. And the desire to get what he wanted no matter the cost.

"Get on," he said, and Holly jumped on behind him.

The bike roared to life, and she wrapped her arms around Kane's waist. He wove through cars, watching the rearview mirror as Enzo wrestled a bike from one of the other kids and came after them.

Chapter Eighteen

"Here," Holly shouted over the engine of the motorcycle. Thanks to Kane's driving skills, some of which had her shutting her eyes and hiding her face against his back, they were ahead of Enzo. Not so much they'd lose him but enough to buy them a few minutes of planning, now that they were at the property her family called home.

She prayed time and home-turf advantage was enough to stop him. She wasn't losing anyone else. Especially not Kane.

"Over there," Holly said, pointing toward a path to the right. He killed the power, and she hopped off as he pushed the bike down the path and ditched it behind a giant scrub oak. Lights came into view, and they both dropped to the ground.

Enzo was closer than she'd thought.

"Where to?" Kane whispered as the mobster flew past them.

They dusted themselves off. "This way," Holly said. Taking his hand, she guided him along the path toward the main facility, relying on her memories and the moonlight that lit up the land.

They jogged up the rolling hill separating the entrance to the facility from the main training area. Below, the lights of Enzo's bike lit up the night. He'd stopped outside the gates.

She knew what he was reading, The Acrobats Extraordinaire. Welcome. She and her mother had hung the midnight blue sign, silver script highlighted with gold leaf, the day the troupe arrived, finishing their long trek from Pensacola, Florida, to the west coast.

Her family. She'd asked her mother for the "full production" in order to get the full distraction potential when she broke into the penthouse, which meant they should all be gone.

She sure hoped so, or this was going to get even more difficult.

She refocused her attention back on their pursuer. From their vantage, she watched Enzo in the light of the bike, checking out the area. Had she made a mistake by leading him here? She knew if she didn't capture him tonight, it was possible he'd come back and hurt them.

Good luck with that. Still, the idea he might try was a powerful motivator.

"We don't have to do this," Kane said, as if reading her uncertainty. "We can call the police. Let them take care of it."

Tempting.

Except for Tammi Lynn. Her soft drawl as she begged for her life. The torture of knowing she was going to die and being unable to even make an attempt to save herself and run because of what she'd done.

Holly stared into the darkness.

"I'm calling the police," Kane, taking her hand in his and pulled her to him. He stared into her eyes, begging her to listen. "It was Enzo who pulled the trigger. You have to remember that."

She wanted to believe him. Wished she could brush off what happened. She couldn't. This was her fault. Her mess to clean up. Her killer to catch.

"I won't risk anyone else," she whispered. "If we do this right, he won't be able to hurt anyone. Ever."

He hesitated and she hoped he was done with his attempts at persuasion. A few more tries and she might give in, but he gave her a sharp nod instead of more argument. "Lead the way."

Thank you. She started back along the path. It cut over the hill, then down a steep slope, bypassing the winding dirt road that skirted the hill and entered the facility from the back. With the family gone, the main lights were off, and only the soft glow of solar lighting marked out the paths among the training areas. Sticking to the edge of the trees, they worked their way along the edges, watching for their quarry.

"Wow," Kane whispered as they reached the flying trapeze, one of the five main training arenas. Even in the dim light, the ladder leading to the platform glimmered. Set at forty feet, it was taller than the average platform, but that's what sold tickets and brought work—taking chances. "This is a circus," he said, his voice tinged with awe. "A real circus."

"Of course it is," Holly said, trying not to feel paranoid. Right now, she needed to focus.

They passed the single-point trapeze, used for singular, dancelike acrobatics. "Wow, this is…" He hesitated, craning his neck upward to follow a set of cables to their termination point four stories up.

"Dangerous?" Holly filled in.

"Yeah, but it's also—" Gravel crunched. Holly paused mid-step, her foot still in the air, and Kane cut himself off mid-sentence. More crunching sounded through the night air. Someone else walked through the arenas.

Enzo. It had to be. He passed in front of one of the path lights, making it flicker. She held her breath, waiting for him to pass. The sound of him walking faded, and she put her foot on the ground and allowed herself to breathe again.

Kane pulled her into the trees. "That was too close. Tell me you have a plan."

The plan was to get Enzo here, and now, but she had no idea. "Sorry. Not sure. Yet."

The shadows hid his expression, but she imagined it was less than pleased. "I can always try to shoot him," he said, more than a little serious.

As much as she appreciated the offer, she wasn't going to ask him to kill for her—even if it was putting down a murderer. "No one dies, not even him."

"Then we better come up with something before your family returns."

Her gaze darted from building to building. Arena to arena. Now that the moment was on her, she wasn't sure what to do. If she were in the air, she'd know. Skyscrapers were her arena. Harnesses and carabineers her weapons.

But Enzo had a gun, and what use was a rope against a bullet? She pressed her hands against her temple, trying to hang on to a single idea long enough to give it an honest evaluation.

"It's okay," Kane said, pulling her close and wrapping his arms around her. She let herself rest against his chest, like she had at the hotel. The security of his embrace calmed her mind. Ideas and plans formed and reformed at a pace less frenzied until she locked on the flying trapeze.

Air was her weapon.

If she could get him to follow her to the platform, she'd come up with something. She wasn't sure what but something. "If we lure him to the trapeze, I think I can take him" She said.

"How?"

She swallowed hard, uneasy at what she needed to do but not seeing an alternative. "All I have to do it is hook him to the ropes and I can push him off. He'll be left hanging midair. Helpless."

He squeezed her hard. "That is the dumbest idea I have ever heard," he whispered.

For a beat, she wondered if she'd heard right. She leaned back, leaving the safety of his arms. "Excuse me?"

He stroked the hair back from her face. "You're overthinking this. There are two of us and one of him. That gives us the advantage. We lure him into a trap and ambush him. Much easier than trying to get him to climb a forty-foot ladder."

A week ago, she'd have fought the idea. Protested and done what she wanted. But he made sense, and she needed his steadiness and his experience.

"You okay?" he asked. "I know that sounded harsh, but we don't have time for a debate."

She rose on her toes and kissed him. "I'm good. "Now

c'mon, I know the perfect place for an ambush."

· · ·

"The stables?"

They stood outside the building, pressed flat against the wall to hide their silhouettes. There was an array of buildings Holly could choose from. Why pick the one that was most likely to be filled with manure?

"It's perfect," she whispered. "Contained. Plus, there's a loft. You can get the drop on him from above."

A ten-foot drop to try and land on someone? Sounded painful and unnecessary. "You've seen too many movies. I'll tackle him as he runs past. Less chance of me breaking my leg."

"Fine, do it your way," she snapped.

His way? He'd shoot the thug.

He appreciated Holly didn't want to kill the man, but as far as Kane was concerned, Enzo was more rabid dog than human. But Holly's face when she heard Tammi Lynn's death stayed his hand and kept his gun in his back pocket.

For Holly.

Of course, if Enzo pointed his weapon at his girl, all bets were off.

"Slowly," she said. Opening the side door, he followed as she made her way to the main aisle running between the stalls. The stable was pitch black compared with the outside. Even when his eyes adjusted, it was difficult to see.

Definitely no shooting. He'd probably hit a horse.

"What's the plan" Kane asked once they took up post in an empty stall.

"I'll lead him here," she said, sounding less determined. He wondered who she was trying to convince. Him or herself. "You tackle him."

As long as Enzo didn't kill her. "No."

"What do you mean 'no'?" She crossed her arms, and he knew she was glaring at him. Mouth tight. Chin jutting out. Let her be pissy. She wasn't going to play bait to assuage her guilt.

"I'm not going to have you shot."

She sighed in exasperation. "I'll be running in the dark in a location I know like the back of my hand. I'm fast. He doesn't stand a chance."

"I don't like it." Shooting Enzo was starting to sound better and better.

"Neither do I," she said, "but I don't see us as having a lot of choice."

He should have called the police as soon as they arrived.

Too late now. Even if he did, Holly would do what she wanted anyway. He'd worked with her enough to know that much. They were in the thick of it, and the best course was to end it as fast as possible.

"Use the ear piece," he pulled out the communicator from his pocket and turned it on. "Let me know when you're close."

She nodded, at a loss for words. "Thanks," she said, her voice low. "For what it's worth, I'm glad you're always prepared."

Warmth washed over him, but he pushed it back. Later. "Just be careful," he insisted. "No chances."

"I won't."

He'd heard that before. More than once. He wrapped his

arms around her, lifting her off her feet. "I mean it."

"I don't have a death wish," she assured him, leaning her forehead against his. Her breath hitched in her throat. "I want him caught. That's all."

He believed her. "I can do that."

He found he couldn't let her go and buried his face in her hair. *I love you.* He wanted to say the words. To whisper them in her ear or scream them from the top of the stable, but a declaration would only distract her. There would be time enough for love when Enzo was subdued, and Holly was safe.

Instead, he showered her with tiny kisses. Working his way from her mouth to the tip of her nose and to the sweet, curved spot where her neck met her shoulder.

He loved her laugh but needed her focused. He set her back on her feet. All business — it was what would keep them both alive. "As soon as you run past, I'll have him."

"Counting on it," she said. She hesitated then slid back out the door.

Be safe. Don't die. Kane shut his eyes and focused on the job. The job. He still hated the plan, but as long as Holly, for once, followed his directions, it might work out.

Get Enzo on to the trapeze.

He smiled at the sheer lunacy of the idea. She'd obviously never been in the field, where the main idea was to keep it simple. The more complicated a plan, the more chances it had to fail.

He knew that all too well.

One of the horses made a snuffing sound, and Kane tensed. Something scuffed the straw. A steady beat. Footsteps. Human footsteps. Had Enzo come in through the door?

Kane readied himself, crouched low and watched as a

dark silhouette worked its way toward him. Then past.

Now.

Kane ran at the man, legs pumping, and dove onto him, taking away any chance he would fire a shot. Enzo hit the ground with an *oomph*. He wrestled the man's hand behind his back, pinning his wrists and shoving an elbow into his spine.

Enzo screamed and Kane froze.

The scream was shrill. Frightened. Feminine. Whoever he'd tackled, it wasn't Enzo.

• • •

"Mom. What the hell are you doing here?" Holly had barely rounded the far corner of the barn when someone entered the door. Thinking it was Enzo, she'd held still then followed only to hear her mother's scream.

A shrill cry of pain and fear that was sure to bring their target to them while everyone was in a convenient-to-shoot pile on the floor.

"I came home right after I talked to you," her mother said, as Kane rolled off of her and pulled her to her feet. "I didn't feel well. Then I heard someone in the barn and came out."

Light shone outside the main barn door, beams filtering through the spaces between the boards.

Shit. Enzo was fast. Taking cover behind a stall, she pulled her mother with her in case Enzo took a shot at them. "You've got to get her to safety," she whispered as Kane joined them. "Get her out of here."

"I know you're in there,' Enzo yelled. "Now come out and bring the chip."

"The plan's blown," Kane said, his grim expression telling her more than in words. He pushed her and her mother toward the back door. "It's time to call the cops. Stay low. I'll distract him."

He pulled out his gun, all warrior. Ready to do battle for those he swore to protect.

No. No. No. Screw this. She knew what she had to do. She met Kane's gaze and hoped that if she failed, he'd forgive her. She shoved her mother into his arms, almost knocking them both over. "Keep her safe," she shouted as she sprinted out the door.

"You want the chip, come and get it," she screamed, leading the thug away from her mother and Kane, daring him to follow.

Her heart pounded in her ears as she found herself heading toward the trapeze. Kane was right. Stupid idea. Complicated. But it was all she could think about as she ran. There was no room for anything else. Just the here and now.

A split-second decision.

She found herself at the base of the ladder and started climbing.

A bullet glanced off the railing near her head. She screamed, almost losing her grip. Only a few more feet, and she'd be safe on the platform.

Until he came up.

The ladder shook as he climbed behind her. She didn't dare look down as she reached the platform.

Safety.

Thick, strong fingers wrapped around her ankle.

A shriek of fear burst from her throat before she could stop herself. She kicked out. Once Twice. Her foot connected with something hard. She hoped it was his head.

Enzo shouted and let her go. She crawled on to the platform and felt for the clip that secured the bar. She needed to get into the air. Her fingers closed on the metal clasp. *There*. The bar released. She gripped it like a life preserver.

Strong hands grabbed her from behind. "Where's the chip, bitch?" Enzo growled in her ear as he lifted her off her feet.

She was going to die.

Tammi Lynn flashed through her mind. Helpless on the floor. Begging. Too scared to fight back. Too weak to try and survive. She didn't want to be that person. The one who let death take them without a battle. She wasn't weak. She wasn't fragile and helpless.

She wasn't Tammi Lynn.

Still gripping the bar, she struggled. Kicked. "Let me go," she screamed, flinging her head back to break his nose.

He dodged the blow and wrapped an arm across her chest to subdue her. "Stop it and give me the fucking chip."

His forearm. Mouth wide, she lunged down and sank her teeth into his skin. The salty taste of blood flowed over her tongue, and she bit down harder, determined to make him hurt.

Enzo screamed and let her go.

One hand on the bar, she swung into the air, the sudden weight of her body almost breaking her grip before she could reach up with the other hand. Then she was flying through the night.

"Holly," it sounded like someone was over her shoulder. "What's happening? Are you okay? You weren't answering."

The earpiece. She'd been so scared, so focused she hadn't

heard Kane.

"I'm fine. Good. Where are you?"

"Down here."

She chanced a glance below as she floated through the air. He was standing at the edge of the net.

"Did you think I'd let you do this alone?" he asked.

A piece of her had. Of course, now she knew that was a foolish idea. If their places were flipped, she'd be at his side. How could she have thought he'd offer less? "Of course not," she lied.

Enzo stood on the platform, gun out, barrel glinting in the moonlight. "Get back here. Now."

"What's the plan?" Kane asked.

She couldn't make out the details, but she knew Enzo was tracking her with the gun. Hitting a moving target in the dark with a handgun was almost impossible, but she didn't want to take any chances. "If I kick him off the platform, can you take him?"

"On it. Just be careful."

"Aren't I always?" she asked, pumping her body to increase her arc and take her back toward Enzo.

"We'll discuss that later."

She turned her attention to the task. *Focus*. She was getting closer now.

"Hang on," Kane said in her ear." I'm going to give him something else to think about besides you."

A shot ripped through the air.

She swung faster now. Flying through the air.

Kane fired again.

Enzo fired back, but she fixed her eyes on her target, refusing to be dissuaded by the thought of death by bullet.

Another shot from below.

There.

Her eyes met Enzo's as she ran into him, knocking him off balance. She wrapped her legs around him before he fell backward. He clutched at her, the combination of her arc and bodyweight pulled him forward, dragging him off the platform.

For a split second, they floated through the air.

He didn't deserve the joy. The freedom.

She unlocked her legs from around his waist and let him fall mid arc. He clutched at her again, but gravity was stronger. He fell.

Holly landed on the opposite platform. Alone.

Below her, the net was gone. A bundle writhed on the ground, wrapped in the material. Enzo. Kane must have cut the net right after he hit.

Her knees went weak, and she sat on the platform with a thud. Head in her hands. It was over. They were safe. No one else had to die.

"Holly?"

Kane said again, but not in her ear this time. Behind her. She raised her head as he kneeled next to her. "Are you all right? Did he hurt you?"

She shook her head "How's my mom?"

"Friendly. And armed. I gave her the other gun for protection." He wrapped his arms around her, pulling her close.

"Thanks," she replied, taking a deep breath to regain her composure. The Boreckyis always said that breathing was as important as strength when tackling the trapeze. The body needed the oxygen to keep the head clear and combat the flight mode that came with risking one's life.

"You could have died," Kane said.

Another breath. "But I didn't," she said, reassuring herself as well as Kane. "I'm okay. My mom's okay. And my family is safe."

A third, deep breath and the shaking stopped, and the adrenaline slowed. *Finally*.

"But you could have," he insisted.

Now that she was calm, she heard the fear in his voice. The anger. And she didn't know what to say to make it better. "But I didn't," she repeated, trying to reassure him.

She felt his shoulders tighten, and she knew she'd missed the mark.

"You're a thief. Not combat trained. You can't do this again," Kane said. "I won't let you."

She knew he carried the guilt from his lover's death. That kind of loss left scars.

But that didn't mean he got to dictate her life. "I know you're upset but you're not my boss so you don't get to tell me what to do," she replied.

Abruptly, he stood. She was sure if the platform were larger, he'd pace.

Instead he crossed his arms over his chest. "I'm the leader of this op, so yes, that's exactly what I get to do."

And there he was, *Kane the Pain*. Again. She thought he'd gone away, but it seemed he'd only been hiding. Slowly, she rose to her feet, anger and frustration overriding any residual fear.

She looked up at him, meeting his anger with hers. "This op is over," she replied.

She climbed down the ladder, leaving him on the platform. Alone.

Chapter Nineteen

Sitting in her mother's Winnebago, Holly drank coffee and stared out the window at the thirty-acre, outdoor lot the troupe called home and contemplated how she'd almost lost everything that mattered.

Her mother. Her family.

Kane.

His voice drifted through the window—he'd been talking to the FBI since sunrise. Giving the details of how Enzo killed Tammi Lynn but leaving out the bit about how she broke into a hotel. Not that they cared. They had Enzo in custody and a charge that might stick.

Coupled with the retrieval of the chip, it seemed to be enough for them.

"You love him, don't you?"

Holly jumped at the words. Her mother stood in the tiny kitchen, hair still damp from her shower and pouring herself a cup of coffee.

"What?"

"You can lie to yourself, but I'll always see through it, Cookie. You know that."

"I don't love him. I think he's an ass," she replied, remembering their last confrontation on the platform. And regretting it more than she wanted to admit.

"You can do both," her mom countered.

Holly sighed and rubbed her tired eyes. Her mother was right, damn her. She loved him, but he was such a jerk sometimes. "Should I tell him?"

"Which part?"

"Both?"

Her mother laughed and took a seat across from her. "I would."

Holly wished she could be as sure. Now that their mission was well and truly over, he might want to move on. To work with someone who wasn't as erratic. Perhaps to have a normal girlfriend who didn't lie and steal for a living.

Or come a hair's breadth from getting killed.

"I don't know," she finally replied.

"I think you do. I know something is holding you back but you need to get over it."

Holly leaned back in the seat, letting her head fall back. "My job makes it difficult. If you knew—"

"Stop." Sarah slammed her hands on the counter, making Holly jump. She'd never seen her mother angry before. Not like this.

"I'm not an idiot. The Feds are here. We were chased by a mobster. I know you don't do makeup for Hollywood films. I don't know what you do, don't even know if it's legal, and I don't care. This is about love. Not work."

Holly stared at her cup. She'd been careful to keep her cover story for her mom. It was part of the job. But she should have known she'd see through it. "You love him," Sarah said, composure regained and spooning sugar into her cup as if her pronouncement were the most normal thing in the world. "Don't lose him because you're too scared to say the words."

She was so good at taking risks, but love meant letting someone be important, and she hadn't done that in a long time. At least no one outside the family.

Her mother made it sound so easy.

"I worked with him two years ago for one night. When it comes down to it, I've known him less than a week."

"Do you think love runs on a timetable? Especially yours?" Sarah laughed. "I knew your father for less than a day when I knew I wanted to marry him. I knew. Like you know about Kane." She took Holly's hand in hers. "We're not that different, you know."

"I've tried before, and you know how that ended," Holly said. "I know he feels something for me, but between his baggage and mine, I can't see this going anywhere."

"You can't fix his baggage," her mother replied. "But you can fix yours and give this a fighting chance. So spill. What's this giant amount of baggage that keeps you from love?"

Crap. What was she supposed to say? Her family was baggage? "Outsiders just don't get us. They never do. Even you have to admit that."

Sarah sighed. "Some do. Some don't. *You* have to admit that."

Holly rolled her mug between her palms. "I've yet to

meet the guy who didn't run once he realized that accepting me meant accepting my family as well. All of you."

Sarah frowned. "You can't live the rest of your life and make decisions because life sucked as a teenager. Now, grow the fuck up."

Holly stared, unsure of how to respond. First anger and now swearing. And the F word? "What?" she finally managed to squeak.

Sarah rose, taking her coffee with her. "Go talk to Kane."

"About what?" he asked, opening the door to the Winnebago. The vehicle rocked as he climbed the few stairs. His eyes were bloodshot, he smelled of sweat and straw, and his clothes needed to be burned.

She'd take a live, grimy Kane over a dead, perfect one any day of the year.

But now that the worst was over, did he want her? All of her and what that meant?

Sarah pushed past him. "Talk to the wuss in the chair."

"I'm not a wuss," Holly muttered as the door slammed shut.

Kane slid into the seat across from her. She tried to read him and found nothing. No anger. But no joy. Just a blank slate. What did that mean?

"I have some good news," he said.

Work. If that was what he wanted, she'd deal with it. "Enzo's getting life?"

"No." He said. "Tempe called. There's someone waiting for you back in your apartment."

"Who?"

He reached across the Formica table top and took her hands in his. Her heart felt as if it skipped a beat.

Stupid heart.

He continued, "Four legs? Stinky fur? Has a tail that wags the dog?"

"Mr. Wiggles." Thanks goodness. "Did the vet say how he was?"

"Needs some TLC, but your roommate seemed eager to help. She also said to get home as soon as possible, and that she doesn't pick up poop."

Holly snickered. Eva was good people.

"So, what is it you need to tell me?" Kane asked.

Was he over whatever had held him back from loving her? If so, *maybe* she could take a chance as well. She'd avoided love for a long time. Avoided anything real.

She didn't want to do that anymore. She wanted the gritty, annoying reality of loving Kane.

If he'd have her.

Do it. Just do it.

"Holly, the cops want to talk to you again if you have a minute," Alyssa, the bearded lady, stuck her head in the trailer. Though her friend was billed as a bearded lady, she had hypertrichosis, also known as werewolf syndrome.

She nodded toward her. "I'll be right out. Just give us a minute."

"Sure thing," Alyssa said before disappearing.

Holly turned her attention back to Kane and met with his surprised, and somewhat shocked, gaze. She knew that look. She'd seen it every time a date met her family. It wasn't just Alyssa. It was Fernando. Santos. All the artists.

Seeing Alyssa had just made Kane realize that her family was different. And she was different.

And for someone as strict and straight as Kane, all that

difference was just too damned much—no matter what her mother wanted to believe.

The *maybe* she'd been entertaining turned into a firm, *negatory*.

Her heart ached at the reality of the situation, and it took an effort to not press her hand to her chest. But at least she'd been spared the humiliation of declaring her love before he ran. That was new.

"So, what's going on?" Kane asked.

She braced herself with a reminder that if she didn't do this now, it would only hurt more later. "I wanted you to know how much I appreciated working with you. We're a good team. And we did some amazing, crazy things."

Kane gave her a suspicious side-eye glance. "I hear a 'but' coming."

Deep breath.

"*But* it's over now, and I think we need to acknowledge that what we had in the field was based on adrenaline and excitement. We're back in the real world now, and while I appreciated our time together, I think we need to go back to just being friends."

Kane's hands slid from her, and he sat back, staring at her, his face a mask of confusion. "What?"

"We're friends. Nothing more and nothing less. Coworkers. I've given it a lot of thought, and it's for the best."

Kane shook his head. "I have no idea what's going on in your head, but we need to talk about this."

Holly rose, knowing she couldn't hold out much longer. "No. We don't. There's nothing to say, and I have to go talk to the Feds." She ran out of the trailer before he could say any more and ruin her resolve.

• • •

"Staring at the phone won't make it ring," Sarah said. "Just call him and tell him you made a mistake. He'll understand."

Holly jammed her cell phone back in her pocket and tried to get comfortable on the wooden bench that was just outside the trapeze arena.

She glanced up at the platforms, backlit by the setting sun. Had it only been two weeks ago that she and Kane had captured Enzo? It both felt like yesterday and years since she almost died.

Since she last saw Kane.

As the rest of the troupe sauntered over to the set of bleachers, Holly leaned against her mom, putting her head on the older woman's shoulder. "I wish I could believe you, but I didn't make a mistake. You should have seen his face when he saw Alyssa. He was freaked out."

"Well, it is startling the first time you see her," Sarah said.

"Maybe," she conceded.

Her mother patted Holly's arm. "He seems like a nice man, and I hate to see you make a mistake. Did you ever talk to him about it? About us?"

What was there to say? She glanced at the group that filled the bleachers. They weren't performing, but that didn't stop some of them from dressing in more eccentric outfits that would get stares under more normal circumstances. But here, one could wear either a sequined leotard and feathered headdress or jeans for dinner, and either were considered normal.

But normal here wasn't normal in Kane's world.

She'd known it was a bad idea to introduce Kane to her mom. They weren't even a couple, had never been a couple, really, and her mom was still trying to get them back together. Holly straightened. "Can we talk about this later? Right now I just want to forget what happened." *And how much I miss him.*

He mother patted her arm, "Of course, Cookie. I know this is difficult for you."

You have no idea.

The music she knew and loved started. Holly settled in to enjoy it and put Kane out of her mind. Stella and Sylvester emerged from the tent behind their trapeze ring, holding hands but parting when they reached the sawdust to head to opposite ladders.

The pair reached their platforms, grabbed the bars, and swung outward.

Holly held her breath as Stella released, did a triple summersault, and seemed to hang in the air.

Then Sylvester was there, his hands found Stella's and they flew through the air, arms locked.

It didn't matter how many times she saw her friends and family perform, it never grew old, was always astonishing, and she felt like a kid again as the rest of the troupe cheered and clapped around her.

"They're spectacular," Holly whispered as Sylvester did a handstand, released and caught the bar as he fell, never losing momentum.

"Wait until you see the dogs," her mother whispered. "The new act is surprising."

Finally, Stella and Sylvester jumped down from their

platforms, landing in the net, and Fernando jogged out from the kennel where he kept his dogs. Wearing sad clown make-up, a large black wig, and over-sized clown suit, he entered the ring as Stella and Sylvester left. Usually working with small dogs, this time, he brought a large yellow lab that refused to listen, and when Fernando tried to grab his collar, the dog ran in circles under the netting, taunting the trainer.

Holly squinted into the fading light. "Is that Mr. Wiggles?"

"Yep," her mother said, looking pleased.

"When did you find time to do this?"

"We didn't. Not really. As you can tell," she said, laughing as Fernando dove for the dog and missed. "But you're gone a lot with work so if you want to leave him here, he needs to earn his keep."

Holly hadn't considered that but it seemed like a good idea. "What about Fernando? Is he okay with this?"

In reply, her mother whistled, a piecing sound that cut through the chatter and laughter of the troupe around them. Fernando turned toward the sound and walked over, Mr. Wiggles finally slowing enough to trot at the trainer's side.

"What's the problem?" he asked, his deep voice resonating.

Holly's breath caught in her throat. The makeup and hair and suit were Fernando's, but that voice…she knew that voice.

And it belonged to Kane.

The troupe grew silent, and Holly turned in her seat. They were staring at her and holding their collective breath.

They'd planned this.

She shook her head. Betrayed by her family. Was nothing sacred?

Stopping in front of her, Kane slipped off the wig and

the oversize clown suit. Someone threw him a towel, and he wiped his face until only a few streaks of makeup remained. He looked once again like the man she couldn't seem to forget.

Around her, the crowd whispered.

Busybodies.

"What are you doing here?" she managed to ask, the words sticking in her throat.

"I told you that we needed to talk, and since you refused, I talked to your mother instead."

"And she cooked this up?" Holly asked, her cheeks burning with a combination of anger and embarrassment. She knew they thought they were helping, but this was high school and humiliation all over again. Her eyes welled with tears, and she wiped them away.

"No, we did," Stella said, emerging from the shadows with Sylvester at her side.

"We all did," Alyssa chimed in. "We're not blind."

Great. Just great. Holly stood as the anger overrode mortification. "I appreciate the thought, but I think I can handle my own life."

"No one is saying you can't," Kane said, kneeling in front of her, "And all I'm asking for is five minutes."

Holly rested her head in her hands, wishing they would all just go the hell away. But when she looked up, they were all still there staring at her. She knew if she didn't give him the five minutes, this would only happen again. "Fine. Five minutes. Now what do you have to say?"

"That you're wrong about me," he said, taking her hand in his.

Her heart pounded harder at his touch. It was as warm

and strong as she remembered, and it took all her willpower to not wrap her fingers around his.

He continued, "I know I spooked you when I first saw Alyssa, and your mom told me about the other boyfriends before me and how they freaked out."

"Thanks, mom," Holly muttered.

"You're welcome," Sarah replied.

"I didn't mean it," Holly said.

"You will. Later."

No, later, they were going to have a discussion about boundaries.

Kane squeezed her hand, drawing her back. "So, after talking to your friends and your mom, we all came to the conclusion that the only person running away from us is you."

Betrayers. "How can you be so sure?"

"You haven't seen me," he said, "because you've been either at work or holed up in your apartment, but I've been here every day. Going to lunch. Hanging out. I needed to prove to them, you, and even myself that I can fit in here. That I am not freaked out by chaos. Or risks. Or you."

Kane rose and pulled her to her feet. Then he kissed her knuckles, and when she met his steady gaze, she saw the truth in his eyes.

And she also saw more. And that 'more' terrified her. She'd had a hard time reading him before. What if she were wrong?

"Why bother?" she asked, dreading the answer but unable to stop herself.

"For someone who excels at reading people, you can be dense." Letting her go, he dug into a pocket of the clown suit, retrieved a microphone, turned it on, and then guided her back to the ring.

Shaking, she turned to face the bleachers, not sure what she'd see in the faces of her family. The entire troupe—her family—filled the first rows. Dressed in a colorful array of Lycra, sequins, glitter, and ribbons, they sparkled in the setting sun, both outrageous and wonderful, all at the same time.

In unison, they gave her a thumbs up. Holly smiled. "How long have they been practicing the timing on that?" she asked, her voice amplified.

"Since I predicted this would happen two weeks ago," her mother shouted. "Now get on with it."

"Now I know where Holly gets her patience," Kane teased, making the troupe laugh.

When they calmed, he pulled her close. "I'm not going to lie," he began, his deep voice booming through the air. "The way you risk your life makes me nervous, but I also know that you can take care of yourself. I only ask one favor."

"What's that?"

"That when things go wrong, and they will, that you let me be the one at your side to help."

He didn't say leader. "You don't want to be the boss of me?"

"Well, sometimes," he replied, his voice only half-serious. "But mostly, I want to be your partner."

He cleared his throat. "I love you, Holly Milano."

He loved her? "Wait? What?"

"You heard me." He put the microphone closer to his lips. "I love you. I love your entire, crazy family. I even love the smell of sawdust."

"You love me?"

He shook his head. "Dense. Really, really dense," he teased. "But I love you even in spite of that."

He loved her. It didn't feel real, yet here he was in clown makeup, standing in the twilight, and telling her that very thing. In front of her family.

He let her hands go long enough to tilt her chin up. "I love you. Now, are you going to say it back, or do I have to make Mr. Wiggles actually do something because that might take a while."

He loved her. "I don't think I can wait that long." Rising on her toes, she kissed him. "I love you, too," she whispered against his mouth, just so he could hear it.

"Say it so they can hear it, or they'll never let us leave," Kane whispered back, handing her the mic.

She turned it off and tossed it. "We're in love," she shouted, loud enough for anyone and everyone to hear.

The clapping started, and Kane picked her up in his arms, swinging her in a circle until she threw her head back, giddy as she shouted the words again, not caring who heard as long as that "we're" included Kane.

About the Author

Sharron McClellan always planned to be a writer of some sort. However, when she went to college, she took journalism and creative writing, and sadly, the teachers sucked the love of writing out of her. So she turned to her next love–science. At first, she wanted to be a marine biologist, but there was the whole shark issue. Frankly, they freak her out.

Instead, she discovered the joys of playing in the dirt—a profession more commonly known as archaeology. For years, she focused on excavating ancient sites that included projectile points, burn pits, and the occasional burial.

Her focus returned to writing when she took a position during the archaeological off-season and ended up answering phones for Princess Cruise Line, a.k.a. The Love Boat. Which, when you consider she writes romance, is somewhat ironic. It was during that time that she took to reading romance. It wasn't long before she fell in love with the genre and returned to her first love—writing.

Five years later, she sold her first book. Five years after that, she landed at Entangled Publishing—Huzzah!

Today, she lives in San Diego, also known as the City of Perfect Weather. She has an awesome husband who supports her passion for the written word in every way possible. They both love to travel, so don't be surprised to find locales they've visited appearing in Sharron's books, and pictures popping up on her website: www.sharronmcclellan.com. It's a big world—both in her head and out there!

Also by Sharron McClellan...

RISKING IT ALL FOR HER BOSS

www.ingramcontent.com/pod-product-compliance
Lightning Source LLC
Chambersburg PA
CBHW031003260626

47169CB00002B/677